DEDALUS EUROPE 1993

Days of Anger

D1549150

Translated from the French
by Christine Donougher

Days of Anger

Sylvie Germain

Dedalus

Dedalus would like to thank The French Ministry of Culture and The Arts Council of Great Britain for their assistance in producing this translation.

Published in the UK by Dedalus Ltd, Langford Lodge, St Judith's Lane, Sawtry, Cambs, PE17 5XE

ISBN 1 873982 65 8

Distributed in Australia & New Zealand by Peribo Pty Ltd, 26, Tepko Road, Terrey Hills, N.S.W. 2084

First published in France as *Jours de colere* in 1989
Jours de colere copyright © 1989 Editions Gallimard
First English edition 1993
English Translation copyright © Christine Donougher 1993

Typeset by Datix International, Bungay, Suffolk
Printed in England by Loader Jackson, Arlesey, Beds

A C.I.P. listing for this title is available on request.

French Literature from Dedalus

French language literature in translation is an important part of Dedalus's list, with French being the language par excellence of literary fantasy.

French books from Dedalus include:

Seraphita – Balzac £6.99
The Quest of the Absolute – Balzac £6.99
The Devil in Love – Jacques Cazotte £5.99
Les Diaboliques – Barbey D'Aurevilly £6.99
Angels of Perversity – Remy de Gourmont £6.99
The Book of Nights – Sylvie Germain £8.99
The Weeping Woman – Sylvie Germain £6.99
Days of Anger – Sylvie Germain £8.99
La-Bas – J. K. Huysmans £7.99
The Cathedral – J. K. Huysmans £6.99
En Route – J. K. Huysmans £6.99
The Phantom of the Opera – Gaston Leroux £6.99
Monsieur de Phocas – Jean Lorrain £8.99
Le Calvaire – Octave Mirbeau £7.99
The Diary of a Chambermaid – Octave Mirbeau £7.99
Torture Garden – Octave Mirbeau £7.99
Smarra & Trilby – Charles Nodier £6.99
Monsieur Venus – Rachilde £6.99
Tales from the Saragossa Manuscript – Jan Potocki £6.99
The Mysteries of Paris – Eugene Sue £6.99
The Wandering Jew – Eugene Sue £9.99
Micromegas – Voltaire £5.99

forthcoming titles include:

The Experience of the Night – Marcel Bealu
The Dedalus Book of French Fantasy – editor Christine Donougher
Night of Amber – Sylvie Germain

The Medusa Child – Sylvie Germain
The Year 2440 – Louis Sebastien Mercier
Abbe Jules – Octave Mirbeau
La Marquise de Sade – Rachilde

Anthologies featuring French Literature in translation:

The Dedalus Book of Decadence – editor Brian
Stableford £7.99
The Second Dedalus Book of Decadence – editor Brian
Stableford £8.99
The Dedalus Book of Surrealism – editor Michael
Richardson £8.99
The Myth of the World: Surrealism 2 – editor Michael
Richardson £8.99

THE AUTHOR

Sylvie Germain was born in Chateauroux in Central France, in 1954. She read philosophy at the Sorbonne, being awarded a doctorate. From 1987 until the summer of 1993 she taught philosophy at the French School in Prague. She now lives in Paris. Sylvie Germain is the author of five novels and one collection of short stories. Her work has so far been translated into fifteen languages.

Sylvie Germain's first novel *Le Livre des nuits* (*The Book of Nights*) was published in France to great acclaim in 1985. It has won six French Literary Prizes as well as the Scott Moncrieff Translation Prize in England. The novel ends with the birth of Night of Amber and his story is continued in *Nuit d'ambre* (1987), which Dedalus will be publishing in 1994. Her third novel *Jours de colere* (*Days of Anger*) won the Prix Femina in 1989. It was followed by *L'Enfant Méduse* in 1991 (Dedalus edition in preparation for 1994) and *La pleurante des rues de Prague* (1992), published under the title *The Weeping Woman on the Streets of Prague* by Dedalus in 1993.

THE TRANSLATOR

Christine Donougher was born in England in 1954. She read English and French at Cambridge and after a career in publishing is now a freelance translator and editor.

Her many translations from French and Italian include Potocki's *Tales from the Saragossa Manuscript*, Boito's *Senso* (*and other stories*) and Octave Mirbeau's *Le Calvaire*. Her translation of Sylvie Germain's *The Book of Nights* won the Scott Moncrieff Prize for the best translation of a Twentieth Century French Novel during 1992.

Her current projects include editing *The Dedalus Book of French Fantasy* and translating Sylvie Germain's *Nuit d'Ambre*.

Christine Donougher lives in Venice with her husband, the writer Roderick Conway-Morris.

THE BOOK OF NIGHTS

Dedalus published Sylvie Germain's first novel *The Book of Nights* to great acclaim last autumn. It was awarded The Scott-Moncrieff Prize for the best translation of a Twentieth Century French Novel into English during 1992.

These are a few of the comments:

'*The Book of Nights* is a masterpiece. Germain is endowed with extraordinary narrative and descriptive abilities ... She excels in portraits of emotional intensity and the gritty realism of raw emotions gives the novel its unique power. *The Book of Nights* is a literary feast.'
Ziauddin Sardar in The Independent

'This astonishing first novel has won no less than six literary prizes since its publication in 1985. The novel tells the story of the Peniel family in the desolate wetlands of Flanders, across which the German invaders pour three times – 1870, 1914 and 1940 – in less than a century. It is hard to avoid thinking of *A Hundred Years of Solitude* but the comparison does no disservice to Germain's novel, so powerful is it. . . . A brilliant book, excellently translated'.
Mike Petty in The Literary Review

'*The Book of Nights* is a moving and powerful book.'
Claire Messud in The European

'This is a lyrical attempt to blend magic realism with *la France profonde*, the desolate peasant regions that remain mired in myth and folklore. Nothing is too grotesque for Germain's eldritch imagination: batrachian women, loving werewolves, necklaces of tears and corpses that metamorphose into dolls all combine to produce a visionary fusion of the pagan and the mystical.'
Elizabeth Young in The New Statesman

ANGER AND BEAUTY

A SMALL VILLAGE

Old folks' madness bides its time. It remains poised, as still as the indistinct, pale shadow of a barn owl in the hollow of a dry tree, with an expression of unfathomable vacancy and amazement behind its blinking eyelids, once the creeping cold, tiredness, and hunger have beset it with a statue-like torpor. But before reaching this state of prostration, madness has to have stolen long before into the heart of the man or woman in whom it will mature, and long inhabited his or her thoughts, dreams, memory and senses, as either a dancing, softly singing undulation, or a stamping, shouting agitation – it all depends.

Madness had burst upon Ambroise Mauperthuis, progressed by leaps and bounds, and then tautened like a bow, with contained violence. A frenzied madness, like a flash of lightning frozen in the sky. A madness that had overtaken him at the sight of a woman he did not know, whom he had only seen dead, knifed in the throat, one spring morning on the banks of the Yonne. But in his memory he had confused the woman's mouth, and those wonderful, parted lips, with the bleeding wound in her neck. He had confused mouth with wound, word with cry, saliva with blood. He had confused beauty with crime, love with anger – and desire with death.

In Edmée Verselay, by contrast, madness had insinuated itself little by little, its progress a gentle trickle, until eventually it came to a quiet halt. A gentle madness, like a patch of delicate blue in a corner of the sky, which no night could ever shroud or extinguish. A madness that had taken root in her heart, too, because of a woman. By grace of a woman – she who was blessed among all women. In her devotion to Our Lady, Edmée had gradually confused her life and her family's with a perpetual miracle granted by the Virgin. She had confused mouth with smile, word with prayer, saliva with tears. She had confused beauty with the invisible, love with mercy – and death with the Assumption.

Both he and she lived to be very old – the madness remained endlessly poised, and did not allow them time to die. They had completely confused death with their lives. And they both spent the duration of this long pause in their madness living in the same hamlet, perched on granite heights, in the shadow of forests. One of them lived at the top of this small village, and the other at the bottom. The hamlet, called Oak-Wolf, was so tiny and so poor that there did not seem much sense in distinguishing a beginning and an end to it. Yet, short though the distance was between these two farms, it nevertheless represented a vast divide. Anything can occur in two different places, however close they might be. And depending on what happens there, either place may be isolated.

This village had no limits – it lay open to every wind, storm, snowfall and rainfall, and to every passion. The only boundaries were those of the forest, but these are moving boundaries, just as penetrable as they are intrusive – like the confines of the heart when madness encroaches upon love. The hamlet was not signposted. It was just a place whose name was known by word of mouth; a place whose force of being passed from one body to another, thriving in obscure glory in the flesh of its inhabitants.

Rarely did any stranger go up there. It was the people of Oak-Wolf that on Sundays and holidays, on market-days and when labour was being hired, came down into the nearest commune with a church, town hall, square, and bars. So rarely did any stranger venture up there that the villagers they descended on regarded these taciturn visitors as somewhat primitive beings, and the local priest even suspected that the Word of God had not quite managed to reach those semi-barbarians of the forests.

And yet it had travelled all the way up there, admittedly burdened by the mud along the paths – a mud steeped in the old beliefs, in ancient fears and obscure magic, and tangled with roots, branches, and tree-bark; wind-buffeted and rain-lashed, like the thick, dark, shadowy leaves.

Oak-Wolf had five farms: five squat, austere buildings with adjoining cowsheds and barns, strung out along the road that climbed up to Jalles Forest, overhanging the river Cure. Ambroise Mauperthuis and his two sons, Ephraim and Marceau, lived in the first house that one came to along this road. It was called Threshold Farm, because it stood right on the edge of the hamlet, like some doorstep leading to poverty and loneliness. This doorstep had been raised and enlarged when Ambroise Mauperthuis moved in, after he had become rich, but it still led to the same loneliness as before. After Threshold Farm came Follin Farm, named after its inhabitants, Firmin and Adolphine Follin, and their two children, Rose and Toinou. Then, by the wash-house, was Middle Farm, where Pierre and Lea Cordebulge lived with their son, Huguet. Next came Gravelle Farm, the home of Guillaume and Ninon Gravelle and their children. And finally, at the top of the road, even more isolated than the others, almost on the edge of the woods, was the farm where Edmée and Jousé Verselay lived with their daughter, Regina. It was called Upper Farm. All the menfolk were loggers, cowherds, and river-drivers during the season when the logs were thrown into the streams and rivers and floated down to be sorted at the ports of Vermenton or Clamecy. The women and children helped with the lopping and barking of trees, gathering sticks and bundling firewood. At certain times of the year, they lived more in the forests than in their houses, and some of them camped on the riverbanks when they were floating the logs downstream.

Their faith matched their lives: it was rude and simple, of few words, but firm and strong. Even on the harshest Sundays in winter, they would assemble at the back of the church, huddled together, with their heads bowed, having come more than three kilometres through the snow and ice to get down there. All the same, the priest and his village flock still regarded them with a stubborn sense of mistrust. Could you really keep your soul safe, living the way they did, closer to the trees, brushwood, and beasts than to other men? Didn't you end up consorting one way or another with witches and the like that haunted the shadows of the forest?

Edmée Verselay's faith differed from that of both the villagers and the rest of the hamlet. It had acquired a scope, intensity and imagination that was lacking in everyone else's. It had even acquired a colour: blue – the light blue of the Virgin's mantle on the painted wooden statue that kept vigil in the glimmer of candlelight near the holy-water basin at the entrance to the nave of the church. Above all, it had also acquired a bold fancifulness. There was nothing that did not evoke the Virgin for Edmée, nothing that she did not place under the miraculous protection of the Madonna's blue cloak. For example, if it snowed on the first of May, Edmée's beliefs on this subject went beyond those generally held. In the years when snow fell on this date, women in those parts would carefully collect it from the short grass, from the cracks and crevises in stones, tree-trunks and on the lips of wells, and keep it in glass phials, for the snow that fell on the first day of the month of Mary, so they said, had magical medicinal proper-ties. Edmée went further: she claimed that snow from the first of May could not only cure bodily ills, but even more the ailments and languour of the soul, for this snow, according to her, was none other than the pure tears shed by the Holy Mother of God, suddenly moved to deep tenderness at the thought of the sinners and unhappy souls on earth.

But her great devotion to Mary had turned to total adoration at the birth of her daughter. For it was to the Blessed Virgin, and to Her alone, that she owed the arrival of her only child, her daughter Regina, her passion, her sole possession and progeny – her entire glory. She regarded as practically negligible the part that her husband, Jousé, had played in this pregnancy. All her gratitude went to the Virgin.

Regina was indeed the very remarkable fruit of her womb, which had long remained sterile. The splendid, late fruit that Edmée had persistently hoped for, and with which she had been rewarded for thousands of Hail Marys, counted off on a rosary of boxwood beads that had become like pearls of marble or obsidian through being polished by her stubbornly fervent fingers. And it was in homage to the Virgin, by whose bounty her womb had been blessed with fecundity when she was more than forty years of age, that she had given her daughter the name of Regina. On the birth certificate she had actually inscribed a whole series of other names that followed like a litany of praise: REGINA, Honorée, Victoria, Gloria, Aimée, Grace, Désirée, Beatrix, Marie VERSELAY.

But this miraculous fecundity granted to her seemed to have further proliferated in the body of her daughter. It had run riot, reaching almost monstruous proportions. It was as though each of the other names that came after Regina, like some majestic train, claimed their own body. And instead of each getting a separate body, these names had taken an ample share of hers. The blessed fruit of old Edmée's womb had turned into a veritable orchard, if not a jungle.

As the years passed, Regina had grown extremely fat. In adolescence she had swollen in size like a ripening fruit, an extraordinary, enormous, luminous fruit whose pulp was perpetually expanding, with a soft, smooth skin. Everyone called her Fat-Ginnie, except for Edmée, who used the noble name that she had given her daughter with such pride and joy. The colossal flourishing of her daughter's body that so intrigued or amused other people never bothered her. On the contrary, it simply increased her admiration for her profuse offspring. Edmée did not at all regard Regina's superabundance of flesh as a freak of nature, but as the Holy Mother of God's continued munificence. And the more her daughter increased in size, the more she gave thanks to the Virgin.

What was most extraordinary about Fat-Ginnie was that it was only her body that swelled. Her face, hands, and feet

17

remained unaffected by this too fruitful bounty. The perfect oval of a minute little face peered out from a mass of red hair and a fantastically bloated neck and throat; a miniature face, like a very delicate, graceful mask, that seemed to have been erroneously set on a gigantic figure. And her hands and feet were the same – finely-wrought marvels of exquisite delicacy, wonderful yet ridiculous appendages to her obese form.

Her eyes had a gentle, often vacant expression, and her eyelids always blinked incredibly slowly, like those of a porcelain doll. From her tiny, deep-red mouth came only babbling sounds and soft, tinkling laughter, and sometimes, too, barely discernible whimpers. She tripped along, rather than walked, quaintly bobbing her head and waving her pretty, little-girl's hands about her plethoric bulk, as if always reaching out for invisible support to help shift her phenomenal weight. Her body was too vast and too heavy to be able to move through space easily, but of such vastness that it was in itself a space – a secret space, a labyrinth of flesh enclosed within her rosy-hued, pale skin, through which she was endlessly groping her way. Her own body was a world unto her: garden, forest, mountain plateau, river and sky.

She dwelt solely within her body, where she reigned supreme, inhabiting her dream-crowded flesh in silence, solitude and slowness. For time passed differently in her body from the way it did outside: it went extremely slowly. And she lived ensconced in her huge palace of flesh, a murmuring pile of pink and golden blubber.

But her inward reign was unhappy. Her body-kingdom was a torment and distress to her, for although she always ate in fantastic quantities, daintily consuming in endless little mouthfuls enormous platters of food prepared by her mother, she never succeeded in assuaging her hunger. Hunger haunted her body. And it was the secret of this persistent famine that she sought in her continual interior wanderings. But she could never catch up with her hunger. It fled in all directions, like some small fearless animal, much too swift for the slow drift of time through the pinguid paths of her being; a little wild animal for ever burrowing deep into her flesh, gouging chasms that she had to keep filling as they opened, so as not to collapse in a faint. A cruel, voracious little creature that gnawed right through to her soul, and with piercing cries from every nook and cranny of her body was always demanding more and more food – those cries smothered by mounds of flesh, and perfidiously transformed in her throat into little purls of laughter.

Such was the life that Fat-Ginnie lived – as sovereign in her own magnificent palace of flesh, in thrall to the whims of a ferocious little beast: her hunger. And that is why there were moments when she would sob in despair and helplessness. But her sobs never reached her eyes: just like the strident cries of hunger, they would lose their way inside all that fat, and come rippling through the golden ooze of her palatial body in a slow, unctuous murmur, causing a very gentle wobbling of her flesh. The gaze behind those doll-like eyelids would then become even more vacant. That look of placid bemusement was her way of expressing the frustration of never being able to seize hold of her enemy, hunger, and wring its neck.

Edmée had no more inkling than anyone else of her daughter's desperation. She was blinded by the stupendousness of that quiescent body, a real goddess of fertility's body, which she took pleasure in feeding and adorning. All day long Edmée slaved for her daughter, who spent her whole time enveloped in the torpor of her being, vainly trying to hunt down her hunger. Every morning Edmée prepared a bath for Fat-Ginnie in a huge wooden tub filled with warm water scented with sweet-smelling roots. Then she would help her to dress, arrange her hair, and beautify her. She would wrap her in big shawls, embroidered with brightly coloured flowers, and pin up her heavy, copper-red hair into a chignon, and slip on to her tiny fingers rings made of deal wood polished until it gleamed like amber. She also wound around her neck long strings of glass beads of translucid blue, like so many clinking rosaries. Then, filled with admiration for this living statue of an obese Virgin, she proudly led her into the kitchen and installed her on a bench by the hearth. And Regina would stay there until evening, quietly bubbling now and then with her pretty, sad laughter, her tiny face bent over some piece of needlework to which she absently applied herself. And so she spent her days, sitting by the fire or at the window overlooking the garden, depending on the season, her graceful fingers daintily embroidering and sewing, while Edmée busied herself with the housework in the kitchen, as well as with the various chores in the garden and the farmyard.

Jousé's feelings towards his daughter were more troubled than those that Edmée experienced and solemnly displayed. Fat-Ginnie inspired him with an obscure mixture of amazement, fascination, and dread. What was to become of their colossal offspring, who devoured more food than ten woodcutters without ever seeming satisfied, and who could do nothing but languidly and dreamily draw a needle? Jousé felt old age weigh increasingly heavily upon his body day by day, and he knew that soon he would no longer be fit to work in the neighbouring forests, or to descend the banks of the Cure when the logs were floated downstream. Who would provide for them then? What man would dare take for his wife this doleful mountain of pink and white flesh with no other dowry but her insatiable hunger? And thus he dwelt on his anxiety, not even able to discuss it with Edmée, who would have been outraged by such remarks – and old age weighed only the more heavily on his weary frame.

ONE MORNING AND
EVENING TWILIGHT

And yet there was a man who desired Fat-Ginnie and wanted to take her for his wife. He was the eldest son of Ambroise Mauperthuis, who owned the forests of Saulches, Jalles, and Failly. No one knew how Mauperthuis, the illegitimate son of a local peasant woman, had managed to make his fortune, and by what obscure deviousness he had succeeded in appropriating Vincent Corvol's timber forests. This inexplicable change of fortune had given rise to a great deal of rumourmongering among the people of the forest communities, but there was also a certain pride that emerged from all this gossip, for it was rare that one of their own, a man of the uplands, should lay hands on the property of a man from the valley. The men of the uplands were as poor as their soil, that granite base covered with dark forests, breached by springs and ponds, and scattered with fields and meadows, enclosed by quickset hedges, and with hamlets nestling among the brambles and nettles. Some uplanders even lived in the middle of the forests, in cabins made of logs plastered with a mixture of clay, moss and straw. And Ambroise Mauperthuis had lived among these men of the forests in his childhood. He was one of them – and even more lowly, for he was only a bastard – but his cunning and ruthlessness had made him their master, the owner of the forests where they hired out their labour. And for this reason they both admired and hated him.

They admired and hated him all the more, because, having become rich, he had returned to Oak-Wolf, to live in the village where he was born. He might never have come back to the place he had left as a boy. He might have chosen to stay in Clamecy, where he had settled a long time ago. He might have moved from the shabby

Bethlehem district, where he dwelt among the log-drivers and their families, into the old town centre, and bought himself a fine house with windows overlooking the street, and a big garden. Yet this was not what he wanted. He was satisfied with the farm at Oak-Wolf. And people wondered whether it was nostalgia that had brought him back, or a spirit of revenge.

In the past, Threshold Farm belonged to the Mourrault family, and his mother, Jeanne Mauperthuis, had been their servant. It was there that he was born, and there that he had grown up. Very soon, he was working with the loggers in Jalles Forest, doing all the minor tasks associated with logging. After the death of François Mourrault, his wife Margot had dismissed her servant. Jeanne Mauperthuis had set off with her son to find work on other farms, in the villages of the Yonne valley. But the boy missed the forests. He did not want to become a farm-hand. His love was neither for the land, nor for animals, but for trees. Since he now lived far from the forests but close to the river, he became a log-driver. And so he was reunited with the trees – as they came downstream, dismembered, without roots or branches or leaves, but trees nevertheless. For a while he even worked as a raftsman's mate, in the days when the logs were still rafted down from Clamecy to Paris. He had descended the Yonne and the Seine on the huge log rafts that doubled, or even tripled, in size as they continued downstream. He had entered the port of Charenton, standing barefoot on these giant rafts, holding the long steering pole that resembled a shepherd's tall crook. For days, from sunrise to sunset, he had helped the raftsman drive his fabulous herd of logs between the riverbanks, negotiating perilous currents, narrow channels, and bridges, and bringing it to safety. But he did not have time to become a raftsman in his own right, before the days of the great timber rafts were over. Now the logs were simply thrown into the river and left to themselves to float downstream.

So he stayed in Clamecy, by the banks of the Yonne,

and lived in the Bethlehem district, among all the other log-drivers. He married and had sons there, the last of whom survived only long enough to be christened Nicholas, in honour of the patron saint of riverfolk. The infant was buried with his mother, who died of fever a few days after the birth. Ambroise Mauperthuis was left on his own with his two boys, Ephraim and Marceau, then aged fourteen and twelve. But the following year, he had moved away from Bethlehem, leaving behind the town, the valley, the river and the riverfolk, and returning to live among the woodlanders. He had gone back up into the forests, to the trees that rose straight out of the granite rock. He had chosen to come back to where he was born. Threshold Farm was empty. Margot Mourrault was long dead, with no heirs to inherit the house that was beginning to fall into ruin. Since the line of succession to it was broken, he was able to buy the farm. He had repaired and enlarged it, had new barns and cowsheds built, and acquired the surrounding land. And there he had settled as master.

St Nicholas, patron of the riverfolk, had not deigned to lend his protection either to Ambroise Mauperthuis' last-born son, who had been named after him, or to the mother who had chosen this name for her child. St Nicholas had turned away from Mauperthuis, and reminded him that he was not a riverman. But what did Ambroise Mauperthuis care, since this disfavour was outmatched by sorcery? In the weeks following his bereavement, he found other protection, offered not by a saint but by some necromantic spirit of the forest encountered on the river-bank. He encountered beauty, and found wealth. Just a brief and terrible glimpse of beauty, as though caught in a flash of lightning. And from that moment, something had grafted itself on to his heart, sinking rugged roots into it, and ensnaring it like some pungent and heady-smelling ivy. He encountered beauty – it had the tang of anger. And this tang of anger had haunted his life ever since.

He did not remarry. He had absolutely no desire to take

another wife. He dismissed every proposition put to him. His choice of wife and lover had been made, once and for all, a choice as unique, final, and imperative as it was impossible. It had been made, suddenly, on a day of beauty, anger and blood. It had been imposed upon him, and it was madness that imposed it.

After he became rich, he engaged an old woman to take care of the house – people called her the Wagger, because she was always wagging her head like a pendulum. All his matrimonial designs became focused on his sons. It was his intention that his elder son Ephraim should marry Corvol's daughter, Claude. He was waiting until they were both old enough to wed. This would be in less than two years' time. As for his younger son, Marceau, he would choose for him a wife worthy of his new circumstances. But it was the marriage between Ephraim and Claude Corvol that mattered most to him. Indeed, it mattered to him more than anything else.

It was not enough that he had enriched himself, and extorted Vincent Corvol's three forests from him. He wanted to take his daughter as well, and uproot her from her home on the banks of the Yonne, and keep her here, in the seclusion of the forests. He wanted to swallow up even Corvol's name, assimilating it into his own. Corvol also had a son, Leger, but he was such a weak and sickly child that there was certainly no danger of his being able to produce any offspring. So when Ephraim announced his decision to take as his wife not the one who had been chosen for him, but that enormous, indolent girl from Upper Farm, Ambroise Mauperthuis was extremely angry. For this was much worse than an act of disobedience, it was a betrayal, an outrage – a theft that robbed him of Corvol's name, losing him the prey that he had been stalking for almost five years. He raged against Ephraim's decision. He threatened to disinherit and disown him. And yet that was what happened.

It happened with remarkable simplicity and speed. They

made bread in the village twice a month. Ephraim fell in love with Fat-Ginnie on the first baking-day in October, and he married her the day after the second baking-day of the same month.

He had gone to Upper Farm because Edmée was famous for her expert knowledge of medicinal herbs and the preparation of salves. The previous evening, Marceau had seriously burned his foot, trying to kick back into the hearth a log that had rolled out. His sock had caught fire and the flames had left the sole of his foot raw. The pain had kept him awake all night long. In the morning, not wanting to leave Marceau's bedside, the Wagger had sent Ephraim to fetch a remedy from Edmée. Ephraim had arrived at Upper Farm very early. The sun had not yet risen, but there was already a red glow at the kitchen window. Edmée was preparing the oven to bake the bread, having kneaded the dough at dawn. When Ephraim entered the kitchen, he was struck by the heat inside and by the rosy reflections rippling on the surface of the walls. Edmée had just lit the broom and dry wood filling the oven. The wood snapped and crackled and curled up, the twigs turning from bright red to translucent yellow, then bursting into tiny fragments, like pink and gold salt crystals. With her sleeves rolled up almost to her shoulders, Edmée was streaming with sweat, as she busied herself at the mouth of the roaring oven. The big kitchen table was covered with wicker baskets containing the dough. Fat-Ginnie lay stretched out on a long bench very close to the oven, with her bust slightly raised. Her little face was turned to the fire, her gaze fixed upon the flames. In fact her gaze was more rapt than fixed. Her pretty, pale-blue eyes, like those of a porcelain doll, stared into the flames, whose brightness made them glisten with the transparency of tears – but tears devoid of any emotion, that neither welled nor trickled from her eyes. Still, gentle tears, like pools of rain-water in the hollow of a rock. Doll's tears.

She had got up early to watch the bread being baked, an oral ritual that enchanted her more than any other. This glowing-red, crackling, blazing oven yawned before her entranced eyes like some magic mouth. A mouth equal to her hunger, where the dough, thrust in on a broad shovel, began to swell and crust and acquire flavour and consistency. Her own mouth became one with the scarlet mouth of the oven and her tongue with the shovel that was soon to slide the dough into it. Saliva came rushing to her lips. And the hunger in her body was excited.

She was still in her night-shirt and had not yet pinned up her hair, which lay spread over her shoulders and tumbled down her back, a long, coruscating wave of copper-brown, with red and honey-coloured glints. Her hair was indistinguishable from the flames of the oven, with the same flickering movement on hair and flames, the same tremulousness, the same blaze of light. Her hair seemed a molten substance, a flow of lava, bronze, and gold. A flow of flesh and earth combined, of saliva and blood streaming from the jaws of some fabulous creature. A flow of mud, sap and sunshine pouring from a tree-god's flanks.

Oven and hair – one same hunger protested itself, writhing and murmuring, in both. A hunger in no way related to want, but to superabundance. A joyous, festive hunger. And Fat-Ginnie's enormous body, clothed in a simple, white linen shirt and langourously stretched out on the bench, was like the balls of dough in the wicker bread-baskets. A soft, white dough, all risen with the fermentation of the yeast. A soft, white skin, all distended with the infinite expansion of flesh. And suddenly Ephraim saw Fat-Ginnie as he had never seen her before. It was no longer the obese girl from Upper Farm that he beheld, but a radiant goddess of flesh and desire.

Oven and hair, dough and flesh, bread and woman, hunger and desire – these all came together in Ephraim's eyes, and in his mouth, all blending and crying aloud within his body. Shimmering gleams danced all around him. Her hair gathered him up like a huge wave. The wood crackled in his muscles, sputtering along his veins

26

and nerves. The heat flared in his stomach and in his back, and the young girl's ample, placid flesh kept rising inside him like a miraculous dough. But what riveted Ephraim's attention more than anything else were Fat-Ginnie's bare feet – her tiny, delicate, white feet that showed beneath her long night-shirt and gently dangled in the air from the end of the bench. Those graceful little feet seemed independent of that heavy, corpulent body; so much so that Ephraim thought he could feel their gentle pressure on his torso, as though they had detached themselves from her body, and were gaily tripping about in space. They drummed on his chest, and he felt his racing heart inside his ribcage beating to the same rhythm as the tapping of those unattached, playful little feet. And he was so flustered that when he announced the purpose of his visit, instead of telling how his brother Marceau had burned his foot on a blazing log, he said that two little feet were burning his heart. He recovered himself, and finally explained his presence.

Since Edmée had started to clear and clean out the oven, which was now at the right temperature for baking, and could not interrupt her work, she told Fat-Ginnie to go and fetch from the greenhouse a pot containing lily petals steeped in camomile oil. And as she dusted the bread shovel with a little flour and tipped on to it the contents of one of the bread baskets, she described to Ephraim how this ointment should be used. But Ephraim was not listening; he barely heard her. He noticed only the sound of Fat-Ginnie's feet lightly touching the ground. She rocked slightly as she walked, an almost indiscernible roll causing the massive body beneath her night-shirt, and her abundant, flowing hair, to sway, while her tiny feet seemed to feel their way forward with the smallest, bobbing steps.

It was not just upon his heart that Fat-Ginnie's little feet now drummed, but also on his back, his stomach, and in the hollow of his groin. Her feet rapped him repeatedly, marking him with invisible, fleeting signs, just as loggers mark the trees destined for felling. And at that moment his whole body yearned for nothing else but to let his entire weight fall upon Fat-Ginnie's wonderfully extravagant body, and to give full vent to the cry of desire soaring inside him until it culminated in a gasp of pleasure. Then, as Edmée quickly closed the oven door, having just slipped the dough inside, Ephraim made a second request. Without any further thought, he asked for Regina's hand in marriage. His desire had suddenly become so profound, so intense, that it vastly exceeded any capacity for thought. His desire had imposed itself as law, fact and necessity.

Her face all shiny with sweat and rosy from the heat, Edmée turned to Ephraim and gave him a piercing look that threw out more sparks than the mouth of the oven. She was sizing him up. For all that he was Mauperthuis' elder son, was this ordinary mortal worthy of taking as his wife her unique and truly wondrous daughter? Admittedly, marriage was in the order of things, and Regina was now seventeen – but was Regina, whose glorious advent into this world was due solely to the grace of the Most Holy Mother of God, subject to the common order of things?

'Have to think about it,' she said eventually, wiping her brow. At that moment Fat-Ginnie reappeared in the kitchen, with little dancing steps, holding the pot of lily petals in her hands. She set it down on the table and immediately resumed her position on the bench, without paying any further attention to the visitor, quite delighted by the sweet smell of the bread cooking.

'Have to think about it,' Edmée said again. 'Come back this evening, when Jousé will be home. We need to discuss it.'

Ephraim returned to Threshold Farm with the pot, which he gave to the Wagger. The ointment soothed Marceau's pain. Then Ephraim went off to meet his father in Saulches Forest. The timber market held at Château-Chinon on All Saints' Day was approaching, and Ambroise Mauperthuis was carrying out a thorough inspection of his trees before deciding on the felling to be done during the winter, bearing in mind what the sales would be. For though he had become a property owner, he still remained a logger at heart - it was in his blood – and he did not rely on any intermediary to value his trees.

It was only on the way back, as the light was beginning to fade, that Ephraim told his father of his decision. Ambroise made his son repeat his announcement three times, as though to convince himself that he was not dreaming, and that Ephraim was serious. Then he said no. His refusal was delivered in the manner of an axe striking at the foot of a tree condemned to be felled. It was an irreversible no, allowing of no discussion and no appeal. But Ephraim said that it made no difference, that his decision had been made, and was even more irrevocable than his father's refusal. Ambroise then turned to threats – of disowning his son, and disinheriting him. Ephraim listened in silence, nodding his head. He knew how sparing of words his father was, that he never said anything he did not mean, and kept every vow he made, for good or ill. His father was about to disown and disinherit him for ever. He accepted this price.

'Do as you wish,' Ephraim contented himself with replying. 'And I shall do likewise. I'm going to marry Regina Verselay.'

Until then, both men had kept walking. But at that moment Ambroise Mauperthuis stopped. Ephraim also stopped. The last glimmerings of daylight were turning violet behind the mountains, and the forests were gathering into a mass of purple, like some gigantic sow's belly, from which the darkness was to rise. The two men stood face to face, their features thrown into relief by the encroaching dusk. In silence, Ephraim's father unfastened his belt, took it off, gripped it by the buckle, then flung his arm back, so as to give greater strength and impetus to his action. He looked his son straight in the eye. Ephraim steadily returned his gaze.

'Renounce!' shouted Ambroise, still curbing his gesture. 'The Corvol girl will be your wife! No other, do you hear, no other!'

'I renounce,' Ephraim replied in a calm voice, 'I renounce

you and your woods. I'm going to marry Regina Verse-lay.'

Then Ambroise let fly his arm, lashing his son right across the face with his belt. It struck Ephraim from his temple to his neck, cutting him all down one side of his face. He was marked. He was the condemned tree, the spurned son. The one destined to fall. But he would come down of his own free will, carried by the sole weight of his desire, and it was upon Regina's body that he would fall. He clenched his jaw and his fists under the onslaught of pain, but said nothing and did not flinch. Blood flowed down his cheek. He seemed to feel again the heat of the bread oven at Upper Farm. He had not averted his gaze from his father's face, but that ugly face, strained with anger, was already receding, growing blurred in the evening shadows, and again his perceptions became confused, everything writhing and swelling in the same reddish glow – the last clouds in the sky, the blood running down his cheek, the blaze of the bread oven at Upper Farm, Regina's hair. He felt simultaneously his present pain and future pleasure, hunger and desire, anger and joy. Ambroise Mauperthuis let his arm fall.

'Well, that's that, Father,' said Ephraim in a dull voice.

'Never call me Father again! From now on, I have only one son. An only son, Marceau. You're dead, like Nicholas. You don't exist any more! And Marceau will marry the Corvol girl, I swear to it. Then he alone will have the woods. And you, nothing! You can sink into destitution, and turn to begging to feed your fat wife! You'll not get any money from me, that's for sure!'

Ephraim started to walk off. Then having gone a few steps, he stopped and turned to his father. 'By the way,' he said, 'how did you steal these forests? At the cost of what foul play, eh?'

It was the first time Ephraim had ever made any reference to the highly dubious obscurity surrounding his father's acquisition of Vincent Corvol's woods. Ambroise Mauperthuis jumped, like a startled animal that yet remained ready to attack.

'Go to hell!' he roared, brandishing his belt once more.

Ephraim turned his back on him and descended to the village, cutting across the fields.

Ambroise Mauperthuis took the road home. His hands were still trembling with anger. But at that moment Ephraim's parting question preyed on him even more than his stubborn determination to marry that fat Verselay girl. Did his own son suspect something? Could Ephraim have succeeded in penetrating the dark secret of his wealth? It was not that it worried Ambroise that his secret might have been discovered, but he was jealous of it, like a lover of his mistress. No, it was impossible. No one could steal it from him. The secret belonged to just two men – Corvol and himself, and it was even less in Corvol's interest than his own to reveal it, even by the slightest allusion. For the secret had a name and a body – a name never mentioned now, and a body that had disappeared. This secret was called Catherine Corvol.

GREEN EYES

Catherine Corvol – Vincent Corvol's wife, whom every-body, both in the valley and in the forest hamlets, believed had gone away. Vincent Corvol claimed that his wife had walked out on him, leaving him on his own with the two children, Claude and Leger, and run off to Paris to join another man. Her departure had not really surprised anyone, for people had always thought that Catherine Corvol was a woman possessed by the devil. She was known to have had more than one lover in the region. After her disappearance, rumour had it that there had been many others besides. Vincent Corvol then became an object of both pity and scorn among local people.

It was true that his wife had left him. She had run away from home one spring morning, before daybreak. She had fled the house on the banks of the Yonne, a provincial life, and above all her husband – a husband that she had never been able to love and had grown to hate. It was true that she had abandoned everything, even her two children with big grey eyes and such pale, silent faces, like masks of sadness. She had fled that little family theatre in which was played out in an unchanging decor only one perpetual scene: her loneliness amid hatred, boredom and sadness. She had fled the numbing of her senses, a somniferous life, the slow petrification of her body.

For it was true that she was possessed by the devil: the devil of desire, movement, and joy. And her beauty had the sharp, luminous brilliance kindled by that enjoyment of living in those whose hearts are enamoured of space and speed.

She had fled, but as fast as she had run that morning, she had not succeeded in catching the train for Paris. Her husband had caught up with her at dawn, on the road to Clamecy, as she was hurrying for the Paris train. They had argued, he trying to force her to return home, she bent on leaving. Corvol had finally dragged her away from the road on to the bank of the Yonne. They had gone tumbling down the embankment, rolling in the dew-spangled scrub. Having picked themselves up, they began wrestling again, but without shouting at each other. The longer their tussle went on, the heavier their silence became. This took place above the narrows at Clamecy, at the time of year when all the logs floated downstream from the Morvan heights reach the town. The night had been mild. The valley's riverbanks were bursting into bloom with the arrival of spring, and Ambroise Mauperthuis, who was one of those whose job it was to keep the logs floating freely, had slept out in the open, by the side of the log-filled, log-reverberating river. It was almost impossible to see the water any more; it seemed to be entirely full of wood. The dismembered bodies of the oaks and beeches from Saulches Forest drifted through the valley, from village to village on the way to town, like some vast, slow-moving, grey herd that made a continuous, low-pitched growling. This was the trees' last song, their sombre lament as they rumbled downstream.

It was beginning to grow light. Ambroise Mauperthuis had woken all of a sudden. He did not understand what it was that had roused him from his sleep. It was a kind of silence: a very strange silence that did not rise from the earth, nor emanate from the water or the timber, nor descend from the sky. There were still the same sounds around, but alongside the rustling of the leaves and the din from the river, an amazing quietness reigned, which seemed to drive all these sounds into the distance. A penetrating, dense and implacable silence that only became more intense. It crept under Ambroise Mauperthuis' skin, like a cold sweat. He stood up, still listening to that silence that was not of land, nor sky, nor water. And suddenly he had seen them. Over on the other side of the river, directly opposite him, a man and a woman were wrestling with each other. It was from them, their tussle, their hatred, that the silence had risen in the rosy light of dawn. Ambroise Mauperthuis could not distinguish their faces. All he could see were two silhouettes clasping each other and pushing each other away in a quick and supple dance. Did this couple exist, or were they just a dream that had sprung from Mauperthuis' sleep? A dream that had escaped his sleep and gone rushing along the riverbank, like the flittering glow of a will-o'-the-wisp.

But the silence radiating from this couple was so dense, almost tangible, that it could not emanate from a dream. Such a silence could only issue from bodies of flesh and blood – and only presage death. Ambroise Mauperthuis noticed at once, through the silence, the stridence of extreme violence. But before he had time to cry out and break this deadly silence, the woman had staggered and collapsed. The man had just stabbed her in the throat. The couple broke apart. And it was at that moment that Ambroise Mauperthuis recognized Victor Corvol, proprietor of the forests of Saulches, Jalles, and Failly. The very same Corvol whose timber, sawn up into thousands upon thousands of logs, each bearing the distinctive mark of their owner – a C inside the shape of a bell – Ambroise Mauperthuis was even now conducting downstream. He had then been seized with a fulminating, vicious joy, suddenly feeling illuminated by the crime he had just witnessed, as though by a storm's harsh, incandescent lightning. He had drawn himself up, and shouted Corvol's name in a glad, ringing voice.

Corvol had stood stock-still, riveted to the bank by the sound of his name called out from across the river – as though he had just been struck in the back by the echo of his murderous deed resounding through the valley. As though the vast muster of floating logs stamped with his initial had started chanting in unison the name of their owner. As though all this timber that made him rich had proclaimed his name. As though all his trees had come down from the Morvan heights to surprise him at the moment of his crime and to denounce him by name to the entire valley. The name of an assassin.

His crime had turned against him, no sooner than he had committed it. At Mauperthuis' call, Victor Corvol had at once felt as if he had been exposed before heaven and earth, before men, birds, trees, God, and above all himself. It was Mauperthuis' call that had turned his crime back on his own heart before he even realized what he had done. And he just stood there, bent over Catherine's body, with his arms dangling, dripping with blood. And while he remained there, petrified, Ambroise Mauperthuis gained the nearest footbridge and crossed the river to join Corvol. And having halted two yards behind him, Mauperthuis told Corvol to leave, to go home, that he, Mauperthuis, would take care of removing the body and all traces of the crime. Afterwards he would come and see him – that evening on the edge of the spinny by Corvol's house on the outskirts of town. Then he would lay down the conditions of his silence. The other man listened without turning towards the stranger who spoke at his back in a voice still blithe and yet so harsh. He listened in silence, then departed. Corvol was already defeated. Like a blind man, he obeyed the orders issued by this person who had appeared from who knows where – from the river, from among the logs of beech and oak, like some obscure water spirit or sylvan daemon, a terrifying genius born of the very crime that he had committed – a cruel and ruthless genius that would never let him go, that gripped his conscience like the jaws of a dog holding its prey by the neck. With a kind of smile.

Victor Corvol slowly walked away, without even turning round, with his shoulders dreadfully hunched. His whole body seemed to have shrunk, as if he were trying to take up as little space as possible. He climbed the bank, with his hands still hanging loosely at his sides, like two dead birds – hands on which the blood that had spurted from Catherine's throat was already drying. And this blood was becoming engrained under his skin, penetrating his flesh right through to his heart. This blood made him feel sick.

Ambroise Mauperthuis watched him go. He noticed how Corvol's rather tall, heavy frame had just changed, suddenly appearing quite stunted and stiff. And Mauperthuis thought, 'This is only the beginning! I shall reduce you the way that a branch is lopped and cut down to a piece of kindling! I shall twist and break you like a dead twig!' And he added with gleeful rancour, 'I'm the master from now on!' Then he turned to the woman lying in the grass.

Her eyes were still open. They were a bright, luminous green, flecked with gold. The kind of green that arouses the wariness of peasants and woodcutters, who suspect women with such coloured eyes of occult dealings with evil spirits and of fatal powers of bewitchment. There were still some old folk who would hastily cross themselves if they accidentally met the gaze of a woman with green eyes. Eyes the colour of mythical serpent's skin that glistens in the waters of streams. A green river-snake.

Her eyes were slightly slanted towards her temples. Her nose was very thin and straight: a pure line that emphasized her somewhat slitted eyelids and the arch of her eyebrows. Her mouth was large, splendid, clay-coloured. Ambroise Mauperthuis had often heard talk of Catherin Corvol's beauty, but he had not suspected how vital it was, how grave and sensual. And how strange. A surprising, troubling beauty that attracted not so much admiration as desire and passion. A beauty that grabbed a man by the throat, like a smothered cry, a husky song, a taste of acid. A beauty not yet spoiled by death's chill. Indeed, the violent death that had just claimed Catherine gave her face an even stronger expression, a look of absolute, bold candour.

Then all the acrimonious joy that had welled up in Ambroise Mauperthuis' heart suddenly blackened, and curdled, and he was again overcome by anger alone. A now sombre, cold anger, against Victor Corvol, who had dared to cut off from the world such beauty. And as he knelt down beside the corpse, to carry it away from the bank and bury it in a thicket, he had suddenly fallen on the woman's body and rubbed his head against her neck. For a moment he held her in his arms, she looking all the more devastatingly beautiful for having just been snatched by death. He challenged death for this beauty, with all the force of desire suddenly stricken with despair. And the sound of the logs floating in the water in that instant acquired a new resonance of terrible deepness and power: as if all the bells crudely carved on the logs had just started clanging in the river and were all tolling in unison with the striking of a single clapper – the letter C inside each one.

C for Corvol, C for Catherine, C for the cyclone of rage and grief that swept over him, as Catherine Corvol's heart, like a bell-clapper, beat out across the water in the wood of all the trees. For one last time on this earth, one last, miraculous time, Catherine Corvol's heart beat against a man's chest. For Ambroise Mauperthuis felt against his breast the woman's heart-beat, he felt in his own heart the beating of hers. It was then that madness breached his heart. Ambroise Mauperthuis had just been seized by madness – for, though she was now his, he could never be this woman's lover.

The blood of her wound was still wet, and he licked it as an animal licks an open wound in its side. He no longer distinguished Catherine's body from his own. Her beauty in death was a wound in his self. The blood that he licked flowed equally from himself as from her, and was as much the blood of life as that of death. He licked the blood of beauty and desire. He licked the blood of anger. He buried his head in the hollow of her shoulder, and his hands in her hair – blonde hair that still retained life's warmth and smell. He kissed her temples and eyelids, he sucked her parted lips.

Then he gently lifted Catherine's body and laid it near some bushes. There he scraped at the earth with a stone and buried the body as deep as possible amid the scrub and thistles. Before covering Catherine with earth and stones, he slipped under her neck a log from the river, and laid Corvol's knife on her breast, like a crucifix placed in a corpse's hands so that the dead person does not enter upon death as a pagan. Or like a coin placed in its palm, so that the deceased's soul is able to pay for the right to pass on to the afterlife. Because there is a price for everything, and Ambroise Mauperthuis made no distinction between this world and the next. He wanted Catherine to be able to accuse her husband-murderer among the forces of the hereafter, and to set as high as possible the price that Corvol would have to pay in retribution.

Before it was completely light, he had removed all traces of the crime – all traces detectable to human eyes, but not to the implacable gaze of those in the realms of the invisible. Catherine, lying dead beneath the earth and trees, held in her hands the knife that her husband had stuck in her throat, and this would become known even to the roots of the trees, the mud, and the creatures that lived beneath the earth and in the waters of the river. Mankind might remain ignorant of this crime, but the earth itself would know of it. From the valley floor to the upland forests, the earth was bound to know, and to take revenge on Corvol, who had stolen beauty.

On the spot where Catherine had fallen and bled, he had lit a fire made of twigs and brambles. The grass and her blood had been turned to ashes, already scattered over the bank by the morning breeze. No one could have suspected what had happened here an hour earlier. And no one would ever know. It was a secret shared only by Corvol and himself. A secret that did not frighten him, as it did Corvol, but of which he was jealous. He knew even more than Corvol, for he alone knew where Catherine's body lay. And even more importantly, he alone knew the taste of Catherine's blood. And he was the last to have laid his head against her throat and put his lips to her neck and mouth; the last to have stroked her hair and breathed the fragrance of her skin.

But what even he did not know, although it was something that was to cleave to him for ever, was that he was the last man to have fallen desperately in love with Catherine Corvol, having seen her lying on the grass bank, looking up at the sky, her almond-shaped eyes, still a brilliant green, gazing at the rosy vastness of dawn. On her slightly parted lips lingered the roar of incredible silence that had preceded the crime, and set into her throat was a kind of second mouth, from which the blood of this mad silence flowed. This image was to remain engraved in him for ever: an eternally enduring image resonant with the clanging of thousands of wooden bells; an haunting image, endlessly, unstintingly proclaiming an extreme beauty – extreme in its violence, desire, pain and vitality. A beauty struck down in all its verve, crushed in its revolt, sundered from its body.

This was what Ambroise Mauperthuis had seen: the ravishment of this beauty from the face that had forged it, gaining it day by day, year by year, elevating it from the viscera of a rebellious, desirous body; the ravishment of this beauty from its own flesh, like a mask of green fire. It was this that he had seen: the fulgurating imponderability of that face on the brink of the unknown, teetering on death; that final blaze of beauty at the moment of slipping into the mystery of extinction. This was all he had seen: Catherine Corvol's beauty exposed in death's seizure. And this was what he had not been able to stop seeing, day and night ever since. At night especially. From the morning when he had encountered Catherine's beauty – and she dead – he had spent every night in bed lying still, with his neck resting on a log like the one that he had placed under Catherine's neck before burying her. But this oak log, taken from the river that morning, bore two identification marks – Corvol's and his own, which he had added. When he became owner of Corvol's forests, he had ordered a mallet to be made for marking the trees with his symbol – an M within a sun.

When he met Victor Corvol that evening, at the place where he had arranged to see him, he spoke to him in an

39

even harsher tone than on the riverbank that morning. A harsh tone that had already lost any edge of playfulness. For in the meantime Catherine's face had taken possession of him, Catherine's beauty bared in death had been revealed to him – like some extraordinary secret, both terrible and sacred – and in the same instant destroyed. And this destruction called for an equal vengeance. Catherine's hatred of her husband, her silent anger, and her fight to the death had overwhelmed him, invading his heart. For him, the jobbing workman, the bastard child, the log-driver from the densely populated outlying district of Bethlehem, it was no longer a matter of simply seizing the opportunity for revenge against a rich man for whom he laboured, season after season, in order to survive, but of wreaking a much graver vengeance. Catherine Corvol's blood was now mingled with his own, carrying a mute cry through his veins, a persistent clamour for revenge. The blood that had blackened on the grassy bank had become a macabre incantation in Ambroise Mauperthuis' heart.

Then he told Victor Corvol that he would keep silent about what he knew on two conditions: that in a year's time Corvol made over to him in the presence of a notary the three upland forests of Saulches, Jalles and Failly, and that he gave his daughter Claude to Mauperthuis' elder son as soon as she was eighteen. This second demand only occurred to him after he had discovered Catherine's beauty. What he wanted by laying claim to Claude was something of Catherine's body; it was to gain possession, through his elder son, of a woman born of Catherine's flesh; and through their children to conjoin their flesh and blood. This was the price of his silence. This was all he demanded, and all he ever would, but if Corvol did not keep these two promises, Mauperthuis would at once denounce him. For he had the evidence, and he alone knew where the body was. Corvol agreed to everything. And he had kept the first of these promises: less than a year later, he made over his forests to Ambroise Mauperthuis.

The surprise prompted by this act of recklessness, which

no one understood, was tempered by the fact that ever
since his wife had run off 'that poor fellow Corvol hasn't
been the same'. People said that when she deserted him,
Catherine Corvol must have carried away in her bags some
of her husband's sanity. He did not go out any more, never
laughed or even smiled now, and no one was ever invited
into his home. He lived as a recluse, in his house on the
banks of the Yonne, with his two still sadder, paler children.
But he did not even talk to his children. He not so much
inhabited his house as haunted it, like some chilly ghost,
remaining locked in his study all day long. And there he
would sit with his hands resting palms down on the table,
contemplating them for hours on end with constant terror
and amazement.

People were not completely mistaken when they said
that by going away his wife had partly bereft him of his
wits. But she had done worse than that: when she fell after
he had stabbed her with a knife, she had deranged what
little of his right mind he was left with. And the sound of
Mauperthuis' voice calling his name across the river had
crystallized that derangement for ever. What Mauperthuis
did not understand was that Corvol had accepted the price
of his silence without any argument not through fear of
being denounced but in order to surrender himself directly
to a punishment that matched his crime in its vileness and
offensiveness. His own crime so horrified him that no
prison could have contained it. But this woodman with his
rough, set face, fierce eyes, and harsh voice, who had risen
from the river like some evil spirit, a dark genius of the
forests – this brute resembled his misdeed. Corvol saw in
Mauperthuis the embodied essence of his crime come to
torment him without end, and not to judge him. He
needed to be tormented, humiliated, and despoiled, but not
to be judged. No one could have judged him more severely
than he judged himself. He was not answerable to the
laws of men, he had transgressed far beyond their jurisdic-
tion. He was now answerable only to some obscure law, a
mad, much crueller law, that assailed his heart and soul

41

incessantly, raking them over like a pile of ever-glowing embers. Mauperthuis embodied this law, this expiatory madness, and Corvol submitted to it.

AN OCTOBER WEDDING

When he reached the village, Ephraim stopped at Upper Farm. He found Edmée and Jousé sitting at the kitchen table. Fat-Ginnie was dozing on the bench by the hearth. She was wrapped in a big, flowery shawl, with her hair up in a bun. When Edmée and Jousé saw Ephraim come in with a long, raw weal down the left side of his face, they rose to their feet. Fat-Ginnie, lost in her daydreams, had not noticed Ephraim's arrival. She gazed absentmindedly into the fire.

'I'm back,' said Ephraim. 'I've asked my father, and this was his reply.' He raised his hand to his face. Then he went on, 'I've come to ask for your daughter Regina's hand in marriage. But I've nothing any more, not even a roof over my head. My father has turned me out of the house.'

Jousé went up to him and took him by the arm. 'Sit down and let's have a drink. Edmée! Bring us some glasses and the brandy. The fact that you're here, son, is cause for celebration, and we must drink to your health. Mauperthuis certainly didn't hold back. He's had a proper go at you there. Edmée! Some compresses, something to treat him with . . .' Old Jousé was circling round in all directions, simultaneously delighted at the arrival of this unhoped-for son-in-law, and worried by the blow he had just received. When Edmée told him that Ephraim Mauperthuis had called that morning and asked to marry their daughter, he had dropped heavily onto the bench and sat there for nearly an hour, beating his knees and saying over and over again, with an idiot grin, 'Well, really! Really and truly!' So there was a man – and one not to be scorned – who was willing to support their daughter. He was completely stupefied with joy. 'Well, really, now fancy that!' He could have danced. It went without saying that he gave his consent. But Edmée was more cautious, and had shown no joy or pride. The honour for her consisted in giving away her daughter, not in acquiring a son-in-law. She hesitated, and all day long mumbled incessantly, 'We'll have to think about it', without even knowing what it was that needed thinking about. As for Fat-Ginnie, she appeared totally unmoved by this development concerning herself. All feelings were dormant in her. There was room only for hunger in her heart and thoughts. Marriage, love, desire – none of these things had any meaning for her.

Edmée had remained undecided until Ephraim's return, but when she saw him come in with the side of his face all swollen, she agreed. The wound that Mauperthuis had just inflicted on the son that he not only disowned but left destitute, was in her eyes a sacred mark that made Ephraim worthy of her daughter. If he had come to make his request, all clean and smart in his Sunday suit, as was the custom, she would still not have thought him equal to the position. Her miraculous daughter transcended all custom. But thus wounded and rejected, Ephraim seemed ennobled to her, and even sanctified, as if Eprhaim the orphan, the pauper, the homeless, was now under the Madonna's sole protection. As for Jousé, he did not shrink at the news of Ephraim's disinheritance. It was pity, of course, but he knew Ephraim well, and knew his strength and stamina for work. That was enough. And besides, they had always been poor, they could very well continue to be. They could shift to make room on the farm for the newcomer. The main thing was that there should be someone to carry on.

Edmée sent Fat-Ginnie out to the greenhouse again, then prepared some compresses with churned milk mixed with medicinal herbs to apply to Ephraim's temple and cheek. Meanwhile, the two men drank, sitting face to face across the table, in front of an earthenware demijohn in which Jousé kept his plum brandy. Then Jousé told his daughter to come and sit with them. She meekly came and sat next to her father. Ephraim asked her if she would marry him. She finally looked up at him with her transparent blue eyes, gave a faint smile, and contented herself with a slight nod of the head.

Ephraim remained at Upper Farm. Until the day of the wedding, he slept in the barn. Ambroise Mauperthuis did not visit the Verselays, not even to threaten or abuse them. Whenever he passed in front of their house, he would turn and spit at their door, as a sign of contempt, and then continued on his way. When he met his son on the road or in the forest, he did not even greet him with the brief and guarded acknowledgement that a stranger is warily accorded. He did not greet him at all, as if Ephraim did not exist, or had become invisible to his eyes. And when people tried to reason with him about the marriage, he would stare at them with a look of surprise and reply curtly, 'Who on earth are you talking about? What do you mean? I've only one son, Marceau. I don't know this fellow Ephraim, and your stories are of no interest to me.'

In her devotion to the Virgin Mary, Edmée was grieved by Ambroise Mauperthuis' glacial wrath, and every evening she bathed Ephraim's bruised face with a cloth moistened with melted snow that had fallen on the first of May, so that this humiliated son's wound should not strike root in his heart and give rise to evil with the smack of revenge. She bathed his hurt, both visible and invisible, in the tears of the Most Merciful Mother of God.

Ambroise Mauperthuis did, however, let Ephraim work in his forests, hiring him like any other jobbing woodcutter, but he checked his work more closely than anyone else's and made him do the hardest tasks. He treated like a slave the man who should have been his heir.

The wedding took place before the end of the month, shortly before All Saints' Day. Jousé, Edmée, Regina and Ephraim set out at dawn in a donkey-drawn cart to go down to the main village. Edmée had made a white robe out of some sheets for her monumental daughter, and tied a blue ribbon round her neck – of the same blue as the Virgin's mantle. No one from their own village accompanied them, everyone being fearful of Ambroise Mauperthuis' wrath. But all eyes were watching from behind the curtains as the cart went by. Only the Wagger had quietly toddled down to the edge of the hamlet to embrace Ephraim and give him a few coins from her savings. When the party returned, darkness was already falling. Once again, they traversed the deserted hamlet in silence. But again, people watched from behind their windows. All they could see through the evening mist and freezing drizzle was the broken-winded donkey drawing the cart, its hooves slipping in the mud, and the indistinct figures of the passengers. Three dark figures sat close together in front, with the large white shape of the bride floating along behind like a colossal snow-goddess come to announce the arrival of winter. Amid the silence of falling sleet, they could hear nothing but the faint jingling of bells attached to the ass's harness – a pretty sound, like the tinkling laughter of a somewhat sad child, just like Fat-Ginnie's strange peals of laughter. And perhaps her laughter was mingled with sound of the old ass's harness-bells.

The marriage had been celebrated, and everything regularized. Between Ephraim and his father, too, things were regularized – Ephraim had just legitimized the reason for Ambroise's anger, and made it irreversible.

So he settled down at Upper Farm for good. Ambroise Mauperthuis had wanted, through him, the elder son, to swallow up Corvol's name, and have his own name triumph as master. Eprhaim had given his name to Regina, sharing it with her. He now bore a name that was deprived of power and wealth. He had allied his name with that of the Verselays, shedding the burden of his name by wedding it to the gentleness of the name of Verselay. For Regina's sake, he had lost everything – his status as son, his entitlement to the three forests, his fine home at Threshold Farm, with its huge yard, barns and cattle sheds. He had only recently escaped poverty, and was now cast back into it. But he regretted none of these things. With Regina he had found peace and happiness – what he had found with her was a great deal more extensive than all those tracts of forests, and a much more spacious home than Threshold

Farm. It was a boundless, open land, free of shadows, without any shady transfer of property rights, a deep, soft land, where he loved to lie hidden and dream. It was a sweet palace of white- and rosy-complexioned flesh, in which every night he buried himself to the point of oblivion, forgetful of his fatigue, poverty and daytime loneliness, forgetful especially of the bottled-up hatred against his father that had so bedevilled his heart. And this hatred did not only date from the evening when his father had disowned and cursed him, and lashed him across the face with his belt. This hatred was older. It was a lifelong hatred. For his father had always been brutal and overbearing, his bitter heart full of pride, and with anger in his soul. A heart so hardened that it had not been even slightly affected by his wife's premature death. And this indifference towards his mother's death was already something for which Ephraim had not forgiven his father. But since his father's mysterious enrichment, he had felt an even greater sense of unease about him, an unease steeped in suspicion and loathing. His father had never explained the reasons for Corvol's incomprehensible gift of property. He had never answered any questions put to him on the matter.

'That's the way it is, and that's all there is to it. There's nothing wrong, everything's in order. Corvol and I have been to the notary. I'm the rightful owner of the forests now.'

This was his surly retort to anyone who dared question him, even his own sons. And if they insisted, he would simply flare up in anger. Ephraim sensed that these reasons that his father so obstinately refused to discuss must be dubious, even base and terrible. Right from the start, this suspicion had never left him, developing inside him into waves of nausea. He did not know Victor Corvol's daughter, Claude, whom his father had vowed to make him marry. She might well have been charming and good-hearted. But he could not have loved her. However pretty she might have been, by her mere presence she would have continually kept alive and even fed this unease and loathing

47

inside him. With Fat-Ginnie, on the other hand, he found forgetfulness – of everything. He felt unburdened of his suspicions, purged of his nausea, and delivered of his hatred. Body and hair, flesh and skin – Fat-Ginnie was to him a palace, a land for his possession, a forest of oblivion, and deep in that forest he buried himself, surrendering to the thrill of all his senses, as if the continual hunger that haunted Fat-Ginnie's body blazed labyrinthine paths of perpetual desire through his own flesh. Hunger and desire were for him confounded in a single flaming vortex.

But for Fat-Ginnie, there was no confounding of hunger and desire; they strove against each other. For there was a conflict within her, a silent, bitter and invisible conflict, as though hunger wanted sole dominion over this vast body it had invaded. As though it wanted to excavate an ever keener and sharper hollowness, clearing an inner space in which to establish an absolute virginity, in expectation not of being taken in desire by a man's body, and not of the rapture of flesh and blood. The insatiable hunger that gnawed away at Fat-Ginnie was in fact nothing else but expectation – expectation made flesh and implanted deep inside her. And the yearning was not for a man's body but a body of a completely different order – glory incarnate, a white illumination. And Fat-Ginnie became even more tormented within her palace of flesh, and her long-lasting state of somnolence gave way to a dream-state. She began, as yet very vaguely, to waken to this indefinite expectation that harried her body and soul unsparingly.

And this expectation was so indefinite that she was destined to continue for a long time like this, drifting on from one delay to the next, frantically dividing herself between the bodies around her that, however numerous they became, were not sufficient to her fulfilment and failed to grant her peace at last. For Fat-Ginnie was to bear nine children. The fecundity of her superabundant being was destined to proliferate beyond her own flesh. In the course of time, each of the first names that her mother had given her acquired its own separate corporeality. The big male body that fell upon her every night in search of oblivion and relief from its weariness, poverty, anguish, and silent anger, caused a new fertility to flourish within her.

In the year after her marriage, Fat-Ginnie gave birth to a son. He was born in the first hour of the day on 15th August. And it was always on 15th August that she gave birth to her sons, as if this same day continued to run its course from year to year. Only the hour in which they were born differed. The eldest was born on 15th August at dawn; the fifth child, on 15th August at midday; and the last child in the night of 15th August. Fat-Ginnie and Ephraim's nine sons marked the hours of a single day like some Marian time-keeping device. There were the sons of Morning, Noon, and Evening. Each bore, appended to his first name, the name of Marie, in honour of the Virgin, to whom Edmée had dedicated her miraculous daughter. And in fact, according to Edmée, this line of sons, all born on the day celebrating the glorious Assumption of the Immaculate Mother of God, was simply the repeated echo of the Virgin's gracious response to the countless Ave Marias that she had addressed to the Madonna. And when Regina's last son was born on the night of 15th August, and Edmée noticed that he had a deformity, far from being upset about it, the old woman rejoiced, for she did not see it at all as a misfortune but, quite the contrary, as a final manifestation of the sacred mystery that she had never ceased to live. The child had a harelip. From this, too, Edmée realized that he would be the last, that Regina would bear no more children after him. For this harelip was a sign graven on the child's mouth at the moment of his birth by the Angel of the sacred mystery, so that he, the youngest and last-born, should keep the secret that had been revealed to him in his mother's womb, the secret that had always dwelt in his mother's womb – the secret of her hunger.

For hunger remained an ever-throbbing presence in

Fat-Ginnie. No more than Ephraim's body did the bodies of the nine sons that she carried, bore, and brought up, manage to appease her hunger and fulfil her expectation. But in the course of all those years punctuated by regular childbirths, the dream-state to which marriage had brought her continued to disengage itself from the somnolent torpor in which she had spent her adolescence and youth, and to tend little by little to a greater lucidity. Fat-Ginnie very slowly came close to the surface of consciousness, the dream-haze that had inhabited her gradually clearing. And the prodigious bulk of her body did not weigh so heavily on her as before. She learnt to busy herself, to apply herself to a task, although still with immense deliberateness and infinite precautions. She learnt to live in her dream-state like a sleepwalker, getting about with slow, rather uncertain movements that sometimes appeared even to be painful, and no longer lying all day long stretched out on a bench by the warmth of the hearth. But in the evening after supper, which inevitably left her hunger unsatisfied, she still liked to lie down for a moment in front of the fireplace, and stare into the blue flames. For she was always susceptible to the dream-haze that sprang from her hunger, and to the indefinite expectation that trembled in her heart. And her eyes, with their gentle, absentminded gaze that was always a little melancholy, acquired the transparent blueness of the flames.

It was also during these years that, after a lifetime devoted to self-effacement, Jousé effaced himself totally. He did not wait for the line of his descendants to be completely established. He died before the birth of Fat-Ginnie's third son. He went to bed one evening, and when he closed his eyes for the night he knew that he would never open them again. And this conviction that he was to drift off that night, not into the arms of sleep but death, did not worry him at all.

'I've lived long enough,' he thought. 'I've had my share of this world, and my time has come. My daughter's married now, the children are already growing up, and

50

there's another on the way. There's someone else to carry on – yes, Ephraim and his sons are well able to carry on! Anyway, we're still very poor, and short of space besides. It's only right to make way for others.'

Then he had turned to Edmée, lying beside him. After all, she had been his companion for almost half a century – he owed her one last look before he closed his eyes for ever. Then he had turned his face to the wall. For there are some things that require modesty, and for Jousé, death was one of them.

AN APRIL WEDDING

Having granted Victor Corvol a stay of execution before taking his daughter away from him, Ambroise Mauperthuis did not wait until the period of reprieve had fully elapsed. He waited only until the end of winter. Ephraim's disobedience had exhausted his patience. He could not run the further risk of Marceau's rebelling in his turn, and getting infatuated with some other local girl. So things had to be speeded up. As soon as the snow started to melt, he yoked his two finest oxen, Bachou and Marjolet, to a newly painted cart, and drove down to Clamecy with Marceau. Marceau had no will of his own: he neither wanted nor refused this marriage to which his father compelled him. Since his brother had been driven out of Threshold Farm, and his father had strictly forbidden him to speak to Ephraim, Marceau had been been totally isolated in his loneliness. Just like Eprhaim, he had always felt a sense of unease with regard to his father, but an unease tinged more with fear than loathing. On the other hand, the affection, trust and even admiration that he felt for Eprhaim were absolute and unreserved. And now suddenly that attachment, of such complete openness, was forbidden to him. His father had introduced gloom where before there had been only light, forcing him to take Ephraim's place and steal his entire inheritance. And this was even more painful to Marceau since he felt responsible for Ephraim's downfall, for it was because of him that Ephraim had gone to Upper Farm to ask Edmée Verselay for something to soothe the pain of the burn on his foot. The calamity dated from that day. But he dared not rebel, he dared not say no to the father who so frightened, even terrified, him. All of this past winter he had been wretchedly unhappy, left alone with the old Wagger and his ever broodingly angry father. And now he was being dragged off in his Sunday best to a marry a girl, just as young as himself, who was totally unknown to him.

Victor Corvol welcomed Ambroise Mauperthuis as one might welcome a punishment expected for a long time: the fact that it was early did not make much difference, and that it was harsher than anticipated came as no surprise at all. For Corvol's son, Leger, refused to be parted from his sister, and preferred to go and bury himself in that remote village on the edge of the forests rather than stay without her in the house on the banks of the Yonne. Since his mother's disappearance, he had transferred to his sister all his hurt and betrayed love. And since the day when his mother had run away from home, leaving them behind, he had stopped growing. Time seemed to have been arrested inside him, fossilizing his child's body. At the age of twelve, he looked like a seven-year-old – as if he were awaiting the return of this prodigal mother and feared that when at last she came back she might not recognize her little boy in short trousers, with his thin, white knees. When his mother came home, she had better be made to believe that nothing had happened, that she had only been gone on a short trip to Paris, and not run away for such a long time. She had been gone now for five years. Only with his sister could Leger find the energy to continue his desperate wait. If Claude were to leave him, too, then all his strength would flake, all his hopes would shatter. His little body in its suspended development could only survive if grafted on to his sister's. And so it was that Victor Corvol lost both his children together. Ambroise Mauperthuis had no use for this timorous and sickly child, but he was bent on robbing Corvol of absolutely everything, and on increasing his loneliness and suffering. So he seized this unexpected opportunity and agreed to take the boy.

As for Claude Corvol, she complied with her fate silently, without a word of complaint. Not, like her father, out of morbid submissiveness, but indifference. She really did not take after her mother at all. There was not the faintest resemblance between them, either of appearance or personality. Her eyes were grey, like her father's, her mouth thin, her lips rough, her beauty insipid. She had no spirit, no radiance, no impulse to flee, but rather an austere calmness. The mask of sadness, slipped over her face in childhood, was now an inalienable part of her. The mask her mother had refused to wear. A rebellious, spirited mother, while she, her daughter, seemed to have been born resigned, to loneliness, silence, and boredom. Her mother had run away from the house by the Yonne, from those bedrooms with the stifling, sweet smell of the flowers in the garden, and the languid sound of bronze pendulums slowly ticking away the hours in clouds of ever more suffocating dust. Claude, however, found peace here. She liked to read, walk along the river, do some gardening, and daydream in the shade of the magnolia tree her father had planted for her on the day of her First Communion, or among the trinkets set out on the dark furniture as though in tribute to the stillness that reigned in this quiet provincial house. In the evenings she played the piano in the now deserted drawing room. No one ever visited them any more, and their father never received guests.

But now, after all these years of reclusiveness, her father was receiving a visitor. And without even discussing it, he was willing to entrust her to this rough-mannered person with an uncouth tone of voice. Well, so be it, let this visitor who looked like a common wood-merchant take her away then, but he might as well have taken a dead branch, or some knick-knack, for she would keep her heart closed and her soul hidden. She would remain aloof from these people with whom she consented to leave, preserving her distance.

The wedding was celebrated in Clamecy at the church of St Martin. Ambroise Mauperthuis had insisted on thus drawing attention to the incongruous marriage between his son – the descendant of poverty-stricken woodcutters, and ever the backwoodsman in his ways, with a poor and halting command of speech – and Claude Corvol, of distinguished appearance, the pale and delicate daughter of a ruined bourgeois father, her hands unsuited to any other work than the art of flower-arranging and piano-playing.

He had insisted that the bond that was to unite the Corvols to the Mauperthuis should be sealed publicly – for this bond was a chain, a halter, a whip lash, intended to choke Corvol's pride, and drag his name, like a dog on a leash, to a forest village, and to suppress it there by exacting its submission to the name of Mauperthuis.

But there was another, much more obscure bond that he wished to create by this marriage: a grafting of his scion on to Catherine's stock. Catherine's ancestry and bloodline. An ancestry that had lost its spirit, and a blood grown pale and sluggish in her daughter, Claude. But Ambroise Mauperthuis hoped to see children descended from Catherine wrest themselves from the womb of the girl he had at last acquired as his daughter-in-law, children who would restore vigour and colour to her bloodline. Once having seen Catherine's beauty cast down on the banks of the Yonne like the mask of a pagan goddess, he had been left with a perpetual desire to see her again, to see her over and over again, to the point of rapture. She could not fail to reappear, to come back and dazzle him. For five years he had lived with this frantic hope, this obsessive expectation.

While the very incongruous marriage of Corvol's daughter and Mauperthuis younger son surprised and shocked the burghers of Clamecy, and set their tongues wagging, it caused much greater amazement among the peasants and woodcutters of the forest hamlets. For they were stunned when they saw Mauperthuis' extraordinary wedding carriage ascending the pink granite road, between the brambles and ferns on either side. The two huge, plodding oxen, Bachou and Marjolet, with their light coats and their ivory-coloured horns garlanded with roses and lilies, drew the brilliantly white cart that, as well as the bride and her brother, carried a pile of chests and trunks, and a grand piano. Following behind came a second dray, which Ambroise Mauperthuis had had to hire in Clamecy. A rust-coated ox whose broad, flat brow was crowned with ivy, pulled a large dung-cart on which stood the magnolia dug up from the Corvol's garden. Claude had not wanted to be parted, in her exile, from either her piano or her majestic tree.

The cortege proceded slowly through the village, in bright April sunshine. Walking at the same pace as the oxen, Ambroise and Marceau Mauperthuis each led one of the conveyances, Ambroise the bride's and Marceau the one with the magnolia. Claude, looking even paler than usual in her delicate bridal lace, sat at the front of the cart, with her brother close beside her, gravely playing with a red wooden cup-and-ball. Without even knowing why, the peasants doffed their hats as they went by, as if this were some kind of religious procession, while the children squealed with glee, thinking that what they were seeing was a travelling theatre. All the people of Oak-Wolf, with the exception of those from Upper Farm, were waiting for the wedding party at the edge of the village. But at the sight of the strange caravan they forgot to offer the cheers of welcome with which they had intended to greet the young bride. They stared open-mouthed at the precious lace, the child with the cup-and-ball, the varnished wooden chests and leather trunks, the wonderful tree with its branches already sprouting countless half-open blossoms amid its big, shiny leaves, and above all the huge, black piano from which the odd muffled note escaped. The Wagger, who, like the others, had never in her life seen a piano, raised her hands to her face in terror, thinking that Mauperthuis' daughter-in-law had brought a family coffin with her. Rich folk often have such whims, even about death, thought the Wagger, and what with the Corvols being ruined now, perhaps it was the only valuable thing left to the girl. This big, misshapen coffin of gleaming black, as though laquered with perpetual tears, mournfully sounding with the smothered, doleful plaint of the unquiet soul of some ancestor anguished by this posthumous exile – such was the Corvol girl's entire inheritance, her total dowry. The Wagger crossed herself three times in dread, before returning to the yard of Threshold Farm, where the procession turned in.

It was in the yard that Claude immediately had her magnolia replanted. In the middle of the yard, facing due south so that the boughs could spread themselves in the sunshine. She ordered a big hole to be dug, which was later filled in with a mixture of earth and dung, then covered with turf, and finally scattered with St-John's-wort seeds. Having been thus dug in, the tree would be able to sustain the rigours of Oak-Wolf's soil and climate. And it was not long in displaying the splendour of its fragrant, ivory-coloured flowers outside the front windows of Threshold Farm.

Ambroise Mauperthuis did not like his daughter-in-law. There was nothing about her to remind him of Catherine. She was the living image of her father, a likeness matured and preserved in the gloom of the bedrooms and drawing-rooms of the Corvol's big family house. Mauperthuis had not even succeeded in burying her name in oblivion. Although she was now Madame Mauperthuis, all the local people, whenever they spoke of her, called her La Corvol. For she came from too far away, from the valley, the town, from an old family who until recent years had always been well off. She was too much of a stranger to them to be able to assume a name as familiar to them as that of Mauperthuis, for all that he might now be rich. And anyway, they found her odd; she only ever went out to take a stroll to the edge of the forest, always with her brother at her side, that timid freak of prolonged childhood who was always playing with his cup-and-ball. No one ever heard them laugh, and they never spoke to anybody. Claude seemed not even to notice people. When she was at the farm, she spent all day long in the drawing-room that she had arranged to her own taste, with ornaments brought from the house by the Yonne. The lovely, sad tunes that she played at the piano could be heard at every hour of the day, until late in the evening.

The Wagger said that La Corvol did nothing when she was at home but shut herself up in the drawing-room whose windows looked out over the magnolia tree, and there she sat in front of her big, sonorous catafalque, letting her hands dance over it, playing music that was so unsettling that there were days when even the Wagger herself lost the will to work, and was all but drained of the will to live. What Claude Corvol loved, the Wagger concluded, was not her husband, for sure, but only that spellbinding piano of hers. Truly, it was not life that she loved, but soulful melancholy – nothing but sadness. She was bewitched. And people said to each other that basically La Corvol was the same as her mother – 'the kind that was not like the rest of us'. Except that the mother, who was all fire and passion, with her fiendish beauty and serpent eyes, had cast her spell over men, whereas the daughter, with her ash-grey eyes and delicate, ghost-like appearance, had bewitched herself with the sound of her heart-breaking melodies.

As the years passed, Ambroise Mauperthuis' feelings towards the damned Corvol woman with her inextinguishable name even turned to resentment, for she did not produce any children, while that other one, Edmée's fat daughter, in her hovel at Upper Farm, gave birth to yet another son every year – sons bursting with health and vigour. Already at the age of five, the eldest, Ferdinand-Marie, was capable of pushing his younger brothers around in a wheelbarrow, to accompaniment of great cries. He was known as Ferdinand-the-Strong and it was said that when he grew to manhood he would be able to uproot oak trees with his bare hands. Ambroise Mauperthuis was seized with anger every time he encountered Ephraim's sons- those brazen little devils with their straw-coloured mops of hair and bright-blue eyes, who were always bawling and shouting.

Fat-Ginnie had just given birth to her seventh son when Claude Corvol finally became pregnant. She had to stay in bed throughout her pregnancy in order to bring her child to term. The Wagger and everyone else suspected that this infant would be made of the same stuff as its melancholy mother and dwarf-uncle – delicate and pale, and lacking in spirit and fervour. It was not so. Claude Corvol gave birth to a strong, healthy little girl.

Claude felt no fondness for her child, and what is more she announced that she would never have another. This pregnancy and confinement had been too distressful an ordeal for her. She felt disgust for the human body, and a horror of sexuality. As soon as her daughter was born, she moved into a separate bedroom and never again opened her door to her husband. Marceau made no attempt to knock at the door behind which his wife had retired. He knew too well how devoid of pleasure her bed was, and how lacking in tenderness her body. His wife's bed was even more like a catafalque than her big black piano. They had conceived their daughter in embittered silence, without exchanging the least kiss or gesture of endearment – she enduring this act as a tribulation, with a sense of violent aversion, feeling as though she were suffocating beneath the loathsome weight of her husband's body; and he doing the deed as a duty, with a sense of profound dismay and boredom. So they were the first to be astounded by the character of the child born of their mute, cold, compulsory union: the little girl was playful, merry, and boisterous, and blessed with a sensuous, luminous grace. She was christened Camille.

The energy that Camille put into her enjoyment of life soon came not merely to astound her mother but to annoy and eventually repel her. This repellence only worsened as the years went by. As Camille grew up, she reminded Claude more and more of her own mother, the Jezebel who had abandoned them all – her father, brother and herself – to give full gratification to her body's animal craving for seduction, amusement and pleasure.

So she turned away from her daughter, who revived all too strongly the ever painful memory of her mother. Claude went back to her piano, devoting all her time to it, not taking care of her little girl at all. The Wagger, who had grown too old to assume the job of nurse, left the Mauperthuis' service. Actually, she was far too superstitious to carry in her arms any child with serpent eyes. For it was true that the little girl took after her grandmother, Catherine Corvol. She had the same slightly almond-shaped eyes of a bright, golden green, and the same wide mouth. Snake-green eyes, the Wagger said warily, and added, 'There's the Evil Eye sparkling in those eyes, and woe betide anyone who looks into them too closely.' Then she decided to leave, for it was better to go and die in peace, a pauper, among her own family, in her own village, than to carry on living at Threshold Farm, with a woman that looked like a ghost, who sat all day long at her catafalque-piano extracting sobs and laments from the dead, and a girl-child with serpent eyes. The Wagger was replaced by Adolphine Follin, known as La Fine, who agreed to look after the little one. She had been a widow for two years, and her children, Rose and Toinou, were already married: Rose to Mathieu Gravelle, and Toinou to Celine Gravelle. When it came to marriage in Oak-Wolf, there was not much choice for young people. They married whoever was old enough to become a husband or wife, and the choice available was restricted to Follin Farm and Gravelle Farm. Huguet Cordebugle, who since the death of his parents lived on his own at Middle Farm, had already acquired the manner and idiosyncracies of a surly old bachelor, determined not to marry. Green-eyed or not, all women seemed dubious, even dangerous, to him. He suspected them all of having dealings with the devil, and a madness in their blood ready to break out at any moment. A recluse by choice in his crabby bachelorhood, he tolerated no other company but that of a cockerel as bad-tempered as himself, to which he had given the name Tatave.

It mattered little to Ambroise Mauperthuis that his daughter-in-law would have no other child. He was satisfied with Camille. Through her, Catherine returned to him. She came back to him as a child, to start again right from the beginning, her beauty developing day by day. For there was in this child the promise of the self-same beauty. In Camille, the miracle of that beauty was restored. In her, beauty and desire re-entered the world. And this beauty wrested from death and oblivion was going to grow up at home with him, in his house at the edge of the forests. And already he bore the child a passionate love full of pride, the love of an insanely jealous lover. 'Look at that child with her serpent eyes,' everyone said, 'she already has the old man infatuated with her! There's no denying she's pretty, and with her boldness, she'll be just as much of a seductress as her grandmother from the valley!' And the prediction for when she was older was not that she would uproot oak trees with her bare hands, like Ferdinand-the-Strong, but that she would be capable of bewitching even the trees of the forest, by the sole charm of her serpent-green gaze.

HYMNS

THE BROTHERS

They were men of the forests. And the forests had shaped them in their own image, of like strength, solitude, and hardness. A hardness deriving from that of their common ground, the pale-pink granite rock, millions of centuries old, bubbling with springs, pitted with pools of water, and everywhere jutting out among the grass, ferns, and brambles. Both men and trees were possessed of the same song: a song that had confronted silence and rock since time immemorial, a tuneless song, a brutal song, with the seasons' harshness – oppressively hot summers, and long, snowbound winters. A song composed of cries and calls, resonances and stridences, a song that expressed both joy and anger.

For, with them, everything, even love, acquired a note of anger. They had been raised more among trees than men. They had fed since childhood on the fruits, plants and wild berries that grew in the underwood, and on the flesh of animals that dwelt in the forests. They were familiar with all the courses of the stars across the sky, all the paths that wound their way through the trees, brambles and bushes, with foxes, wild cats and roe-deer slipping through their shadows, as well as the tracks made by boars – these dirt tracks among weeds and thorns as though mirroring those of the Milky Way, and replicating, too, the route taken by pilgrims from Vézelay to Santiago di Compostella. All the age-old byways forged by animals, men and the stars were known to them.

The house where they were born had very soon proved much too small to accommodate them all, and what is more, too poor to feed them. They were the sons of Fat-Ginnie and Ephraim Mauperthuis. All his life – a life as needy as it was unobtrusive – old Jousé Verselay had never taken up much room, and when he left the farm to journey down to the village cemetery, he freed only a very small amount of space.

Every year for nine consecutive years, another boy had been born in that one bedroom at Upper Farm. As these births followed one another, Ephraim had converted the roof space for the older ones, first of all in the attic, and then in the barn, and eventually the older boys had built themselves a cabin made of logs, clay and branches, in Jalles Forest, where they slept on beds of straw. These older boys were the sons of Morning, born between dawn and midday on successive 15ths of August. They were sturdily built, with reddish-fair hair. The ruggedness of their features and their weather-beaten complexions heightened their fairness and the very pale blue of their deep-set eyes beneath their prominent brows.

Ferdinand-Marie exceeded his brothers of the Morning in size and strength – in this, as a man, he lived up to the legends that he had already inspired as a child.

Adrien-Marie exceeded Ferdinand-the-Strong in the force of his laughter. For his was an extraordinary, huge, resounding laugh that it took very little to provoke. And when he laughed, with one of those tremendous outbursts, his eyes became so bright that their colour intensified to a brilliant blue, causing him, by association, to be nicknamed Adrien-the-Blue.

Whereas it was his eldest brother's exceptional strength and the second's exceptional laughter that had given rise to their nicknames, Martin-Marie's sobriquet focused instead on his uncommon reserve: he was called Martin-the-Sparing. Not that he was sparing of any possessions or of his money, for he was far too poor to be able to hoard anything. It was of himself that he was sparing. Sparing of words, feelings, and self-expression, sparing even of his dreams. Fear, hope and doubt were alien to him. He seemed to have been rough-hewn all of a piece, and to have no more inner life than a stone. At work, he never wasted the least movement or effort, which meant that he was remarkably precise and adroit in his actions.

As for Germain-Marie, he was named the Deaf, because he had actually become so, neither by accident nor as a result of an illness, but so as not to hear any more. To stop the pain of hearing. Because from his earliest childhood, all sounds and voices were a torment to him. He could not bear the least noise, not even a whisper or a sigh – in fact, especially not faint sounds. It was as if he had been endowed, or rather afflicted, with hearing of abnormally acute sensitivity. As if each sound broke down inside his ear into countless piercing shrills. In the depths of every sound, he seemed to hear a lamentation, a smothered cry, a sob. Even in silence he discerned confused murmurs, an imperceptible weeping. And everywhere, all the time, he thought he could hear a call – a stray, stark voice emitting a suppliant stridulation, like that of some invisible glass insect. And this call, as incomprehensible as it was persistent, he perceived with particular intensity in the voices and breathing of other people: a haunting, plaintive vibrancy. He had always been distressfully alive to the gentle purly laughter of his mother, Fat-Ginnie, to which others paid so little attention. And even when he had gone to join his three older brothers in their cabin in Jalles Forest, he had continued to suffer from noises, sounds, breathing and voices. Everything reverberated in his ears. The silence was woven with a constant muted murmuring. The night was a riot of whispers, and the trees continually rustling, sighing, creaking, fluttering, whistling or whining. From their roots to their topmost extremities, every tree was for him a sound-box filled with resonances. One day when he was cutting down a beech with Martin-the-Sparing, just as the tree was about to topple he had felt something overturn inside him, at the same speed as the tall, lopped trunk came down. As if the tree had fallen inside him. His axe had slipped from his grasp and he had dropped to his knees on the ground, lifting his hands to his ears and uttering a cry. Then there was a momentary silence, that brief silence that always gathers suddenly around a felled tree after the tremendous noise of its falling. And then Adrien-the-Blue's thunderous laughter had shattered the silence. For this was his way of marking the perfectly executed felling of a tree.

But this time his brother Germain had not heard that great burst of laughter. The dense, heavy silence of the tree-fall had frozen inside him. The felled beech-trunk had come down on his hearing, striking him deaf. And from that day forth, he had remained deaf.

Simon-Marie, the fifth son, the Noon child, was a herdsman. He looked after Ambroise Mauperthuis' oxen that carted the timber from the forests to the banks of the Cure when it was time to float the logs downstream. He lived partly in the cowsheds at Threshold Farm, and some-times went and joined his Morning brothers in the forest. He was called the Hothead, for being as quick to anger as he was easily fired with enthusiasm, and impatient and unrestrained in his words, deeds, and flights of passion. Even Ambroise Mauperthuis was fearful of his fits of anger, but continued to employ him, knowing that he could not have found a better herdsmen in the vicinity. And besides, there was something about Simon-the-Hot-head that he found disquieting, for he recognized more of himself in Simon than in his own sons, Ephraim and Marceau, and at the same time was aware of a resemblance to Camille. Simon's eyes were of a very light hazel, dusted with gold, but he had the same gaze as Camille – a gaze both bold and luminous that settled unveeringly on things, animals and people. Both shared a candour often bordering on insolence, and their vitality was similarly intemperate.

Old Mauperthuis' feelings towards Simon were con-fused, a secret admiration mingled with envy and animos-ity. He could not help having greater esteem for him than for his own sons, and at the same time feeling hostile towards him. The likeness to himself that Ambroise Mau-perthuis detected in Simon-the-Hothead – a likeness both physical and of character – simultaneously brought out the differences between them, for what was warped and hidden and twisted in the one showed itself with impulsiveness and candour in the other. The older man was incessantly devious with his feelings, brooding on his anger and hatred, intensifying them and making them obdurate and vengeful, and he admitted to no one, not even to himself really, his sole, obsessive passion for Catherine Corvol. A tortuous passion that he continued over the years to transfer to their mutual grandchild. The younger man, by contrast, gave free expression to his feelings.

Simon had started working for Ambroise Mauperthuis at about the age of twelve. He, like his brothers, did not think of him as their grandfather. The old man was simply their employer. He was master of the village and of all the other surrounding villages, and owner of the forests where all the men and young lads of the neighbourhood came to hire themselves out as woodcutters. He was a hard, taciturn boss, watchful that the work was well done; a man who inspired neither friendship nor the least sympathy, but who commanded a certain respect for his success, and for the efficiency with which he was able to conduct his business. Yet this respect was always tainted with suspicion and a vague hostility, as the secret of his wealth had never been penetrated. All that Ephraim's sons had in common with him was their name. He had too violently severed any relationship with them even before they were born for them to be able to regard him as their grandparent. Since the evening when he had struck Ephraim across the face, he had never addressed another word to him, except to issue orders when work demanded it. And he treated all his grandsons in the same way, like hired hands on his estate, and he only spoke to them to tell them what to do. His anger towards Ephraim had long ago cooled, but although it had lost its purpose since Marceau's marriage to Claude Corvol, and especially since the birth of Camille, he had not revoked it. His anger towards Ephraim had simply fossilized, and his repudiation of him had become a habit. He was far too proud to go to his son and suggest any reconciliation, particularly as he suspected that Ephraim did not even wish it. He thought that Ephraim harboured a lasting resentment.

In truth, the resentment that had for so long irked and borne down on Ephraim had eventually ebbed away. After initially rankling and festering in his heart, the broken tie of kinship had simply withered away, and this brutal and unjust father now meant nothing to him. He had found so much tenderness and peace at Upper Farm with Edmée and Fat-Ginnie, and then so much joy in his sons that all that had passed between them ceased to weigh on him. He accepted his destiny uncomplainingly, and he had never had cause to regret the choice he made that far-off October morning. So his father could go his own way, and he would go his. Sometimes his sons would rage against Ambroise Mauperthuis, who only ever approached them in the forest to check their work and shout orders in a harsh and scornful tone of voice, and on more than one occasion they had questioned their father about his past, and the reason why he had been disowned. But then Ephraim would content himself with replying, 'That's the way it is. The old man's nothing but a boss to us. He's a rich, hard-hearted man, as unfeeling as a stone. He's the boss, and nothing more. It's no use expecting anything of him – nothing good. He gives us work, and that's sufficient. We're no longer part of his family, you and I. He was the one who wanted it that way, and it's turned out just as well. You should never have any regrets.'

Ephraim did not have any regrets, and he certainly did not envy his brother, Marceau, who had married La Corvol in his stead – the wife who invested all her pride in remaining a total stranger in the village where she had been living now for a quarter of a century. With that cold, haughty woman, he would never have found peace, oblivion and happiness – all of which Regina gave him in abundance, by her mere physical presence, by her huge, calm and loving body, by the gentleness of her voice, her smile, and her movements. And he was proud, moreover, of his sons, especially the sons of Morning, and the one of Noon. He admired the elder boys' strength and stamina at work, and the fifth son's beauty, his radiant freedom of being. These five grappled with life without worrying about their poverty, or minding about their tiredness. It seemed to Ephraim that all the power of his love for Fat-Ginnie had found the incarnation of its vitality in these sons, and in Simon-the-Hothead the visible expression of its joy, beauty and glory.

His feelings towards his other sons, the sons of Evening, were more tinged with astonishment and unease. These sons did not have the extreme vigour of the older ones, nor the radiance of the fifth. The twilight of their evening births seemed to have stolen inside them. They had brown hair, dark eyes, and more anguish than ardour in their hearts. They were neither woodcutters nor herdsmen, although they sometimes worked in the forest when the trees were being marked; they were mainly woodcarvers. Not adept at wielding the axe, their hands were very skilled at fashioning clogs, and wooden kitchenware and implements that they sold at markets and fairs. This quieter, more solitary work suited them. For their desire for solitude was great, and in Leon-Marie even excessive.

As soon as Leon-Marie finished work, he would set off, never in search of company but to penetrate deep into the forest on his own. He so fiercely cherished his solitude that he was called Leon-the-Loner. His passion was for hunting. He had made himself some decoys and was a past master at imitating the calls and song of every bird, and he had also made a bow for shooting fowl. He never ate the flesh of all these birds that he would bring back to the farm, night after night, but he was adamant about plucking them himself. This was a ritual as sacred to him as the chase itself. Afterwards, he would gather up all the plucked feathers, sort them, and then lock them away in a chest in the attic, to which he always carried the key.

Just like Leon-the-Loner, Eloi-Marie would leave the village at every opportunity, not to plunge into the forest seeking birds to kill, but to go and sit by rivers and ponds. There, he liked to remain still and silent, fishing and dreaming. For he never tired of dreaming – dreaming of imaginary and impossible elsewheres. Not that he wanted to leave his village and go and live in a town, or in some other place; the elsewhere that he pined for was not a place. It was an unidentifiable landscape, immense and flat, like a flooded plain. He did not even want to see the sea: the waves, the tides, the swell – all these things would have scared him. What he continually dreamt of was a boundless, gleaming expanse of translucid, still waters, stretching away, level, as far as the eye could see, glinting with silvery reflections. A pool of rainwater, extending to infinity. And this liquid tract would be planted with thousands of trees, but not all clustered together: a scattered host of trees, each one mirrored in the water. Aspens, birches, and beech saplings – a whole company of trees, with tall, slender trunks of silky grey or satiny white, with supple branches, perpetually bound to their own reflections, steeped in soft silence and a gentle light. In the distance would rise a bunting's brief song, the whistling of a grebe, or an oriole's melody, and just as every tree would be eternally mirrored by its double, so every bird's song would be matched with an echo, and in the water every fish accompanied by its own shadow. This dream that he took pleasure in endlessly reconjuring had first come to him long ago. It had stolen inside him one August morning, in the village church where he went to mass every Sunday, together with his brothers, and their father, preceded by Edmée and their mother, who drove down in the donkey-drawn cart. Their Sunday procession always amused those who passed them on the way: the two women seated in the cart, Edmée wearing a black shawl wrapped round her face, and Fat-Ginnie looking voluminous and airy in the Madonna-blue shawl that floated about her body; Ephraim walking beside the donkey, holding the reins; and the nine sons following behind. 'There go 'Phraim and his tribe to pay their respects to the Good Lord!' people would say as they passed.

That morning, the reading from the Gospel had captured the attention of the usually distracted Eloi-Marie. The priest read from the Gospel of St Matthew, describing how

Jesus had walked upon the waters. This account had both astonished and delighted him. So it was possible, then, to walk on water. This idea had suddenly made him delirious with joy. Could he, too, who so loved to play beside rivers and to fish in ponds, go gliding over the water? He already imagined himself crossing Settons Lake barefoot, running and dancing on the surface. As they came out of church, he had cried, 'I want to walk on water, too!'

His older brothers had laughed at him. 'You? But you're much too easily scared! You'd sink like a sodden log quicker than St Peter!'

And Edmée had said, 'Now, that's enough, these things are not to be joked about. Walking on water is something that saints do. And you and I are not saints. To be a saint, your soul needs to be lighter than a dragonfly.'

So Eloi had kept his dream to himself, but this dream had never left him, occupying his mind constantly and making him more distracted than ever. And whenever anyone asked him what he was thinking about when he appeared to be lost in reverie, he would reply, unruffled, 'I'd like to be elsewhere.' Elsewhere to him meant that magic place of luminousness, with its calm, clear waters reflecting trees and clouds; a watery expanse between heaven and earth, stretching away to infinity, on which he would be able to walk barefoot, and run and dance and glide. And ever since then, he had been called Eloi-Else-where.

The nicknames of the two youngest sons were self-evident, dictated right from the start by the boys' natural defects - although Louis-Marie, whom they originally called the Daft, because he was simple-minded, had over the years become Loulou-the-Bellclinker.

He prattled on in a reedy voice, settling upon everything and everybody his gentle idiot gaze, gesticulating quaintly all the time, and switching at any moment from high-pitched laughter to the most sorrowful tears. When he reached the age of puberty, he was taken with a strange fancy, from which he had never recovered. He decided that he was not really a boy, but a girl. His slight, thin body with its long, frail limbs, his shrill voice and whimsical manner, the way he laughed and cried for no reason at all, and the way he skipped about, if not actually capered, could in fact have suggested a ludicrous attempt at girlish behaviour. But his claim to be a girl was, for him, utterly serious. He began talking about himself in the third-person feminine. He dressed most of the time in old skirts and shawls, and wore his hair, which he had grown long, in a pony-tail or plaited in a braid.

He fulfilled the role at Upper Farm of a general maid, because he could not do anything properly. But there were three jobs that he loved to do: sweeping (and if no one had stopped him, he would have swept not only the forest, but the streams and sky as well); helping his mother, the sight of whom filled him with radiant joy; and ringing the bells in the village church. Since he could not go down to the village every day, he had hung a carillon of bells of various shapes and sizes from the branches of an elm behind the farm, and he would set them ringing three times a day: for the morning, noon and evening angelus. And every time, the chimes of his jangling bells would send him into peals of gleeful laughter.

As for the youngest, Blaise-Marie, the harelip that disfigured his face had earned him the name of Blaise-the-Ugly. This deformity had also made him his grandmother Edmée's favourite. He was the last-born, who had come into the world at the dead of night, bringing to a close that strangely extended 15th August that had run its course over nine years – Edmée regarding this nine-times repeated date, with its Marian associations, as a single day. This last-born child had been blessed even in his mother's womb, still floating in the maternal waters. The Angel of the Lord had laid his finger on the infant's mouth, both as a blessing and injunction to keep to himself the burning secret that inhabited his mother's heart and flesh, and which it had been his privilege to discover. Angels' fingers are so gentle, so imperceptibly light, that their touch is terrible, and those whom they deign to bless in this way bear the mark on their flesh all their lives, like some marvellous, unhealable wound.

Edmée had never otherwise interpreted Regina's prodigious obesity: it was a flourishing of her daughter's flesh at the miraculous touch of the Almighty's messenger, the Archangel Gabriel, who stands in the presence of God and whom God sent first to Zacharius to tell him that his wife would bear a son in his old age, and then to Mary, with the greeting 'Hail, Mary, full of grace, the Lord is with thee.' And this was why Edmée beheld with such wonder and delight the hugeness of her daughter's body and her youngest grandson's harelip. Both had been chosen to receive a visit from the Archangel Gabriel. Both, more so than any of the others or herself, were the Madonna's well-beloved, for she had sent to them the Archangel of the Annunciation. The physical anomalies that afflicted them were for Edmée the visible signs of supernatural beauty. For, as she saw it, the beauty of blessedness had nothing at all to do with prettiness; rather, it was a kind of awe-inspiring monstrousness.

However wonderful Blaise might have appeared to his grandmother, he was none the less totally ugly in the eyes of others. He knew this, but it did not distress him. He had received a gift as great as his physical ill-favouredness – the gift of words. He spoke in a lovely deep voice with such melodious inflections that no one could hear it without being amazed and stopping to listen. And he spoke as no one else around knew how to speak, with words like so many images, feelings, flavours and colours. He was the only one who had learned to read, and he had an extraordinary memory.

Blaise-the-Ugly kept bees, which in those parts were called honey-flies, and the hives were called honey-fly boxes. These hives consisted of bell-shaped structures made of straw woven with thick bramble stalks and hazel twigs, set on a piece of wood covered with rye-straw thatching. It was the custom at Christmas to take from the hearth a piece of charcoal from the log lit on Christmas Eve, and put it inside the hive for luck; and on Palm Sunday, to bring home from mass the first branch of boxwood to have been blessed, and to stick it in the thatching of each hive. But just as his grandmother had greatly elaborated on the religious beliefs of all the other old women, so Blaise-the-Ugly took local customs to much greater lengths, and every ceremony celebrated in honour of the Lord, the Virgin Mary or the Saints, was for him the occasion of some ritual to be observed with his bees.

He had placed his hives behind the farm, not far from the bell-hung elm that his brother set ringing three times a day. He liked this craze of Loulou-the-Bellclinker, to be for ever ringing bells accompanied by shrill squeals of laughter, for the bees' song, he said, 'is bright and gay, a sunny song that flits and dances in splinters of light, and my bellringer-brother's merry music enchants them. In reality,' he said, 'the bees are nothing less than the angels' laughter.' He believed in the invisible presence among men of angels whose joy at having seen God was so great that they wanted to share it with every other creature, sending it throughout the world in gentle chuckles of fire and gold. He also said that he owed to the bees the eloquence of his crooked mouth. They came and settled on his hands, shoulders and face. They even settled on his lips. 'The bees,' he said, 'deposit on my mouth pollen they have gathered from flowers, and an ardent dust gleaned from the light; they fill my mouth with sugar and fragrance, with all the flavours reaped from the earth. The taste of sugar is sweet only to those not mindful of it; it is fact terribly and violently hot. This is what my words are made of – they are moulded in all of the earth's sugar and fragrances, they flow inside me like pure honey, they glisten and whirl like a cloud of larks besotted with space and sunshine. The bees speak in my mouth, they dance on my tongue, they sing in my throat, they blaze in my heart. They are my joy, my light, my love.'

This was the response of Blaise-the-Ugly, the last-born of Ephraim and Fat Ginnie's nine sons, whenever anyone wondered at his strange manner of expression. And their surprise only increased, triumphing over any desire to mock. This was also why there was greater confusion than pride in Ephraim's heart with respect to his sons of the Evening. He did not understand anything of their strange fancies, and their mentality, whether preoccupied with wandering, solitude, or an elsewhere, whether overshadowed by imbecility or, on the contrary, all too enlightened. But Fat-Ginnie derived from them a comfort that allayed her pangs of hunger. When Leon-the-Loner came home in the evening and tossed on to the kitchen table the birds he had just killed, and sat down to carry out in silence the slow ritual of plucking them, she felt the cruel ferret that was her hunger suddenly retreat into the deepest recesses of her sad flesh, as if its furtive voracity had been momentarily arrested. In Eloi-Marie's absent gaze she glimpsed the ineffable elsewhere that so haunted him, and she vaguely discerned a bare landscape so deeply submerged under fresh water that even her hunger could have drowned in it. And when Loulou-the-Bellclinker amused himself by standing under the elm, ringing his bells and laughing happily, she thought she could detect in this carillon the innocent, gay flurry of her own laughter, at last freed from the oppression of her body.

As for Blaise-the-Ugly, she listened with such amazement to his incomprehensible speech strewn with strange words that she forgot for a moment her obsessive craving. Through the transparency of the words and images that melodiously issued from the deformed mouth of her last-born, she perceived a field of radiance, a realm of weightlessness. Within the confines of these words, she glimpsed a dazzling vista of unencumbered lightness. And her body, monumental though it remained, seemed not so heavy, and in the course of time managed to acquire a nimbleness and ease that she had never known before. As all these children born of her flesh became independent grown men, each forging for himself a strong and vital spirit, they gradually assuaged her hunger.

Despite all these differences that distinguished the brothers of Morning, Noon and Evening, there was a profound understanding between them, much more profound than in any other family in the village or any of the surrounding villages. Such were the closeness and warmth of their relationships with one another that they even aroused suspicion in some people – anything was to be expected of a tribe of savages as solidly united as this, in whom strength was allied with eccentricity, not to say crankiness. Admittedly, when they all gathered on Sundays to go down to church, and on holidays and festivals or family occasions, they presented quite an amazing spectacle. The Morning brothers always walked four abreast, ambling along slowly like dray-horses, with Simon-the-Hothead leading the way, going too fast to keep pace with them, and the Evening brothers following behind, with Loulou-the-Bellclinker trotting after them, doing a little hop, skip and a jump every three paces, whimpering with pleasure. In church, they would stand with their father in a group at the back, while their mother and Edmée sat in the last pew, and at the elevation of the Host they would all kneel down together, bowing so low their foreheads almost touched the ground, then they would solemnly file up to the altar, one after the other, to receive communion. And they sang powerfully, heartily – Blaise-the-Ugly's melodious voice gradually rising higher and higher above the bass tones of his elder brothers' chorus, while Loulou-the-Bellclinker trilled away, like a sparrow hopping about. After the service they would all go to the bar in the village square. They drank with gusto, apart from Martin-the-Sparing and Loulou-the-Bellclinker, the one because he hated to lose control of himself, even to the smallest degree, and the other because alcohol went straight to his head and made him even dafter than ever. But Ferdinand-the-Strong and Adrien-the-Blue drank enough for all of the brothers put together. Ferdinand always knocked back his drinks in a single draught, downing one glass of brandy after another until he had not a sou left in his pocket and his mind was completely befuddled.

The older brothers played cards, with the exception of Martin-the-Sparing, who was loth to gamble and contented himself with watching them play, silently circling round their noisy table. Seated at another table, Blaise-the-Ugly told stories that held his audience spellbound – an audience that always included Leon-the-Loner and Eloi-Elsewhere. Loulou-the-Bellclinker, who could never sit still, frolicked among the chairs, or danced attendance on the waitress, eager to help her serve.

But it was on the really important feast-days that the tribe of Mauperthuis brothers made their presence truly felt, in the most remarkable – and indeed, for some people's taste, worrying – way. For on these occasions they would turn themselves into an orchestra. But their sense of music was so peculiar that their impromptu performances were always characterized as much by the strangeness as the loudness of the din they created. The older brothers had no notion of melody whatsoever; on the other hand, they enjoyed an incredible sense of rhythm. Their instruments were quite rudimentary. Ferdinand-the-Strong alternately clapped his hands, slapped his palms against his thighs, and stamped the ground with the heavy clogs on his feet, while Adrien-the-Blue, Martin-the-Sparing, and Germain-the-Deaf rapped sticks of various sizes against each other. Even Germain-the-Deaf excelled at this percussion: he watched his brothers, and the rhythm marked by their movements invaded his entire body, penetrating his limbs and muscles, and by mimicking them he managed to keep in perfect time.

Leon-the-Loner played a bizarre instrument of his own devising, and which he called a 'nine-stringed bow'. This was like a drum-cum-guitar-cum-xylophone, a bit of this, that and the other. It consisted of a finely polished, oval-shaped, wooden bowl, across which he had stretched nine

79

metal strings of decreasing thickness. From these, he extracted sharp, sonorous vibrations, either by striking them with thin metal rods, or by plucking at them with two fingers. He wore his nine-stringed bow slung across his shoulder and resting on his hip.

Eloi-Elsewhere played a small accordion, and Loulou-the-Bellclinker jingled a set of shrill-sounding, high-pitched bells attached to a tall hazel-staff that he held in his hand. Blaise-the-Ugly beat a metal gong with a little wooden mallet.

Simon-the-Hothead revelled in the glory of turning his breath, amplified by brass, into a pure, penetrating sound of sparkling liveliness: he played the trumpet. And he played it with the same ease, passion and brilliance that he brought to everything.

Every important feast-day gave them an excuse for their music, but particularly the Feast of the Assumption. Then the enthusiasm, happiness and boldness of their playing knew no bounds. At one and the same time they celebrated in joyful confusion the Virgin, whom they had been brought up by their grandmother to revere; their own mother, Regina, who was the incarnation of the Madonna's grace; and their nine birthdays that were also their name-days – each of them bearing the name of Marie tagged to his first name, like some talismanic bulwark against evil, sin and death.

OUR-LADY-OF-THE-BEECHES

The day came that saw the culmination of their joy, when they gave vent to it in a tremendously resounding performance – so inordinately resounding that it caused a scandal, but a happy and even glorious scandal. It was on the occasion of the consecration of a statue of the Virgin dedicated to Our-Lady-of-the-Beeches, in the middle of the vast clearing at an intersection of woodland paths between the forests of Jalles and Saulches. This ceremony took place one 15th August, at midday. All the woodcutters and peasants from every little out-of-the-way village on the fringes on these forests were there with their wives and children. Mingling with this crowd of poor folk there were also tradespeople and even some local worthies who had come up from the bigger villages and towns to take part in the event. The priest from the church attended every Sunday by the Mauperthuis family was accompanied by priests from four other neighbouring parishes, surrounded by a host of choirboys in starched, white lace surplices, carrying candles and censers. The clergy led the solemn procession, walking ahead of the sky-blue velvet canopy, spangled with gold and silver stars, covering the statue of Our-Lady-of-the-Beeches that stood on a litter, also covered with blue velvet, borne on the shoulders of six men. The swarm of choirboys flitted around them in clouds of incense, their immaculate, stiff surplices gleaming like the wing-sheaths of some white insect. Behind this sacred procession came the crowd: first, the children, then the young girls, followed by the older women, and last of all the men. Everyone was carrying flowers, sheaves of corn, or baskets of fruit.

Camille walked among the bevy of young girls. For

once, old Mauperthuis, who was also present, had allowed her to appear in public and join the crowd. But this crowd had a dignity that justified this departure from his usual practice of keeping his granddaughter in seclusion. He had brought her up in total isolation, spoiling her like a little princess held captive within the spacious confines of his farm. He had succeeded in curbing Camille's unruliness and curiosity by imprisoning her within a sweet idle dream. She knew nothing of the outside world, having always lived like a bird in a cage. A cage that he had contrived as a lovely large aviary so that she might not grow bored. On her alone, he had heaped his love and attention. And until that day Camille had been content with this easy, monotonous and cosseted life.

Ambroise Mauperthuis was not a believer, or if he was, he believed more in the devil than in God. He only deigned to go to mass at Easter and Christmas, just so as not appear a total miscreant in the eyes of others. And he had obliged both his son Marceau and Camille to follow his example. But this ceremony was a moment of glory that he claimed for himself. Our-Lady-of-the-Beeches was to be enthroned in the heart of his forests. With Marceau at his left, he walked with his head held high, and as much through vigilance as admiration did not for a moment lose sight of Camille. Demurely dressed in white, with her hair pinned up in a chignon beneath a white silk veil embroidered with white flowers and birds, she walked with the other young girls of her age, her hands clasped round a big bouquet of white, yellow and orange-coloured roses. And moving at the same slow, steady, almost funereal pace as everyone else, she sang the Magnificat in unison with the choir.

But old Mauperthuis was not the only one to have his eyes fixed on her. All the men cast their gaze much more in her direction than that of the blue-velvet litter floating at the head of the procession. For no one was fooled: it was no use Camille keeping step with her eyes lowered, and singing in chorus, studiously behaving like a dutiful and retiring young girl, her beauty asserted itself none the less in all the spiritedness of her flesh and blood, and her eyelids merely hid a sparkling serpent gaze. She was not meant to be dressed in white, but to deck herself out in bright colours, nor was her hair meant for a chignon and veil, but for dishevelment. Her docile gait seemed unnatural, her whole body trembled with contained emotion, with a secret desire to skip and dance, and her voice had an accent too husky and sensuous not to betray a lively disposition for laughter, shouting and songs. She was like a little wild horse cobbled with silk, satin and lace, and all the men sensed behind those airs of an artless and well-behaved young lady the hidden mettlesomeness of that impetuous little horse named desire. And deep down, all the men envied old Mauperthuis for having such a lovely girl in the house.

'The old fox!' they said to themselves. 'It wasn't enough for him to extort from Corvol his forests and his children, he's also robbed him of this beautiful creature. She must take after her Corvol grandmother, the one with a weakness for men, who ran away, so they say.' And to console themselves for not having such a lovely young girl under their own roofs, they added, 'But try as he might to keep that Camille of his on a leash, sooner or later she'll give him the slip!' And having already deemed Camille bold and flighty, some of them even carried consolation so far as to imagine themselves the happy beneficiaries of her lovely body.

It would never have occurred to anyone to think of Camille as Marceau's daughter. She was, of course, but so domineeringly had the old man interposed himself between his son and his granddaughter, so effectively had he excluded the lacklustre Marceau, that no one considered him of any account, as he knew only too well. Just the day before, his spinelessness had led him once again to obey a humiliating order from his father, in another act of cowardice that he could not forgive himself. The old man had sent him to Upper Farm to tell his brother Ephraim that he and his nine sons were absolutely forbidden to attend the 15th August festivities.

'Go and tell him yourself!' Marceau had dared to mutter, sickened and wounded by such treatment of his brother. But old Mauperthuis had immediately railed against him in a fury, and once again fear had got the better of Marceau's spark of rebellion. He had gone out, taunted by his father, and trudged up to his brother's place, bearing his message like a pack upon his shoulders and his heart. He had not gone into the house at Upper Farm, but spoken to his brother in the yard, in an indistinct, halting voice, with his eyes fixed on the ground. Not for one moment had he dared to look up at Ephraim. Had he done so, the tears that made his throat ache would have scalded his eyes. Without uttering a word, Ephraim had let him speak. All that the older brother had said at the end was, 'I shan't be going. That old godless thief and bully has no business to be following the Virgin's statue. It's disgraceful! And it's not a sight that I want to see. You can tell the old man that. But my nine boys will do as they please. Because I, for one, don't harass my sons – they're not my slaves, they're free men. And you can tell that to the old man, too!'

And he had turned his back on Marceau, leaving him alone in the middle of the yard. Marceau was so miserable, so defeated by his own weakness, so mortified in his secret affection for his brother, that he had felt completely dazed, as though he had taken a beating. And there had been a stabbing pain in his foot, like a recurrence of his old childhood burn. And he had limped home, cursing himself even more than his father.

Neither the sons nor their father were among the men in the procession, and the absence of the Mauperthuis tribe, universally known for their extreme and singular devotion to the Madonna, intrigued everybody and roused curiosity. On the other hand, no one was surprised by the absence of La Corvol and her aged infant-brother. She was known to be much too proud, and as usual she would not have wanted to mix with the rabble of peasants and woodcutters. She had surely preferred to remain at her musical catafalque, endlessly extracting from it the sobs and laments of her ruined family's displaced dead.

However, Edmée and Regina were there, unconcerned by any orders and threats from that old sinner Mauperthuis. Edmée, who was soon to turn ninety, trotted along spryly on her daughter's arm. Old age had merely wrinkled and wizened her skin, but not penetrated her heart. She had preserved intact a heart radiant with a childlike devotion, for ever enamoured of the Most Merciful Madonna. And her gaze did not wander to right or left, nor did she take sidelong glances at anybody. She kept her eyes fixed on the sky-blue velvet litter, with a blissful smile on her lips. Fat-Ginnie sailed along beside her, gently pitching from side to side, a similar rapture lightening her weight. Besides, both of them knew that the boys were going to come and pay homage to Our-Lady-of-the-Beeches.

At the forest crossing known as Beech-Cross, the crowd split up, with the women on one side and the men on the other, gathered in semi-circles round the stone shrine in the middle of the crossing that was to house the statue. The sky was a deep, dazzling blue. An enormous blazing sun directly overhead beat down on the clearing. The grass was dry, crackling underfoot; and there was the sound of chirring insects. The air thrummed with the heat, redolent with mingled smells – spicy and honied, sweet and bitter, acidic and sugary – the smell of incense, the fragrance of fruit and flowers, the odour of sweating bodies. While all the little girls held posies of wild flowers in their hands, and the older ones came with bouquets of roses in their arms, the women clasped to their bosoms clusters of brightly coloured blooms from their gardens, and the old ladies carried the finest fruit from their orchards in little wicker baskets. The boys bore branches of hawthorn, honeysuckle and woody nightshade, picked from the hedge-rows and bound together in long drifts garlanded with ivy, while the men brought sheaves of wheat, rye and barley.

Everyone came to offer the best that their hands had sown, cultivated and reaped from the earth, and the children brought what they had found while playing in the fields or ferreting along the paths.

The statue was placed in its niche, blessed and censed, then the most senior of the priests delivered a sermon on the Assumption of the Blessed Mother of God and the sweet mystery of her Dormition. The crowd listened, at once somnolent and meditative in the befuddling heat of the clearing, with its heady smells and buzzing of flies and wasps. Many people seemed to be quietly dozing on their feet. Heads nodded, and eyelids grew heavy. Then the crowd moved off again, languorously following the churchmen and choirboys, like a troop of sleepwalkers lazily chanting:

> *Ave Regina caelorum,*
> *Ave Domina Angelorum:*
> *Salve radix, salve porta,*
> *Ex qua mundo lux est orta . . .*

It was then that they appeared, entering the clearing by a path opposite the one down which the crowd was retreating. They came seven abreast, with their instruments in their hands, wearing their Sunday-best trousers and a plain white shirt decorated with either poppies or butter-cups at the neck for a tie. Loulou-the-Bellclinker led the way, dressed as a girl, with his long hair tied up in a pony-tail on the top of his head. He shook his bell-staff, making pretty little high-pitched sounds. Leon-the-Loner brought up the rear. He was wrapped in a huge cape covered with bird feathers. The crowd slowed its pace almost to a halt, and the chanting died away in a confused murmur:

> *Gaude Virgo gloriosa,*
> *Super omnes speciosa:*
> *Vale, o valde decora,*
> *Et pro nobis Christum exora.*

The children eventually came to a complete standstill, so as to watch the newcomers. Despite their parents' efforts to drag them away, they remained, round-eyed, rooted to the spot. But the parents tugged at their sleeves without great conviction; everyone was burning with curiosity. The crowd had just been wrested from its torpor. Another ceremony was about to begin.

Ephraim's sons advanced briskly towards the middle of the clearing without paying the slightest attention to the crowd. Loulou-the-Bellclinker jingled his bells with increasing gaiety, while the Morning brothers began to beat a slow rhythm and Eloi-Elsewhere quietly played his accordion. Blaise-the-Ugly struck his gong and the nine brothers shouted in unison. Then Blaise stepped forward and preceding the rest of the group began to declaim in a loud voice:

'And the Temple of God was opened in heaven, and there was seen in His Temple the ark of His Testament . . .

'And there appeared a great wonder in heaven; a woman clothed with the sun, and the moon under her feet, and upon her head a crown of twelve stars; and she being with child cried, travailing in birth, and pained to be delivered. And there appeared another wonder in heaven: and behold, a great red dragon, having seven heads and ten horns, and seven crowns upon his heads. And his tail drew the third part of the stars of heaven, and did cast them to the earth: and the dragon stood before the woman which was ready to be delivered, for to devour her child as soon as it was born. And she brought forth a man child, who was to rule all the nations with a rod of iron: and her child was caught up unto God, and unto His throne. And the woman fled into the wilderness, where she hath a place prepared of God . . .'

He fell silent for a moment, and the Morning brothers brought up the sound of their tattoo, while Leon-the-Loner drew sonorous vibrations from his nine-stringed bow, and Loulou-the-Bellclinker shook his bells more frenziedly than ever. The crowd on the other side of the clearing listened, open-mouthed.

Then Blaise went on. 'And I heard a loud voice in heaven, saying: Now is come the salvation, and the strength, and the kingdom of our God, and the power of his Christ.'

Blaise struck his gong once more, and the others started to play quietly again, with their rhythmic beating of sticks, accordion, nine-stringed bow, and an increasingly gay carillon of little bells. They had drawn near to the statue of Our-Lady-of-the-Beeches, encircling. Loulou hopped up and down, shaking his bell-staff with the greatest rapidity, while the others intensified their rhythm. And suddenly there came the soaring sound of a trumpet, a splash of gold surging from Simon-the-Hothead's body, bursting from the earth and rising straight up to the sun to underscore with its dazzling clarion the joy and splendour of that day. Then the others gave free rein to their energy and enthusiasm. Ferdinand-the-Strong bounded across to Simon, and began to speed up the rhythm, slapping his hands and stamping his feet ever more violently, and releasing great cries as he did so. Ha! Ha! Ha! And his brothers re-echoed these cries. Simon-the-Hothead drew all their cries, sounds and resonances in the wake of his trumpet's flamboyant blasting. He wrung the breath from their entrails and throats, propelling it skywards to revel in the full light of day. He swayed as he played, now bending forward, now leaning back, and his brothers danced about him, spinning round and leaping in the air, laughing, and performing with great exuberance. This was their offering – not just the flowers and fruits of the earth, but their energy and youth, their hearts' impetuousness, their wonderful fullness of breath and hilarity. They came as messengers of the trees among which they had always lived, and which Our Lady had come to honour with her statue and protect with her name. Our-Lady-of-the-Beeches. She was theirs. So closely were they bound, body and soul, with the trees, they belonged to the tree tribe, to the tree kingdom. They were princes of the realm of trees, dancing musician princes, wild and playful princes, greeting their queen.

Some people in the crowd began to murmur: Really! The way Ephraim's sons were behaving wasn't Christian! They were creating a barbaric rumpus and showing no respect for decent folk! Was not this blasphemous, all this shouting and stamping round the Virgin's statue that the priests had just blessed in accordance with the age-old rituals?

Ambroise Mauperthuis was beside himself with rage. So these underlings engendered by his disowned son and that fat Verselay woman from Upper Farm had dared to disobey his orders! Maybe they thought they were on their own ground in the midst of these forests that belonged to none but himself? He turned to look at Camille. And what he saw provoked his anger beyond all measure.

Although apparently still, she stood as though about to spring forward into the middle of the clearing, her shoulders quivering with the desire to dance. The old man saw her in profile, her face strained towards the group of brothers. He glimpsed the intense sparkle of her green eyes and the moist redness of her parted lips. He sensed the irregular beating of her heart, the extreme tension of her muscles and the slight raspiness of her breath. And then came that gesture – she tore off her veil and with an abrupt shake of her head loosened her hair. This sharp and rapid gesture was like a slap across his face. Camille was slipping away from him. Desire had infiltrated her heart, taken possession of her body and alienated her from him. She resembled Catherine even more closely, showing the same intemperance and impatience, the same ardour and impudence, the same unique beauty. Everything that he had contrived to keep hidden from the eyes of others had just burst into view, right here in public, and all because of those ragamuffins born one after another, amid the squalor of Upper Farm, delivered of the teeming womb of the Verselays' fat daughter! His rage was such that he could not contain himself any longer. He walked straight up to Camille, pushing aside all who stood in his way. He seized her by the arm, gripping her tightly, and said to her curtly, 'That's enough! We're going home!'

Without even turning towards him, she bridled and tried to free her arm with a wrench of her shoulder. Then he pulled her, tightening his grasp. She had to submit, but the look she gave him was furious and haughty.

'Put your veil back on!' he commanded her in a low voice as he dragged her away. Her sole response was to drop the veil on the grass and grind her heel in it.

'Little hussy!' he hissed between his teeth. 'Just wait till we get home!'

'It's here that things are happening!' she retorted in vexation.

Not only was Camille slipping away from him, she had suddenly started to rebel. She was standing up to him without the slightest fear, and before long she was going to turn against him. Realizing that it was pointless and even dangerous to try to quarrel with her under his breath in front of all these people, he redirected his anger against the five priests who had hung back a bit. Why were there just standing there like that? What was keeping them from putting a stop to this racket, and driving these barbarians away? He came and planted himself in front of them, still dragging Camille by the arm. 'God damn it!' he shouted at them. 'Why don't you do something! Here are these hooligans stamping around and bellowing in a holy place, and you don't say a word! Just look at them real devilish swine fit for slaughter, and you let them carry on like that! For God's sake, this rumpus can't be allowed to continue!'

The priest turned to look at him coldly, while the choirboys, who could not believe their ears, stared at him, wide-eyed with amazement. For in his anger Ambroise Mauperthuis had just blasphemed twice, without even realizing it. One of the priests, Father Monin, the one who had delivered the sermon, eventually spoke.

'If there's been any transgression, sir, it lies with you, and not with these boys. With your coarse swearing, you profane the name of the God before his servants, whereas I see no harm in these young men who have come to sing their faith, however uncouth their song. I detect no evil intention in their exuberant behaviour, extravagant though it may be. I discern in them a great impulse of joy, which is a rare thing. And what is even more rare, they are familiar with the Holy Scriptures. Would you, sir, be capable of reciting from memory a passage from St John's Book of Revelation, as this young lad did?'

The other priests were less well disposed towards the Mauperthuis brothers, considering their wild demonstrations to be scandalous, but faced with the old man giving them murderous looks and grimacing with rage after having sworn at them, they were more inclined to support their fellow-clergyman. At that point Simon-the-Hothead's resounding music and the frenetic pace of his brothers' rhythm began to die down; the sound of the trumpet became softer and the beat grew lighter, heightening the crowd's attention all the more. The brothers were catching their breath. In fact they were creating a new opening, leaving the way clear for Blaise-the-Ugly's melodious voice, which started to chant the Litany to the Virgin. The crowd listened, no longer dumbfounded as they had been a moment before, but enchanted.

Blaise's voice flowed so gracefully that it seemed to flutter in the air, to swim in the light, to ripple through the whole area.

'Mother of light, Mother of life, Mother of love, Mother of mercy, Mother of hope . . .'

And as he sang, he gently swayed, while his brothers supported his voice with their soft playing.

'Virgin full of grace, Virgin most holy, Virgin most humble, Virgin most lowly, Virgin most pure, and obedient to the Word . . .'

His voice took on modulations of entreaty. Obedient to the Word: in the depths of his wretchedness, he the deformed knew what that meant – with his ugly, twisted mouth visited by so many words that even he could not always fully comprehend.

'Virgin of devotion, Virgin of suffering, Virgin of joy, Eve reborn, Daughter of Sion . . .'

The finger that the Angel of the Mystery had laid on his lips like a fiery tip had left, behind the horrible wound in his flesh, a transparent bright flame that danced in his heart and mouth.

'Queen of heaven, Queen of angels, Queen of patriarchs, Queen of prophets . . .'

Tears of tenderness trembled in his exquisite voice, wonderfully poised on the highest notes. His brothers kept up their muted beat. Edmée and Regina treasured inside themselves the rush of happiness that ravished their hearts, while the crowd held its breath, and old Mauperthuis bottled up his rage.

Not until long after Ambroise Mauperthuis had gone, dragging Camille away, with Marceau following behind, did everyone else depart, leaving the clearing of Our-Lady-of-the-Beeches with gladdened hearts. Even those who had originally been hostile to the nine brothers, after they had appeared so blatantly in the clearing, had undergone a change of heart. The beauty and sweetness of Blaise-the-Ugly's singing had overcome all resistance and indignation, especially as the priests – including the local parish priest who had always been wary of these woodcutters whom he regarded as semi-barbarians – had finally approached the Mauperthuis brothers in a show of appreciation. This recognition from the very people who might have condemned them had thus changed the initial impression of outrage into a sense of pride and joy.

But the brothers cared no more for this recognition than they worried about the anger of the old man who was their employer. They had done what they had to do. They had sung their ritual praises to the Virgin, they had professed their joyful dedication to Mary, their simple faith in God, their jubilant belief in the invisible presence of angels – a belief and devotion in which were mingled their love of the earth and their passion for the forests. They had proclaimed their gladness with unstinted zest, such that the hearts of all those men, women and children who had been witness to its display had been swept along by it. And when Father Monin expressed his admiration for Blaise-the-Ugly's knowledge of the Holy Scriptures, and for his exceptionally pure voice, the young Mauperthuis contented himself with replying, 'I deserve no praise. It's not I that speak and sing, but the bees. My mirth is their abode, they sleep in my heart and illuminate it with their dreams – their beautiful dreams of gold and brightness gathered from the laughter of angels. Their light, delicate bodies are born of angels' laughter. And my deformed mouth with its twisted smile that inspires nothing but disgust or derision in other people does not frighten them. Far from fleeing my ugliness, they come and sweeten it, consoling me even until I rejoice in it. I'm a stranger to envy, hatred, rancour, jealousy or the spirit of vengeance. Even pain and distress are unknown to me. I'm happy. Yes, I, the last-born child, in all my ugliness, am happy, happier than anyone else, because I'm bound by a completely transcending joy to attest the beauty of the world, life's blessings, the earth's splendour and the infinite love of God.'

'What you say disturbs me. There are terrible accents of pride in your humility,' the priest remarked, astounded by such language from such an uneducated person, and almost appalled by this self-assurance.

But Blaise-the-Ugly softly laughed, and continued: 'My speech has only the accents dictated by the joy and wonder conferred on me through pure grace. I have no other pride but my love of God, of the land and my family. All my pride is in loving – in loving more than I am capable of by myself, for I have been blessed with a dream by the Angel that visited Mary. And that's not pride, it's gratitude.'

'Do you know what you're saying?' the priest asked.

'If I really knew what I was saying, I wouldn't be able to speak any more. I wouldn't be able to find the least word worthy of that knowledge. It's only men that speak, because of something that trembles inside them, something that stirs within their flesh, that moves in their hearts. They sense this, but they don't understand it. So they speak. They keep on speaking, to track down word by word this strange thing that flits and floats within them without ever allowing itself to be caught. The angels do not speak. When they come to address mankind, they use a language that is swift and concise. They themselves have no need of words. They are inhabited by light, they are made of brightness, they are transparent beings. They do not even have names. If asked what they are called, they reply without names, for their names are Wonderful. But I have to search and pick my way through words, step by step. If I were fully cognisant of the things I spoke of, I couldn't live any more. I would die from their exorbitant splendour and grace. Just as I love more than I would be capable of by myself, so my thoughts go beyond what I am aware of thinking, and what I say falls far short of the song that makes itself heard within me, through me.'

'And your brothers?'

'Each of us has received his share of light – just a glimmer, but a vital glimmer.'

'And also his share of anger!' the parish priest interjected, recalling some of the Morning brothers' outbursts.

'And anger, too,' Blaise-the-Ugly calmly admitted. 'But this anger is devoid of all rage and there's no evil in it. This anger is never fury. Is there not madness in all beauty, boldness in joy, passion in love? Tenderness itself is intense and impulsive – a burning flame! Light is violent, the wind is a strong, moving force that rushes along – how it rushes! See how this 15th August sun beats down on the earth! All is fervour. And the cry of new-born infants? Everything begins with a cry, a rending. The creation of the world began in that way, and that's how the world will end. My brothers and I live close to this primitive cry, which also means close to the last cry. We live among the trees, on poor, hard soil, directly at the mercy of a sky that casts in our faces its rains and storms, its snows and sunshine, its winds, frosts and lightning. Our bodies are marked by all this. It's in the grain of our skin, and our hearts are filled with it. And our souls rejoice in it. This is how we're made

– we are the way we are, and we'll not change. With this love of the land and trees grafted onto our flesh, with this boundless joy, and this faith driven deep into our hearts, we'll always live close to the world as it emerges from the hands of God. So it is. Each of us has received his share of light – as strength and anger for the older ones, as songs and dreams for the younger.'

'What about Ambroise Mauperthuis? He's your grandfather, I believe?'

'He's our employer. He denied his son, and all the rest of us thereafter. He's severed all ties with his family.'

'And with God?'

'That is not for me to judge.'

THE CIRCLE OF ANGELS

Ambroise Mauperthuis had severed all ties with his son and grandsons only to bind himself closer to Catherine and to Catherine's image. And those ties that he had so ruthlessly established with Camille, taking care to keep her away from everyone else, devolved from this unique bond with Catherine. A bond from which all else originated. The years before Catherine did not count. He had only begun to exist, to be truly alive, since his encounter with this woman on the banks of the Yonne, through the jolt of her beauty laid low. Through Camille, he hunted down Catherine's image, prowling about like an animal at bay, perpetually fanning the flames of his brief ravishment of long ago. But now this image was suddenly escaping from him, at the very moment of its most dazzling radiance.

Camille now shunned him. She no longer laughed, nor sang, nor ran to meet him and take him by the arm when he came home from making his rounds of the forests, or returned from his trips to Vermenton, Clamecy, or Château-Chinon. She no longer came and walked or sat beside him to talk to him the way she always used to. Since the interrupted festivities in the clearing of Our-Lady-of-the-Beeches, Camille had kept her distance. Nor did she seek out anyone else's company, neither La Fine's, nor that of some local girl. The only company she craved was forbidden to her: that of the nine brothers. She had a burning desire to see them again, to be close to them. She knew that she was like them. She wanted to be their friend, their sister.

Camille did not think, she felt things – passionately, with all the strength of her being. All her senses were newly envigoured. From its first arrival in the middle of the clearing, the statue of Our-Lady-of-the-Beeches had worked a miracle, a very simple miracle that was thoroughly, magnificently human: with marvellous suddenness, Camille saw others and her own life with new eyes. Her body had broken free of itself in an outward, forward rush. Desire had surged into her flesh and seized her heart.

The unforeseen had swept into her previously well-ordered life, like a gust of wind, and set ablaze this prodigious force of desire that had always been smouldering inside her, but which her extremely vigilant grandfather had taken such pains to keep dormant. An unhoped-for, sudden gust of wind, so wonderful it made her want to cry with joy, a sunny gust of wind – Simon's brass-amplified breath. Simon, the humble cowherd who worked for her grandfather; that always dishevelled and dirty rustic, who would fly into a temper over the slightest thing, and become equally jubilant over another trifle. The distracted and even rather haughty way that she had always regarded him, as well as all the other sons from Upper Farm, had now changed. Her eyes suddenly focused on them with keen attention.

The strange words that Blaise-the-Ugly had declaimed when he advanced to the centre of the clearing continued to resonate within her.

'And the Temple of God was opened in heaven . . .'

It was the earth that was opened before her. The temple that exists on earth: the forests.

'And there appeared a great wonder in heaven . . .'

A great and dazzling wonder had appeared in the forests. Nine young men had imparted flesh and movement to the Virgin's statue, had caused it to rise from its stone shrine, and invited it to dance barefoot on the sun-scorched grass.

'A woman clothed with the sun, and the moon under her feet, and upon her head a crown of twelve stars . . .'

Camille could see this woman. She could see the clearing of Our-Lady-of-the-Beeches opening before her, the streaming sun turning the grass golden. The statue assumed flesh and blood and vitality; it got up and danced towards the trees. It danced and skipped, a living light striking the ground with its heels. And each time it did so, roses sprang up in the grass – granite roses with flaming hearts. And the woman cried out, consumed with a joy as profound as the day, greater than the world. Her cries flew up to the treetops, and settled on the branches – multitudes of flame-red birds. The branches bowed beneath their weight, beneath the splendour of those cries; they swayed with a terrible, voluptuous languour.

The trees wrenched themselves from the soil, and began to move. Their branches laden with birds, cries, fruits, and flames, writhed like the arms of men in the throes of desire. They gleamed incandescently. The woman, a figure of mud and light, whirled among them, and the granite roses that everywhere perforated the ground rolled in the grass, chased by the wind, pecked by the birds. And the trees intoned a rough-voiced song - a song of pure joy.

The words of the Litany of the Virgin chanted by Blaise-the-Ugly sounded with a new ring inside her.

'Mother of light, Mother of life, Mother of love . . .'

Mother of the earth, Genetrix of the earth's happiness. Woman bearing the earth's beauty in her arms, like a child. Camille felt herself to be one with this woman. She was her daughter and her sister. Sister of light and life. She bore desire in her embrace like an armful of flowers – roses and flame-red poenies. And it hurt her not to be able to share these flowers, to scatter their petals with those who had inspired her with such immense and profound joy. It grieved her not to be able to proclaim this mad happiness that wrung her heart and entrails, nor dance in her gaiety and cry out her desire, with them – the brothers.

There had appeared a great wonder on earth. The forests where the Mauperthuis brothers had always dwelt had been enchanted. The Madonna's statue had made her solemn entrance into these woods and her presence now filled the place with light, making it rich in wonder. They, the brothers, had gone rushing to meet her, and greeted her as their sovereign. All that they held dear came together in her image: their faith in God, whose blessed servant, daughter and mother she was; their affection for Edmée;

their love for their mother; their pride in their father, who had sacrificed everything without a moment's hesitation in order to pursue his desire to the limit; their passion for the forests. Their lives revolved around this image more than ever before. They drew their strength and happiness from it. But they were not satisfied with having acclaimed its arrival, they wanted still to honour its presence in the midst of the forests. They had an idea.

One morning, at the first glimmerings of dawn, all nine of them set out for the clearing of Our-Lady-of-the-Beeches. There, they chose thirteen trees set in a circle on the edge of the clearing, facing the statue. And they set to work. In the trunk of each tree they carved an angel. In the beech that stood directly in front of the Madonna they fashioned an angel whose arms were filled with fruit, in honour of their mother, and to the left of it, an angel with open hands carrying its heart in the hollow of its palms. This was the sons' homage to the love their father had borne Fat-Ginnie. To the right of the angel-with-fruit, they carved an angel with its hands joined together and a smiling face, deep in prayer: this was the adoring-angel, in honour of Edmée. Next to it, they created an angel with its eyes closed: the sleeping-angel, in memory of Jousé. Then on either side of these four trees they sculpted angels with their own distinguishing characteristics. In the trunks of five beeches to the left of the angel-with-the-heart appeared the figures of angels representing the brothers of Morning and Noon: the angel-with-the-axe, the laughing-angel, the stern-angel, the angel-with-ears (rolled up like ram's horns), and the angel-with-the-trumpet. To the right of the sleeping-angel, the figures of angels in the image of the Evening brothers emerged from the tree-trunks: the angel-with-birds, the angel-with-fish, the angel-with-bells, and the angel-with-bees. And they had worked the wood in such a way that when the wind rose it was caught in the holes, grooves and crevices hollowed out of the wood. The wind that swept through the clearing stole into the angels' mouths, whistled upon their lips, between their fingers and their wings, and in the folds of their gowns. Moaning, shrieking, howling, whispering – the clearing sang, the wind soughed, its themes sometimes lively and sometimes slow; the light rippled on the sculpted trunks, and the trees quivered at having been thus cast in the mould of angels.

When old Mauperthuis found out what Ephraim's sons were up to this time, he finally gave vent to the fury that had been festering inside him since the 15th August celebrations. These trees belonged to him, no one had any right to meddle with them at will. He came into the clearing one morning. The nine brothers were there, working at their sculptures. But the threats and abuse that he hurled at them served only to provoke the elder brothers' anger. It was he who took fright – he even drew back when Ferdinand-the-Strong came straight at him, with Adrien-the-Blue and Martin-the-Sparing at either side. But even as he shrank from them, he shouted, 'I'll have those trees cut down. That's enough damage you've done, you bunch of scoundrels! These are my woods and I'm not going to let you destroy them in this way!'

Brandishing the axe that he always carried, Ferdinand-the-Strong replied, 'Then we'll do the same to you. Not even strokes of lightning frighten me. And I'm no more scared of you than I am of lightning.' It was true that he had no fear of lightning. When a storm broke in the forest and thunder rocked the skies, Ferdinand would raise his felling axe, slicing the air with it as though to cleave the flash of brilliance.

'These trees are mine and I'll do as I please. Villains! Thieves! I'll drive the lot of you out of my forests,' the old man ranted.

Simon-the-Hothead sprang forward and shouted in his face, 'If anyone here is a thief, it's you! Everyone knows that you stole these woods! After all, they weren't yours when you were born, were they? No one even wants to know how you came by them, it must have been such a nasty business. For you've a nasty, wicked heart! You drove our father from your house, and you've always worked us to death, and we've never said a word, though we do the work better than anyone, as you well know! But this time we won't keep silent. These aren't anybody's trees. They're no more yours than ours. They belong to the Madonna.'

'He's right,' said the Blaise-the-Ugly, coming forward in his turn. 'These trees belong to none of us. Look, they're marked with the signs of angels. They're here to keep guard round Our-Lady-of-the-Beeches. She's come to find a place in the heart of your forests and you're not even willing to allow this simple homage to be paid to her? You've nothing to hold against us. We've always served you honestly. But we've other masters above you. We're the servants of the Lord's Handmaiden. Do you not fear God? Will you refuse to offer Him these few trees?'

The old man sole response was to spit with anger, and turn his back on them, then he went off cursing, with his fists clenched. The brothers returned to their task.

For the second time Ambroise Mauperthuis had to beat a retreat. He had a burning desire to drive out of his forests every one of these rogues spawned by that fat Verselay woman, but even though he had the power to do so, he still dared not act upon it, for ever since that cursed 15th August he sensed that local opinion had swung in their favour. Even that terrible band of priests had sided with them, approving of the scandalous racket they had made and admiring the dronings of that ugly rat-faced lad, and criticizing him – Mauperthuis – in public! He did not want to put himself at odds with the entire local population, so he would wait for his revenge. For he would certainly claim it one day. He would bide his time, with the fearsome, cold patience of a beast of prey watching for the right moment to devour its victim.

Yet during the following week his vengeful wait was temporarily deflected. Something happened that suddenly took him back to his oldest enemy, and revived his original underlying hatred. Victor Corvol emerged from the darkness into which Ambroise Mauperthuis had cast him. From the bottom of the valley, from the depths of his house on the banks of the Yonne, where for more than thirty years he had been expiating his crime in loneliness and terror, old Corvol now summoned him.

Escorted by Marceau, Claude and Leger, Ambroise Mauperthuis descended with great ceremony to Clamecy, his heart girded with rancour and malice. Camille was not allowed to accompany them. Under no circumstances was she to get involved with the Corvol clan. She was to remain totally ignorant of this man who was once and for all doomed to oblivion. La Fine was instructed to keep the strictest watch over Camille at Threshold Farm.

DIES IRAE

Dies irae, dies illa,
Solvet saeculum in favilla:
Teste David cum Sibylla.

Quantus tremor est futurus,
Quando judex est venturus,
Cuncta stricte discussurus!

The choir intoned the *Dies Irae*. The church of St Martin was packed. But the crowd in black, standing in the amber light filtering through the stained-glass windows that September morning, had come not so much out of loyalty or affection towards the person whose funeral was being celebrated, as out of curiosity. Yet there was nothing to see – only the coffin draped with a long black velvet pall, set on trestles facing the altar, at the end of the nave. The dead man's initial, embroidered on the black velvet in silver thread, gleamed dully, with a murky brilliance that held the congregation in thrall.

Tuba mirum spargens sonum
Per sepulcra regionum,
coget omnes ante thronum.

Mors stupebit et natura,
Cum resurget creatura,
Judicanti responsura.

There was nothing to see. But everyone was consumed with the desire to see. They had all heard about the deceased's last wish. A crazy, monstruous wish. It was said that just before he died he had summoned the notary to his bedside and dictated his last will, making him swear on the crucifix hanging on the wall above his bed that he would see to it that this request was carried out to the letter. And the notary had kept his promise. Since nobody actually knew the details of this strange testament, there was all the more speculation. The only thing known for sure was that the deceased's remains had been mutilated according to his wish. So everybody invented the details of this mysterious mutilation. While there was nothing to see, there was frightful scope for the imagination. And it was for this reason that all eyes stared so fixedly at the black-velvet-draped coffin, as if everyone were trying to penetrate the opacity of the velvet and wood in order to see through them the maimed corpse.

> *Liber scriptus proferetur,*
> *In quo totum continetur,*
> *Unde mundus judicetur.*
>
> *Judex ergo cum sedebit,*
> *Quidquid latet apparebit:*
> *Nil inultum remanebit.*
>
> *Dies irae! Dies irae!*
> *Dies irae, dies illa,*
> *Solvet saeclum in favilla:*
> *Teste David cum Sybilla.*

But there was one man in the congregation who knew. He knew everything. He sat in the front pew, belonging to the deceased's family. That man was Ambroise Mauperthuis, related to the deceased by their children's marriage. He, too, stared at the coffin, but not, like the others, trying to guess what mutilation maimed the body – for he knew. He stared at the silver letter neatly embroidered on the velvet, the dead man's initial – the letter C.

Victor Corvol appeared before him for the last time, displaying the initial of his name – the name of an assassin – not hollowed out of logs of deeply resonant wood, but embroidered on velvet in silver thread. A dully gleaming

C – a still, now silent, single letter, not as before crudely repeated in countless logs thunderously floating downstream. And yet the sepulchral clamour of the choir singing the *Dies Irae* evoked for Ambroise Mauperthuis that other great clamour, so extraordinary-sounding, of that huge herd of oak- and beech-logs coming down the river, that sombre chant of dismembered trees booming out between the banks and suddenly shot through with a piercing silence, on the morning of the crime. More than thirty years had passed since then, but from that morning ever after Ambroise Mauperthuis had lost the real measure of time, and now that long-ago, spring dawn merged with the present September morning. The two mornings blended into each other, the intervening years notwithstanding, like a confluence of clear, cold waters carrying along with the current these perpetually unchanged bodies: of hatred, splendour, and crazed desire – of Corvol, Catherine and himself – three bodies of extremity, of anger and revenge.

> *Quid sum miser tunc dicturus?*
> *Quem patronum rogaturus,*
> *Cum vix justus sit securus?*
>
> *Rex tremendae majestatis,*
> *Qui salvandos salvas gratis,*
> *Salva me, fons pietatis.*

Ambroise Mauperthuis' vision blurred. He thought he saw the coffin almost imperceptibly move, as if it were about to float away. Was it not made of oak, like the logs that floated in the water? Did it not bear the same initial? C for Corvol.

C for Catherine. What did this coffin actually contain – old Corvol's body, or Catherine's? Catherine, who had remained for ever young, endowed throughout the years with her staggering beauty and her green-eyed gaze. Catherine, who had come to life again under the earth in which he had buried her, and burrowed her way from the bank down to the river, and slipped into the water, and swum upstream to reach the forests on the Morvan heights, Corvol's forests that were now Mauperthuis'.

Catherine, running through the forests, his forests. She runs, fleeing the husband who pursues her. Her dress is torn on the branches and brambles. Catherine leans, naked, against a tree, beating the trunk with her fists until it cracks open and encloses her inside it. And the oak-tree inhabited by Catherine's body wrests itself from the ground and starts to walk, and goes roaming the world, finally coming to rest here, beneath this black velvet pall.

Ambroise Mauperthuis' thoughts blurred. He confused his own body with that of an oak-tree in the forest of Saulches. He was a tree of flesh and blood haunted by Catherine's beauty.

> *Recordare Jesu pie,*
> *Quod sum causa tuae viae:*
> *Ne me perdas illas die.*
>
> *Quaerens me, sedisti lassus:*
> *Redemisti crucem passus:*
> *Tantus labor non sit cassus.*

A tree of flesh and blood haunted by Catherine's beauty – so old Mauperthuis stood amid the clamour of the singing, a stormy clamour, a cry that rose from his entrails. Again, as on the first day, he was overcome by his hatred of Corvol, but it was a hatred intensified by the years, allowed to run riot by his now crazed memory, intoxicated by Catherine; a hatred increased by the solemnity of the place and the splendour of the singing; a hatred dazzled by Catherine's beauty rediscovered in Camille.

The golden light that fell from the windows and was burnished by the candle flames was Camille's fairness mingled with Catherine's. It was the splendour of a single body in its earthly progress, the body of a woman who had traversed death only to rise again younger and bolder than ever, between granite-rock and sky, between trees and water, at his side, belonging to him. The woman Catherine-Camille was his very own – passionately so. Catherine-Camille, his only love, a love frantic with jealousy. And Ephraim's sons, who had turned Camille against him with their wild cries and foot-stamping, now seemed to him to be old Corvol's myrmidons. The same hatred and vengeful fury set his jealous heart against them. His deluded heart. C for Catherine-Camille.

Ambroise Mauperthuis kept his eyes fixed on the coffin. 'No,' he said to himself, 'Corvol's not lying in that oak box. It's been too long since I cut him down to size, reduced him to nothing – an old dry stick. Or maybe his body, that of a murderer, is lurking in there, like a dog. But mind, Corvol! All the oak trees are mine and have been for a long time, and my trees know of your crime and they know of my hatred for you. That coffin is going to shrink in the ground and close in on you, squeezing you like a walnut until it crushes you to pieces. Even in the earth you'll be tormented. Catherine has long since spoken to the roots and the creatures under the ground. The whole earth cries vengeance from its deepest entrails, and it will be revenged against you. Stay where you are, Corvol, languishing in my anger. You're going to rot in my anger!'

> *Ingemisco, tanquam, reus:*
> *Culpa rubet vultus meus:*
> *Supplicanti parce, Deus.*

> *Qui Mariam absolvisti,*
> *Et latronem exausdisti,*
> *Mihi quoque spem dedisti.*

Claude Mauperthuis, standing behind her father-in-law, also stared in silence at the black-draped coffin. Her father's coffin. The letter C gleamed softly – lamentably so. A C the colour of the moon, of frost, ashes, and tears.

Claude slowly took repossession of her name. She remembered that she had been born a Corvol. It was here in this church that it had all begun – the unhappiness, the loss of her name, its degradation in favour of that of Mauperthuis. The misalliance. It had taken place in this church of St Martin of Clamecy. Her father had led her by the arm to the altar. She remembered. The two red velvet chairs. And she in her mother's wedding-dress, disguised in her fugitive mother's ivory lace, humiliated in her mother's treacherous garb. Would Camille in her turn wear this dress, this sloughed skin that made a young girl shed her father's name and assume another unknown to her, of husband and stranger. This garb of falsehood to be cast off on her wedding-night in order to regale a man's boorishness with her naked virgin body. This garb of anguish that heralded her own body's downfall, that doomed it to abject loneliness, smothered beneath the weight of a man she did not know or love, and certainly did not desire.

St Martin cut his cloak in two in order to clothe a pauper. She tore her dress to shreds and threw these at her mother's averted face and in her daughter's face. Mother and daughter – a twin-headed hydra, with the same serpent eyes, the same wide mouth, their lips moist with carefree laughter and immodest desires, full, boldly pouting lips. She tore up her wedding-dress, she rejected her married name. She denied herself so as to reclaim the honour of her maiden name, her name from before this misalliance. That weightless name, Corvol, that she had received at birth and borne at school: a name as light and calm as a bird sleeping in the hollow of one's hand, not burdensome like the name Mauperthuis that had the ponderousness of her husband's heavy body, which had sweated and panted upon her until it made her heavy, too – heavy with another body: her daughter.

> *Confutatis maledictis,*
> *Flammis acribus addictis:*
> *Voca me cum benedictis.*

Oro supplex et acclinis,
Cor contritum quasi cinis:
Gere curam mei finis.

Claude firmly took repossession of her name. There, before her father's coffin, before the big black pall on which her initial softly gleamed. C for Claude Corvol. And memories came back to her – of her childhood, a peaceful childhood in that lovely house on the banks of the Yonne, with its cool rooms smelling of beeswax, and with the sweet fragrance of roses wilting in their vases, and of fruit from the garden, heaped in red or golden pyramids, in porcelain bowls: apples, cherries, pears and plums. Sweet, yellow greengages, which the French have named *reines-claudes* –'Queen-Claudes'. Hers was the name of a fruit, a royal fruit, named for a queen from the banks of the Loire. So why had she thus been exiled, far from her own realm, banished from those tranquil rooms where clocks and pendulums on marble dressers registered the blissful monotony of the passing hours? Why had she been obliged to leave that big garden with its pink gravel path shaded by a long pergola covered with a mass of greenery, of clematis and convulvulus, where birds came to warble? That big garden, with swings under the portico, with its orchard in one corner, and rose bower in another, its tool-shed, lilacs and magnolia. And by the lilacs, the armchair where her father liked to come and sit on spring and summer evenings.

Her father – to whom she had given so little thought in all these years. To avoid the pain, perhaps, so as not to be assailed with the temptation to look back. Her father, whose features, voice and gaze she now sought. Her father, whom she suddenly felt a great desire to see again – to hold him in her arms, to hug him and ask his forgiveness for having left him alone for so long. For having forgotten him.

Lacrimosa dies illa,
Qua resurget ex favilla
Judicandus homo reus.
Huis ergo parce, Deus.

Pie Jesu Domine,
Dona eis requiem.

For, just like her mother, she had forsaken him, and gone off on the arm of another man. But a man that she had never loved. A poor forest bumpkin. And it was not as if she had ever dreamt of any other love. She did not believe in love. Her treacherous, fugitive mother had robbed her of any understanding of love, or inclination for it. She no longer even knew why, or how, she had come to be parted from her father. She was so young at the time. She had allowed herself to be led by her father to this altar one day. Then her father had disappeared into the background, and two strange men had taken her to a little village high up in the forests, on an ox-drawn cart. She had been loaded on to the cart, along with her trunks and piano, like an object, a mannequin. She had already been treated like an object by her mother, left unclaimed, with her father and brother, among all the knick-knacks and furniture, like soiled goods of no value – a mere thing, on the verge of inexistence, with an unfeeling body.

Her husband had remained a stranger to her. And so, too, had the child she had borne him: Camille, who so closely resembled her own mother, it was intolerable. This resemblance had constantly taunted her, as though her runaway mother took delight in saying to her, through Camille, 'You see, I abandoned you one day, never to set eyes on you again, but I've sent you my double to trifle with you further, and betray you once more by soon leaving you!'

She had never become attached to her daughter, and never tried to thwart her father-in-law's stratagems and stop the old man from monopolizing Camille's affections.

She had withdrawn from the lives of all of them – father-in-law, husband and daughter – right there on the farm, where she had allowed herself to be caged. She had suspended time, and put in suspense also her own life, her body, memory and heart. She suspended them in oblivion, indifference and melancholy. The old Wagger, who used to curse her piano so much, accusing it of witchery, might have been right, after all. She had been lulled into oblivion by that piano. It had absolved her from existing. She had shut herself up with the instrument, as though in a tomb. A dulcet tomb contrived of notes, in which her extremely evanescent life had constantly dissolved into absence and grown partial to its annihilation – a falsely melodious, extremely vapid kind of annihilation.

> *Sanctus, Sanctus, Sanctus,*
> *Dominus, Deus Saboath.*
> *Pleni sunt caeli et terra gloria tua.*
> *Hosanna in excelis.*
>
> *Benedictus qui venti in nomine Domini.*
> *Hosanna in excelis.*

Claude took painful repossession of her name. Yes, she remembered that she was born a Corvol. And a loathing for the name of Mauperthuis erupted in her heart. A loathing for all the Mauperthuis clan, her own daughter included. That silver initial that gleamed so softly in the candlelight was hers. She had nothing more to do with the name of Mauperthuis. She was going to cast it aside like discarded rubbish, and take back her maiden name. Her father's name.

It was here that it had all begun. But now there was a coffin instead of chairs, and the red velvet had turned to black. And in the coffin lay her father. Emotion rose in her like the pain and blood of a wound long numbed beneath ice and now suddenly grown warm. Emotion rose in her like boiling water, with mingled shame, tenderness, remorse, pity and grief. She wanted to see her father one last time. It was said that he had asked to be mutilated before being laid in the coffin. It was not that she, like the others, wanted to know what kind of mutilation this could possibly be. What she knew, what she now realized, was that her father had twice been mutilated – first by his wife, and then by his two children.

It was here that it had all begun. And it was here, too, that everything would start again. She was going to leave the Mauperthuis – her father-in-law, husband, and daughter. She would not go back to their primitive village, to their farm with its cattle and pigs, except to fetch her belongings, her trunks and piano. She was going to move back into her father's house, which was hers from now on. She would shut herself up in it with Leger, her infantile brother with the wrinkled face of an aged child, who was snuggled against her. She would shut herself up in her father's house, in his memory, in his large, absent body, and take over his loneliness and silence. She would take back his name, the name that her father's body had left behind, a name with no heirs to be passed on to. Corvol.

> Agnus Dei, qui tollis peccata mundi:
> dona eis requiem.
> Agnus Dei, qui tollis peccata mundi:
> dona eis requiem.
> Agnus Dei, qui tollis peccata mundi:
> dona eis requiem sempiternam.

Claude Corvol took full repossession of her name, with a vengeance, in the very place where she had lost it. She returned to her father. She espoused her father's death. Yes, the Wagger was right: her piano was a necromantic tomb that had bewitched her. A tomb at which she would sit more than ever before, listening for the voice of the dead, and through which she would offer to the dead – to her father – a sacred song, a song of forgiveness, reconciliation, memory and peace. And Leger, her brother with the mind and body of a doltish child, a little boy who never, ever wanted to grow up, and whose hands, already speckled with age, were incapable of anything else but playing with a cup-and-ball or hoop, would live out with her his bleak dream.

C for Corvol. The silver letter trembled on the black velvet like a soft, grey tear-drop, a dead man's tear-drop, shed as a sign of farewell, to purge memory, to wash away the past. Her father's tear transuded through death like a delicate night-star, to show her which path to follow, and where she should live from now on: down there, on the banks of the Yonne.

C for Claude Corvol, Vincent Corvol's daughter. She would make herself a new bridal dress out of the big black velvet pall in which her father was shrouded, and wed herself to the remembrance of the dead.

> *Lux aeterna luceat eis, Domine:*
> *Cum sanctis tuis in aeternum: quia pius es.*
>
> *Requiem aeternam dona eis, Domine:*
> *et lux perpetua luceat eis.*

Who was lying there, wondered Marceau. The bass voices of the men singing the Requiem, the flickering light of the candles, the smell of wax and incense, the amber light from the windows that formed a nimbus over the crowd dressed in stiff black – all made his head swim. He felt ill – his stomach heaved and he felt dizzy. Who was lying there? This question kept drumming in his mind. He had only seen his father-in-law three times in his life: the day of the marriage proposal, the day of the engagement, and the day of the wedding. Three precipitous occasions that followed almost immediately on one another, three days organized in all haste by his father – three cursed days. It was all so long ago. He had only a vague memory of the man who had been his father-in-law: a thin figure with hunched shoulders, and a hunted look in his dull eyes –

113

that was the only impression he was left with. But now he was assailed by queries. Why had this man dispossessed himself, as he had done, in favour of his father? Why had he consented to give him his daughter in marriage? Why had he agreed to be parted from his two children, and why had he never tried to see them again? And finally, what was the significance of this rumour that Victor Corvol had asked to be mutilated after his death? And above all, what secret had bound this man to his father?

His father, his father! Why was he not dead? Why was he not the one lying there, instead of the other man? His wicked-hearted, devious father, who had never stopped coming between him and life, who had deprived him of everything – of his will, his desires, his feelings. Who had separated him from his brother, then forced him into an unhappy marriage with a strange woman who no more loved him than he loved her. A stranger who had remained so – a woman with a heart that was grey, like the colour of her eyes, with a cold skin, and a body as dry as a piece of dead wood – a haughty, hostile stranger.

His father, his father! A jealous and deceitful-hearted tyrant who had purloined the love of his son's daughter. His father, who had settled his inheritance on Camille, passing him over as his direct heir. The old man was constantly cheating him, casting him into darkness, humiliating him and depriving him of his due. But he well knew that he had contributed to his own downfall, and it was this that most grieved him. He had allowed himself to be crushed and treated as a lackey, a dog, without ever daring to rebel. For he was a coward. His meekness was merely his way of admitting to his own cowardice. He had allowed himself to be consigned to oblivion amid general scorn and indifference, because he had grown indifferent to himself. He was nothing since being parted from his elder brother, Ephraim, who had dared to say no to their father, who had preferred to preserve intact his pride, his will and his life, rather than jettison them in order to retain his rights as son and heir.

Libera me, Domine, de morte aeterna,
in die illa tremenda:
Quando caeli movendi sunt et terra:
Dum veneris judicare
saeculum per ignem.

Who was lying there? Marceau the coward, the forgotten, the unloved, stared mournfully at the big black pall. He tried to understand. This coffin seemed as enigmatic to him as all those gapingly empty sarcophagi that for centuries had mutely stood guard around the small church of Quarré-les-Tombes. Whose bodies had they contained, and why were there so many of them? Whose body lay today beneath the black pall? Indeed, was there actually a body under it? He felt so lonely, he could have screamed, he could have wept. This big black pall was like a tarpaulin thrown over his own life, his forlorn heart and servile body that had never known any joy, pleasure or tenderness. He thought of his mother, who had died when he was still a child - the only person who might perhaps have loved him. He thought of Ephraim, the older brother he had always so much admired, now banished to the far end of the village, the far end of the world. It had become impossible for them to speak to each other, and the affection between them was destroyed. His brother had been stripped of his rights, robbed of what belonged to him, and reduced to poverty, but he owned something far greater – a love free of all shadow and all anxiety – whereas he himself was nought but inward ruin and loneliness.

All around Marceau seemed to spin and sway. And he had no one to lean on. If he fell to the ground in a heap, nobody would come to pick him up. Nobody cared about him. When his time came to die, no one would notice. No one would grieve for him or miss him. The light in the church seemed to turn rancid and the coffin looked like a dead tree-trunk borne by the current of a yellow, muddy river. He felt thirsty, so thirsty he could have screamed, and wept. If only he could have sat down at a table with his brother and drunk with him!

> *Tremens factus sum ego, et timeo,*
> *Dum discussio venerit*
> *Atque ventura ira.*

Who was lying there? And feeling overcome by the swell of the choir's singing and the sickening smell emanating from the candles, by the incense and the crowd, he had suddenly exclaimed inwardly, 'But why aren't I lying there?' It was at that moment that the idea occurred to him, in a flash of darkness, of putting an end to his life – a life that served nothing and no one, the life of a coward and a failure. And this idea had reconciled him to himself. He had never been anything but a walking corpse, a lost soul pining within his body, pining for his brother. The name of Ephraim had then enveloped him like a big black velvet pall. Yes, soon he would be a real corpse, a corpse relieved of his burden of shame and remorse, of all distress. A corpse grown so light at being able finally to lie down that it would go wherever the wind took it, floating with the current. Perhaps this was how the sarcophagi of Quarré-les-Tombes came to be open, allowing the dead to escape through the woods, with the flow of the rivers Cure and Trinquelin, like so many invisible birds and fishes. Perhaps it was all those unseen dead that on certain days caused the enormous Rocking-Stone to tremble. Perhaps they were dancing.

Who was lying there? He soon would be. The spirit of the dead had taken hold of Marceau. In the ever murkier glow of the candlelight, he saw all the tombs of Quarré-les-Tombes open up for him, like so many deep, soft beds, in which he fancied himself lying. He fancied himself floating lightly on the clear waters of a mountain stream, flying through the forests, dancing on the heavy slab of stone poised on the rock, lying asleep in the stone, water, forest and wind, dancing on the glorious name of Ephraim.

116

The spirit of the dead had just enfolded his heart - with the consolation, promise and hope of deliverance.

> *Dies illa, dies irae,*
> *calamitas et miseriae,*
> *dies magna et amara valde.*
> *Dum veneris judicare*
> *saeculum per ignem.*

This day and every day of his life was a day of anger, an everlasting day of anger. Old Mauperthuis felt his heart pounding with anger, pounding fit to burst open this coffin, to shatter the bones of the man lying inside it. And he already dismissed the promise that this man had dared to try and extort from him. For Vincent Corvol had written to him just before he died, a sealed letter that the notary had given to Mauperthuis the previous evening, along with two boxes – two boxes containing what the crowd with their eyes riveted to the coffin sought to discover with such avid curiosity.

THE WILL

Sir,

The man who killed Catherine is about to die in his turn. Thanks to you, this man has endured a punishment that human justice, had it learned of his crime, would not have imposed on him with such cruelty. In the moment of that crime, you stood up, not as judge but accuser, as the tormentor of my conscience. You stripped me of my possessions, you took away my children and turned them against me. You condemned me to the darkest solitude, the bitterest poverty – a poverty of heart. It is true that when my wife tried to leave me, I lost my human heart. When I discovered her treachery, her flight, it was with the heart of a dog that I ran after her to stop her and bring her back – the heart of a dog crazed with sorrow, jealousy and anger. But that heart was rent from me when I killed Catherine. It was that lost heart, driven wild with fear and grief, that killed her, and it died in the same instant as its victim. It could not survive her. When you buried Catherine after I had left, at the same time you buried my dual heart – of man and dog. That dual heart has long since rotted in the earth. And no other heart has been given to me. You left me alone, so painfully alone, with an arid hole where my heart should have been.

I have asked that after my death my heart be removed from my corpse, so that my body might descend into the earth with the visible, tangible sign of its terrible poverty. I have also asked that after my death my right hand be cut off, so that my body might be placed in my ancestors' tomb without this murderous instrument. I want my body, parted from Catherine for ever, for ever bereft of her, to be buried thus mutilated, since I amputated her body from mine by killing her. On the Day of Judgement, when the Trumpet sounds throughout the world to summon the dead to appear before God, it is with this mutilated body, twice marked by the infinite anguish of its crime, that I shall rise up and go to meet my Judge. God will judge me. But only Catherine's forgiveness in the hereafter will be able to restore to my body the wholeness presently denied to it.

You should know, sir, that you, too, will have to appear before God, and that he will demand account of you, as well as of me. Think seriously on this as you read the request I make of you, and which I beg you to accomplish.

I have asked that my heart and hand be given to you so that you might place this empty husk that is my heart in the place where you once buried my wife, Catherine, for this heart has never belonged to anyone but her – and more in the grief and remorse I have endured incessantly since committing my crime than in the love I bore her when she was alive. Set beside her this lost and devastated, hollow heart – set it there as a silent supplication. I beg Catherine's forgiveness, even after my death, even under the earth, having begged it for more than thirty years, continually shedding tears of chill, acidic blood.

As for the hand that you failed, or were unable, to arrest before the crime, the very hand that writes to you now, I entrust it to you, to find a suitable place for it in this world. What place, I do not know, and little care. It is enough that it should not disturb the sleep of my ancestors whom I am about to join. But you who so excelled in finding the punishment my crime deserved will surely know what to do with this hand that I repudiate.

You involved yourself in the crime that I committed. You perverted to your sole advantage the justice to which I was answerable. And finally, by setting yourself up master of my shame, suffering and absolute remorse, you have in your own way colluded in the crime. From now on, you'll be the lone bearer of the secret of that murder. Since you chose of your own free will to make yourself responsible for the punishment my crime deserved, I now make you responsible for the memory of that crime – not to obscure it further, but at long last to release it. Grant my request: set my repentant, supplicant heart, which had paid so dearly for its sin, close to her whom I have never ceased to love.

Do not forget, sir, that your own appearance before our Eternal Judge is not far off. And then a reckoning will be made of you, of a severity beyond your conjecture, for the way in which you have behaved.

Grant my request, without delay or default. This is not an order – I am not a man entitled to give orders, my crime having long since deprived me completely of any power. This is much more than an order, and certainly much more terrible: it is an entreaty, which places our souls in jeopardy.

Know this, sir, and take it to heart, and do what it is now yours to accomplish.

May God take pity on us all, the living and the dead.

Vincent Corvol

Such was the letter that Vincent Corvol had written to Ambroise Mauperthuis. It was dated the day before his death. He gave it that same day to his notary, along with his will, in which he bequeathed to his daughter Claude his house and few remaining possessions, and in which he asked to be doubly mutilated, and for his heart and hand to be given to Ambroise Mauperthuis, his daughter's father-in-law, to whom his forests had formerly been made over – an endowment that he did not contest. He had written this letter and drawn up this testament in full soundness of mind, the latter being unaffected by his illness, so that he had remained entirely lucid until the final hours, as the notary could not but admit, despite the terror that this will, read to him by the dying man himself, instilled in him. A terror that Victor Corvol immediately relegated to silence by insisting that the notary, a pious man known to him for his rectitude and scrupulous, uncompromising faith, swore on the crucifix hanging over his bed not to divulge to anybody the contents of the will, and to see that his last wishes were strictly carried out, in secrecy. And

Corvol said to him, 'Don't try to fathom the reasons for this request, which, I can well understand, shocks and even revolts you. Don't try to work out the rationale for it, which, in essence, partly eludes me. Yes, even me. But of which I sense the necessity. Only, be assured that I am not mad. If I am at all debilitated, it's not through any kind of dementia but, on the contrary, an excessive lucidity, which is worse. That is why I am asking you to meet my request in every particular. It is that of a man who has sinned beyond anything you could imagine. It is the request of a man who is about to commit his soul to God in the most extreme sorrow and remorse. I place my confidence in you, and thank you. Now, please leave me. The time is close when I am to be summoned . . . All must be consummated. And all will be consummated – and judged.'

These were Vincent Corvol's last words. The notary withdrew, leaving him alone. And he remained alone until the end. He died the following morning, having watched dusk fall and the darkness set in and deepen, then seen the dawn break and the sky turn rosy, and the day brighten as the birds started singing. And his breathing had gradually grown shallower, becoming hoarse and raspy, and his memory had thrown back wide its gates, suddenly revealing to him a tremendous expanse – that of his seventy years of life. And his consciousness, at its most sharply attentive, had soared over this vast expanse like a very high-flying bird winging above an immensity of fields, towns and forests. He had seen his childhood and his youth, and all those people and places that had marked his horizons, set his life in motion, and made it eventful. He had seen Catherine, the young, fair-haired girl, with green, almond-shaped eyes, and the young woman whose breasts had the bright roundedness and warmth of day, and of the earth, in the hollow of his hands, and whose mouth had the redness of dark roses, and the brilliance of day, and whose body had the day's depth and heat. Earth, roses, earth, day. Roses, fires of the earth, freshness of day. Roses, beauty that came of the union of earth and day.

Roses, the day's plenitude, vitality and silkiness. The day, the day! He had never known any other day but that of Catherine, of Catherine's body, Catherine's gaze. There was day only through Catherine, and in Catherine. She was the earth's day, the earth's beauty. She was the day's body, the day's skin, the day's light. The day, the day, Catherine!

As he lay motionless in his bed, between rough sheets, breathing his last, he saw Catherine at every moment of her life. He saw her even to the point of pain and madness, while prey to a desire that culminated sometimes in ecstasy, sometimes in rage. Of course he had known, he had always known, that she was unfaithful to him. But he had never said anything. He had always been far too afraid of losing her. And knowing that she surrendered herself to other men's pleasure, and not daring to say anything, he had hated her. But his love for her had overtaken his hatred every time, and his hatred had mingled with his passion, the way the waters of a mountain stream come rushing into a river, swelling its course and making it flow faster. His love for her had accepted everything – that she lied to him, that she deceived him, that she laughed at him, and even swore at him - everything, as long as she did not leave him.

When she walked, with that very gentle swaying of her hips, all the space around her seemed to swing, everything seemed to make way for her. When she spoke, in that somewhat husky voice of hers, all surrounding noises gathered into a strange silence, a feverish murmur, such as precedes the clash of cymbals slicing through the sound of strings and woodwind. When she smiled, slightly crinkling her eyes and parting those wonderful lips, it suddenly took your breath away.

Was she now smiling, here, in this room, through the walls? Victor Corvol wondered as he entered his death throes, and his breathing became more and more spasmodic. Catherine's image kept increasing in size, colour, movement and vitality. As dawn began to break, her image acquired even greater substance and presence. He saw her running down a road. Mist rose from the banks of the river, from which came the rumbling of the migrating droves of logs. He heard the dull booming of the timber. And the sound of her footstep, so light and swift, on the road. An almost skipping little step, so pretty and joyful in the fresh coolness of dawn. A dreadful little step that was taking her away from him, out of his sight, out of his reach, wresting her from his body. A gaily fugitive little step. She had crept out of the bedroom, then out of the house, without a sound, running away without taking anything with her. She had left empty-handed. Did she so detest him that she had not wanted to burden herself with a single object, not even a piece of linen or jewellery, from their house on the banks of the Yonne that might remind her of their life together? Did she so hate him that she had not even kissed her children one last time before abandoning them – children that he had fathered? She had made no sound. But he had woken nevertheless. He had just seen Catherine, in his dream, running down a road, running so fast it made her breathless, and not turning back when he called her, as he sank into a swamp teeming with insects and slimy fish. In his nightmare he had cried at the top of his voice, 'Catherine!' And his cry had wakened him with a start. He had then turned to her in bed, still in the grip of anguish. But she was not there. Instead of fading, his dream had become reality. He had hurriedly dressed, and seized from his bedside table the slender, ivory-handled dagger that served him as a paper-knife. He had grabbed it without thinking, and stuffed it into his pocket. He had not even searched the house for Catherine, so embroiled was he still in his dream, which revealed her to him running down the road. He had rushed off in pursuit of her.

He had seen her ahead of him. She was running, bareheaded. Her legs had such a strange lustre – the legs of an adulterous woman, a prodigal mother, the lovely legs of a fugitive, a pitiless lover. How they gleamed in the brightness of dawn! He was intimate with the grain of their skin, their curves, their softness – and the wonderful way they wrapped round his body, and the pressure of those heels in the small of his back in the moment of orgasm. Legs that she was going to prostitute to some other lover. Then, for the first time ever, as he raced to catch up with her, his hatred had overtaken his love, overwhelming and smothering it.

And as he lay suffocating in bed, he watched the first glimmerings of daylight appear through the window. A thin, pale ray stole into the room. So was Catherine returning then, climbing over the sill? How long and slender her leg was, and what suppleness in her movements! He saw Catherine's legs dancing on the wall. And he called out to her, begging her to come back to bed with him, to come and wrap her legs once more round his back, his chest, his shoulders. But already the sound of his voice was limed in his clammy mouth.

Then Catherine had continued to run away, to flee. But his anger was so intense that he managed to catch up with her. He had taken hold of her shoulder, and asked her to come back with him. She had turned away without answering, and walked on. Again he caught up with her, and told her to come home, that the children were going to wake up and would be looking for her. She darted him a look full of fury, as well as pain, then set off again with the same determined step. A third time he had tried to talk to her, and she had spat in his face, exasperated, and hissed between her teeth, 'Let me go. I'm leaving, I'm leaving, I'm leaving! Nothing and nobody can stop me. Least of all you, because it's you I'm running away from! I don't love you, do you understand? Let me go, I'm never coming back!'

Then he had grabbed her by the arm and pushed her off the road. They had tumbled down the slope on to the riverbank. And there they had tussled. They had not spoken again. What more could she have added after that scathing, devastating admission : 'I don't love you!' What more could he have said, when she would not listen to him any more. 'It's you I'm running away from!' she had said.

They had tussled, she trying to break free and escape from him, he trying to detain her. They had tussled only because their movements were no longer in harmony. They were straining in opposite directions, in collision with each other. And in the course of their silent struggle, which sharpened the stridence of their breathing, his love once again triumphed over his hatred. His love for her suddenly seized him by the throat, like a sob, his desire for her made him lose his head. Unable to find the words to tell her the splendour and unboundedness of his love, the magic of his desire for her, unable to find a voice to make itself heard by her, he had found the dagger in his pocket. He had not meant to kill her, he only wanted to get through to her, to make himself heard, when she was so deaf to him. He had not meant to kill her – only to pierce her deafness.

And all of a sudden came that cry – his name called out across the river. And all that blood, so warm and sickening, spurting on to his hands. Where was the blood gushing from? From that cry across the river? From the wood floating in the river? And why was Catherine's body so limp in his arms? Had she finally given in? But no, the day had just toppled into the mire, and harsh reality had torn off its mask: this was no dream, this had actually happened. Irreparably. Catherine was no longer alive. She would not be coming home again. And reality had shown its face – its vicious, coarse and treacherous face, with the harsh and ugly features of Mauperthuis.

Why was there so much light in the room? Because ever since that moment when reality had revealed the horror of its countenance, no other image had materialized, no other event had occurred. Why was there so much light on the wall – for so long now there had been nothing to see. Victor Corvol was amazed by this dissipation and mendacity of light. For he knew that since Catherine's death there had been no day. His heartbeat was inexorably slowing, his breath faltering in a syncopated hiss. He eventually closed his eyes, indifferent to the brightening day that was a mere simulacrum of light. He closed his eyes as he drew his last gasp – with this final fleeting thought flashing through his mind: the thought of Catherine amusing herself by wrapping her legs round his neck and squeezing her knees round his throat.

He died experiencing this sensation, completely forgetful at the last of the Judge in whose name he had written to Mauperthuis, and of whom he had lived in continual terror ever since committing his crime.

ANGER AND LONELINESS

THE BLUE YONDER

Who really cared about this Judge – *Judex et Rex tremendae majestatis* – the Judge whose most holy and just anger had been voiced in song around Vincent Corvol's coffin? Who still feared him? As soon as the Requiem was over, thoughts of the Judge and terror of the Last Judgement faded amid the grey and amber haze of incense and candlelight – only the tang of anger continued to bite in people's breasts, mouths and saliva, a strong and bitter tang that was most invigorating – the tang of human anger.

Victor Corvol had been interred. He had been buried in his ancestors' tomb, unburdened of his penitent, mendicant heart and of his murderous hand. Back at Threshold Farm that same evening, Ambroise Mauperthuis had thrown these two bits of offal into the pig trough, without the least dread of that Judge whom Corvol had invoked throughout his letter. In fact he had barely been able to understand the letter's solemn language, which he had laboriously deciphered, stumbling over every word, clumsily following with his finger the dense, neat, slanting script. He had only learned to read when he became the owner of the forests, so as to be able to keep his account books and to make sense of notices of timber sales, not in order to puzzle over absurdly bombastic letters. What he had understood – and this was enough for him – was that Corvol had had the temerity to raise the subject of Catherine, had dared to claim to love her and, worse still, made so bold as to ask him to place his heart where Catherine was buried. Such liberties, in Mauperthuis' view, were sheer presumption. He had not pursued the effort of trying to understand this outrageous letter. One reading, no less laboured than furious, had sufficed. He had torn up the letter. Not only did he feel no obligation whatsoever towards Corvol – quite the contrary – but he considered himself entitled to infinite revenge and imprecation against him.

Claude had to postpone the decision she had so firmly taken on the morning of the funeral, to leave Oak-Wolf without delay, and return to live in her father's house. Before she even had time to gather her belongings and pack her trunks, she suffered another bereavement, a bereavement that was more of a vexation than a grief to her. Marceau had hastened to answer the gloomy summons that the spirit of the dead had made to him in the church of St Martin. On his return, he had spent the night at his bedroom window. It was a clear night. Outside, in the middle of the yard, stood the huge, spreading magnolia tree. A still-warm breeze very gently stirred its long branches thick with broad leaves, laquered brown and green, that glistened in the cold brightness of the stars. And all around the tree, on the ground, gleamed its fallen blossoms, like a milky shadow of its boughs. There was no moon in the sky, only stars. The moon lay on the ground, down in the yard, a deliciously fragrant, white nimbus. It was the time of year when flowers, fruits and, soon, leaves fell from the trees in silence. They fell soundlessly, then were carried away by the wind, dispersed, forgotten. Fruits and flowers, and now leaves, dropped off, telling the hours like vegetal minutes, and the moon lay on the ground like a crumpled handkerchief, whitened with tears, like a face torn from its body, bereft of its eyes and mouth, washed clean of all its features, hulled of its senses and dreams, and of all hope and desire. The zest for life had faded, leaving only the redolent, sickly smell of flowers in decay.

Earlier that night Marceau had glimpsed his father's figure creeping past the front of the house and disappearing into the pigsty, from which he re-emerged almost at once. Then the old man had gone back into the house: his last image of his father, already no more than an indistinct figure sneaking about, a dark figure secretly infiltrating his heart. The quietness deepened; everyone on the farm was asleep. And sleep overcame Marceau. He fell asleep standing at the open window.

His last dream: he was walking towards Threshold Farm,

but there was no surrounding wall any more, or yard, or outbuildings, just rocky ground and wasteland everywhere. Actually, this farm looked more like Upper Farm than Threshold Farm. It was built slightly askew, as if the ground had heaved. The light was not of day, or night, or twilight. It was a chalky, bluish light. Everything was blue: the walls of the house, the shutters, the door and the roof were painted various shades of blue, tending to violet, green, turquoise or azure. Seated on an old wooden bench in front of the house, watching him approach, was his brother, Ephraim. His face and hands were a very beautiful, bright, royal blue. He was carving a piece of wood. Looking up from his work and settling his gaze on Marceau, his eyes were grave, perhaps a little sad. He was making a pair of clogs out of beechwood.

In the doorway stood their father, a stocky, gnarled figure of a blue so dark it was almost black. Marceau could not distinguish his features, nor even his eyes. He merely sensed them: intransigent, malicious, full of suspicion. Up on the roof, astride the chimney, was Leger, gazing at the sky. He was playing with his cup-and-ball, but instead of a wooden ball there was the sun tied by a woollen cord to the handle of the toy: a large, ultramarine-blue sun that did not shine, but sat heavily in the sky and occasionally bounced on to the end of the stick and then immediately bounced off again. A rusty iron hoop suddenly rolled down the slope in front of the farm, making a harsh, grating racket, but nobody seemed to take any notice. Ephraim continued to carve the pair of clogs, Leger to play cup-and-ball with the blue sun, and the old man to peer out from the shadows. And Marceau continued to stare at them all, and to watch the iron hoop on its zigzagging, unsteady course.

As his father stood there motionless, obscured in the doorway, with one hand resting on the doorframe, a slow worm appeared on his chest, a thin, bright-gold stripe that went streaking off and disappeared between the wall's purple stones.

Glass snakes – that was what they called slow-worms, whose tails, like those of lizards, so easily broke off between the fingers of anyone who tried to catch them. And in its haste, this slow-worm had broken its delicate tail, which was still snagged where the reptile had just vanished: a little golden tear-drop already tarnishing, there on the wall – and scalding Marceau's cheeks.

He woke with his cheeks aflame, and the blood pounding at his temples. He had a fever. The wind had chilled, and was now blowing strongly, gustily swaying the branches of the magnolia and scattering the opalescent flowers across the yard in drifts. There was no moon any more, either in the sky or on the ground. There was, in the sky and on the ground, the same white trail: the Milky Way, where stars were born amid the most pure violence in the close embrace of soft brightness; the scattered, fallen flowers that were losing their lustre and whose perfume was fading. Marceau could have wept. He felt such total, naked distress, like the distress that sometimes overwhelms small children when love deserts them and they feel abandoned. But he knew that he had been abandoned by everybody. And now he was abandoning himself. He felt weary-worn and jaded with loneliness. He could have wept, taking pity for a moment on the man he was preparing to leave, to yield to death, the man no one cared about and no one would mourn. But he was even incapable of this: he could not even manage a few tears for himself. He was emptied, stricken with aridness. He stared at the faded flowers, now the colour of plaster, that skimmed the ground in the wind.

No, he would not hang himself from the branches of this big tree that had shed its blossoms. This magnolia that he had escorted back from his wedding, like some prisoner of noble birth ceremoniously led into exile, had not a single branch equal to his woe. It had too much pride – that of his frigid, haughty, Corvol wife. And suddenly he had wondered what the name was of the big, red-coated Morvan ox that drew the cart carrying the exiled tree, on that long-ago April morning. It had such a placid gaze.

He would take his woe, his heartache, into the forest, to those trees without splendour, without any display of nacreous flowers of balmy fragrance, or any bitterly scornful nostalgia for a lush garden in the valley – to the oaks, beeches and hornbeams, all those familiar trees among which he and his brother had grown to manhood, and worked.

One day, Leger had asked him why the forests always looked so blue when seen from a distance, and changed colour as soon as you approached them. Leger spent hours gazing into the distance. Only what you could not reach remained blue – the sky, the horizon. And that untouchable, indeed unapproachable, blue enchanted him. Marceau was fond of this slightly crazy, aged child, who could be enchanted by no more than the illusory blue yonder.

But no, even from close up, the forests were blue. The further Marceau penetrated into the forest, the bluer the trees became. Maybe the miracle only occurred at this late hour of the night, almost at the break of day. He walked straight ahead, into the blue shadows of the woods, breathing the smell of the trees and ferns. The further he walked, the lighter grew the burden of his affliction. He no longer felt like weeping. He walked on. And again that absurd but insistent question nagged him: what was the name of the red ox that had drawn the magnificent magnolia? Then into his mind came the recollection of the labourers' slow chanting of the names of the oxen drawing the plough, as they trod the furrows: Fragnot, Corbin, Varmoue, Fleuri, Blondeau, Courtin, Chambrun, Teuchon, Chavot, Chamentin . . . He could hear the deep, singsong voices, with almost the cadences of prayer, of the labourers in the fields.

Was it only in memory that he heard them? Then what was that muffled singing, coming from the heart of the forest? Was it a lament, lullaby, sobbing, or a call? It was a little of all these simultaneously. He walked towards the singing. It was truly blue, there, where the singing softly swelled. Very close by now. Here, in the clearing. He had come to the crossing of the forest paths, at the place called Our-Lady-of-the-Beeches. The circle of angels droned in the damply blowing wind. And the same question kept ringing through his mind: what on earth was the name of that placid, russet-coated ox? The beeches in the shape of angels crooned their monotonous melody. Each had its own inflexions, lost in the single, quiet song of their mingled voices. He joined in their humming – a tree among other trees, a brother returned to the fraternity. He went up to each one, stroking their crudely carved angels' faces. He stopped before the angel-with-the-heart - that offered its heart to whom? Whose was this bared heart? This sad heart of grey wood, moist with dew? He climbed half-way up the trunk of the angel-with-the-heart. And the same question climbed with him: what on earth was the name of that red-coated ox with which he had ambled back from his wedding? He took from his pocket the rope that he had slipped into it before leaving the farm, slowly unrolled it, then tied it round a branch. A patch of blue pierced the still-dark sky above the trees, a most intense and gentle blue. It seemed to him, perched up in the beech-tree, quite possible to reach that small patch of blue and touch it with his fingertips. He passed the slip-knot round his neck, continuing to hum. Amid a rustling of damp leaves, the birds started to waken, sounding their first notes. He jumped into space. At that moment the name of the ox came back to him: it was quite simply, Joli! His clogs had fallen into the grass, and as he dangled at the end of the rope, his heels very softly banged against the angel's heart.

THE GIFT

There were no singing, no prayers, none of that, at his interment. There was no mass. He was buried like a pagan. His father, Claude and Camille led the cortege on foot. La Fine and several men came after, but there were few prepared to follow the coffin of a man who had killed himself. Among those few were Ephraim and his sons. They did not exchange a single word with the old man. Not for one moment did Camille raise her eyes to gaze on the faces of those present: there was among them one face that she could not have beheld without turning pale, without looking him straight in the eye and crying, 'Take me away!' She had to keep silent her desire, subdue the passion of her heart, bury as deep as possible the avowal of her love – otherwise all was lost.

Leger did not attend Marceau's burial. Claude did not want him to come, because he had not yet recovered from the trauma of their father's funeral. Not that he had been affected by the death of that father whom he had scarcely known, but the ceremony, the congregation dressed in black, the dirges, and then the procession to the family tomb had thrown his too delicate spirit into terrible distress. Claude had even concealed from him the fact that Marceau was dead, and ordered the others not to say anything. She told him that Marceau had gone away for a few days, that the old man had sent him to Vermenton on business. Then she announced her decision to go back and live in their house in Clamecy, as though breaking to him a most wonderful piece of news.

'What about Marceau?' Leger asked anxiously.

'He'll come and join us there soon.' Claude was well aware that with the passage of time Leger had grown fond of this man who, as far as she was concerned, had always left her in a state of cold indifference more or less tinged, from one day to the next, with disgust or hostility. She sensed that her infantile brother had come to regard as a father a man who was actually no more than a very nominal brother-in-law. But hatred and rancour and scorn were alien to Leger's great simple-heartedness, and this was why Claude lied to him.

'And will Camille come, too?'

'Yes.'

'And Mother?' he had added finally, in a yet more anxious voice.

'We'll continue to wait for her,' Camille had forced herself to reply, this third lie raising her bile, but Leger had only survived the last thirty years sustained by this illusion, and it was far too late now to break the hazy charm of such a falsehood. Leger left her no choice but to perpetuate the deception.

Claude hastened the preparations for their departure, which Ambroise Mauperthuis, far from opposing, gladly approved. He did not care if Corvol's daughter left, taking away that freak brother of hers. Camille was all that mattered. Catherine-Camille, 'my Spark of Life', as he liked to call her. From now on he would be alone with her, he would have her all to himself more than ever before. And surely he would soon reconquer her affection and trust, which she seemed to have withdrawn from him since that blasted 15th August festival. He even agreed to accompany his daughter-in-law, the widow, down to her retreat in the valley. Once again he harnessed two oxen to a cart, loaded with Claude's piano and trunks, and on which she installed herself with Leger.

And Claude left Oak-Wolf just as she had come there a quarter of a century earlier. But this time the cart had not been repainted: it was mud-stained and smelt of cow-dung and mildew. The oxen's horns were unadorned in the grey autumn rain. A piece of canvas covered the trunks and the grand piano that had once so astounded the village peasants. Claude was no longer radiant in white, beneath a long, lace veil: already a little stooped, and even thinner now, she sat wrapped in a big, black velvet cape – the pall that had shrouded her father's coffin. For it was not at all as Marceau Mauperthuis' widow that she left the farm of her deceased husband, but as Victor Corvol's bereaved child that she returned to her forebears' house. No other cart followed behind. The magnolia was left in the yard of Threshold Farm. It had rooted itself too deeply and grown too big to be transplanted yet again, while both the ox, Joli, that had drawn it and Marceau, who had led the animal, had lost any roots they had once had in this world.

Bundled up in a thick, brown, woollen overcoat, Leger clutched in his lap a wooden top painted bright blue. It was Marceau who had made it for him.

The only person who remained completely unchanged was Ambroise Mauperthuis – with the same robust stature, the same heavy tread, the same dull gleam in his eye, the same hard and stubborn air.

Camille had seen off her mother and Leger, accompanying their dismal conveyance to the edge of the village. They formed a procession as silent and lugubrious as the one that had followed her father's body a few days before. After her father, her mother was now leaving. But both her father and mother had so singularly failed to fulfil their roles for their only daughter, both living at such a remove from her childhood, her games, her joys and sorrows, her worries and dreams, her hopes and emotions, that they departed without leaving any real trace or causing any pain. No sense of absence opened in their wake; they had always been absent. Only a thin trail of bitterness was left behind them. Loneliness closed in on her, and at the same time extended around her as vacant space where anything might happen.

But everything had already happened to her – everything. She had already tasted happiness, the robust, fiery taste of insane happiness. Yes, this sour woman, lacking in all tenderness, who had taken the trouble only to give birth to her, might just as well go away never to return – without a word, or a kiss, or even one backward glance. It would not make any difference really. It was enough that

La Fine was staying, who had always been a mother to her. But she would miss Leger. She called him 'Little Uncle', although she actually considered him more as a very young brother than an uncle. A much younger brother who had hardly shared her games at all when she was a child, for right from the start her mother had taken pains not to leave them together, and had always kept Leger with her, like a bird in a cage. An humming-bird, invisibly snared by the languid beauty of the tunes she played on the piano, in the drawing room with the shutters half-closed. A frail, melancholy bird, confined within secret, age-old memories, to which Camille was never allowed access. Yet there were days when they spent a little time together, and those moments stolen from the dual vigilance of Claude and old Mauperthuis, who both contrived in their separate ways to keep them living as strangers to each other in the same house, had always been peaceful, happy moments. Unable to share their games, they had shared their dreams. Leger seemed to have no other occupation, or vocation, in this world but to dream. The dreams that filled his nights continued as daytime reveries. His life was one long, continuous dream, more or less sorrowful, more or less consoling. His dreams fed on the simple images afforded to him by his daily life: the untouchable blue of the sky, the deep, unattainable blue of the horizon, the trees, reeds, grasses and flowers, oxen and birds, and the big black piano. These simple things were magic to him, objects of amazement and transformation - now anxiety, now enchantment.

And his dreams, too, were magical – at least, Camille thought so. At the beginning of summer, Leger had told her of a dream that he had had the night before. They were sitting side by side on the old, semi-dilapidated wall separating the garden from the orchard behind the farm. Tufts of saxifrage, with bright yellow flowers, sprang out between the stones.

'Last night I had a dream. It was strange . . .' He always began his accounts in this way. 'There were sheets drying in the meadows, but the wind rose and the sheets blew away. They were so many of them, you couldn't see the sky any more, or the sun. They flapped in the wind. I heard the sharp sound they made as they flapped, and that sound kept echoing to infinity. It was from these sheets that the light came. They were at once sky, light, birds and clouds. And the light cast by these sheets was white and soft – a morning brightness, that of a fine morning of white linen. The earth smelt of washing. People glided like fish past all those sheets. They swam through the air in slow motion: they were asleep in the sky. They swam and slept among the sheets in silence. They looked happy. The women's hair floated around them, and they smiled in their sleep. The men took the women in their arms, and they began to dance, all of them spinning through the sky. But it was always the same woman and the same man, a single, innumerable couple. I didn't see their faces, but I sensed that they were smiling. And then the sheets tore into thousands upon thousands of little bits of cloth, like white butterflies fluttering in the light. These white butterflies turned into flowers, thousands upon thousands of white flowers that were so sweet-smelling! All the trees in the orchard were in blossom, a magnificent flowering of cherry- and plum-trees, of apple, pear, and rowan. This orchard was much bigger than the orchard on the farm. It was truly vast. And there were other trees besides – chestnut and lilac, and every one of them in flower. And all these flowers twirled slowly in the air, covering the sky and the earth, and people were swimming through the flowers. In my dream I smelt their fragrance, and at the same time I had the taste in my mouth of fruit that would later ripen. And this taste brought a sweet saliva into my mouth. And then the flowers became almost like foam, like the waters of a mountain stream – rushing waters, flowing ever more swiftly. I sensed that swiftness, and I was scared, and at the same time it was . . . I don't know how to describe it . . . You know, it was rather like when you have a high fever: you feel hot and cold simultaneously, you're lying still in bed and yet you have the feeling of moving very fast, of hurtling through space . . . Well, it was strange. And I was very frightened. The water was absolutely freezing cold. And I was lying at the bottom of that water, like a pebble. And through the water I could see the sky, so blue and bright. It was as though I could hear the light tinkling.' He fell silent.

'And then?' said Camille.

'Then? Well, nothing. That's all. I've forgotten, or else I woke up.'

'Nothing very much happens in your dream, but it's a very pretty dream – I like it.'

'If you want, I'll give it to you,' said Leger, who was always ready to make a gift of anything at all – a blade of grass, a snail-shell, a little mother-of-pearl button, a lucky charm from a Twelfth-Night cake, or a dried flower – as if each of these were a rare and precious object. Camille laughed.

'You can't give away a dream.'

'Why not?'

'Because it doesn't exist. Dreams are just images that go through our minds when we're asleep, and then fade away. They're like clouds. You can't give away a cloud.'

Leger reflected for a while, then replied in that always rather worried and grave manner typical of this aged child, 'That's not true, dreams are real pictures. When I was at school, the teacher sometimes gave me pictures, and when I made my First Communion I received some more, to mark the pages of my missal. I still remember all those images, I've even kept a lot of them. When I look at a field, a forest, the smoke from a fire, a squirrel, or a bird, I see a picture, and if I like it, I keep it. I keep everything I see. I think we have plenty of eyes, lots and lots of them. And all these eyes open at night. Dreams are our night-eyes.'

'Well, if I take your dream, what shall I do with it?'

'I don't know. You could make other dreams out of it.'

'Or put it between the pages of a book, like the pictures you got at school and for your First Communion.'

Again, Leger reflected. However frivolous a question might be, however whimsical a remark, he always treated it seriously. So great was his naivety that he was incapable of realizing when he was being teased. But he had not had time to think of an answer to Camille's last question. They heard Claude's voice, calling him from the garden, and he at once jumped down from the wall and went running to her. Camille remained by herself for a while: it was nearly noon, the blazing sun was at its height, and little grey lizards darted over the stones, while wasps hovered over the saxifrage. She gazed at these tufts of flowers with keen attention, and thought, 'This is how Leger looks at everything, even blades of grass and pebbles. It's how he manages to keep so many images.'

Then she went back to the farmhouse. But by the time she had crossed the garden, she had forgotten the dream that Leger had just offered her. It was not until the end of summer that she came upon it again, like something forgotten in the bottom of a pocket. When old Mauperthuis, together with Marceau, Claude and Leger, went to Clamecy to attend Victor Corvol's funeral, Camille had stayed behind on the farm with La Fine. It was the first time that she had ever been left on her own like this, with such a free run of Threshold Farm. She had delighted in exploring the house, going into all the rooms, especially those she had never been allowed into before. She went into her mother's bedroom, her father's and her grandfather's, all of them austere, silent rooms. She had crept into the drawing-room and sat down at the piano, but without daring to touch it. She had merely run her fingertips very lightly over the smooth, cold keys. The music that she wanted to hear was not the piano's languid melodies, only capable of enchanting the dead, but something quite different, something she had heard for the first time at Beech-Cross: music with the nine brothers' rhythm and verve.

WASH-DAYS

It was during those few days' holiday that the ritual of the great annual wash took place, with which Camille helped La Fine. Having left all the household linen to soak for a long time in clean water, they then piled it into the huge washing-tub that stood on a tripod in the back yard by the kitchen door. They placed soap-flakes and sweet-smelling roots between the folds of each layer of linen – sheets, tea-towels, underwear and table linen – then tied it all up inside the old sheet laid at the bottom of the tub and knotted together by the corners. Finally, they covered the whole lot with a big hempen cloth on which they spread a thick layer of oak ash. The first wash-day: a day of cloth and ashes.

The next day was entirely devoted to a slow pouring into the tub of water set to boil on the hearth, and the continuous filtering of water through the wash. The oak-ash cleaned the linen of bodily soil, of sweat and stains. The smell of the oiris roots rose from the wet linen in blue-tinged clouds of steam. There was an interpenetration of all the different textures: of dead trees, human beings, plants and water. And this alchemy of textures, sublimated into a light and fragrant vapour, occurred in every yard in the village. All the women busied themselves around their tubs, their faces and arms imbued with sweat and a bluish mist. All the women gleamed with a warm and watery blueness. The second wash-day: a day of steam and texture and fragrances.

The following day they emptied the tub in the yard and piled the linen into a wheelbarrow, which they covered with a sheet, and then made their way to the wash-house. All the women were gathered there with their wheelbarrows filled with still-steaming laundry. Each one went down on her knees in a little wooden box lined with straw or a folded rag, then leaning over the wash-basin threw into the water a sheet or tablecloth. A terrific din resounded in the wash-house. The women called out to each, laughing and shouting, from all around the wash-basin, over the scrubbing sound of their brushes and the smack of their beetles. Edmée and Fat-Ginnie were there, together with Loulou-the-Bellclinker, who had come to help with the rinsing. The women liked him; he was funny and made them laugh, and was always so eager to please and lend everyone a hand. The water splashed right up to the roofbeams, the drops rising in the light in a dazzling spray, while a brownish scum issued from the sheets. The whole year's grime came out in the ice-cold swirling water in frills of grey. Then, when the water finally was clear again, the washerwomen blued their laundry. Great streaks of azure spread across the basin, clusters of iridescent bubbles danced around the washerwomen's hands. Some plunged their reddened arms to the bottom of the water to retrieve a brush or beetle that had fallen in. Then they twisted the laundry to wring it, still kneeling in the wet boxes, and their arms, too, seemed to twist round. The third wash-day: a day of great noise, of splashing and bluing.

When they came out of the wash-house and were loading their laundry back on to the wheelbarrows, they laughed as they caught sight of Huguet Cordebugle spying on them from his window, with black looks and rolling eyes. He could not stand these grand wash-days, when all the women of the village gathered in the wash-house by his farm. He heard their shouting and high-pitched laughter, and it drove him mad. He was in a fury all day long. But not for anything in the world would he have left his house during those days. Posted behind curtains stiff with dirt and dust, he kept avid watch, relishing the anger that the sight of all these dreadful screeching hussies caused him, with Alphonse (Tatave's third successor, after Baron and Raspberry) perched on his lap, frantically shaking his blood-red comb. Even more bad-tempered than its three predecessors put together, this cockerel seemed indestructible. Going on for thirteen years old, it still squawked as much as ever, though sounding increasingly hoarse and crowing for matins at the wrong time. To bolster his spirits while surreptiously keeping watch from behind his filthy window-panes, Huguet drank one glass of wine after another, swilling it down. It mostly bolstered his anger and dampened his spirits. He ritually fell asleep, dead drunk, in his chair, every evening after laundry-day at the wash-house, with old Alphonse slumped in his lap. But he always woke up in the middle of the night, then immediately went out marauding in people's gardens, leaving a hagard-looking Alphonse on the chair.

His fury turned to jubilation when the women made fun of him in loud voices, and shook their fists at him, laughing, as they loaded their linen on to their wheelbarrows before leaving. For they knew perfectly well that this old grouser, who would spit after them for no good reason, came creeping into their gardens at night to steal their underwear hung out to dry. He stole night-dresses, camisoles, knickers and petticoats. And he stole underwear from the gardens not only in Oak-Wolf but in every hamlet and village he passed through. It was not really known what he did with all this women's lingerie; it was suspected that he must dirty it. No one had entered his house since his parents died, for he boorishly did not open his door to anybody, but he was generally thought to be living in a pigsty.

This was more or less the case, but there was something people did not know. He did indeed live in the most dismal squalor: he had reduced his living space to a single room that served him as kitchen, bedroom, living room, lumber-room, and garden shed combined, where he kept his tools, logs and kindling, as well as his food supplies. Suspended from lines stretched across the room were pieces of meat, mushrooms and plants that he was drying. His few clothes hung from nails on the walls. Everything was impregnated, even saturated, with a fetid stench, in which the fumes from the fire mingled with the smell of dust, mildew, pork fat, and the straw in his mattress that he never changed. But there was another room at the back of his house: it was small and almost always locked. This room was spotlessly clean. At the windows, whose shutters he invariably kept closed, hung white cotton curtains fringed with lace that he had made out of night-dresses. Similarly, he had made table-mats, sheets, pillowcases, and a bedspread, by cutting up and sewing together all the women's underwear that he had filched from here and there. Far from soiling this stolen linen, as people suspected, he treated it with great care. He spent his evenings diligently cutting and sewing, using the needlework kit inherited from his mother. Over the years, his secret room had become a veritable young girl's boudoir, all draped in white and fragrant with aromatic plants.

For a whole month, he would not wash or change his clothes, sleeping fully dressed on his damp straw pallet, covered with dirty old sheets, and with Alphonse the cockerel perched on the back of a chair at his side. But at every new moon, he underwent a radical transformation. He took off the clothes he had been wearing for a month, sluiced himself clean, then put on a gorgeously extravagant night-shirt and went to sleep in the immaculate bed in the little room, having warmed the bedclothes with a warming-pan filled with hot coals. He slept right through the night – a long, delicious night – enveloped in the soft whiteness of fine linen, immense sheets of skin made of cloth and lace, the delicate slough cast by women's bodies that he instilled with new warmth and life. The very next day he put on his old clothes again, and did not wash at all until the next new moon.

La Fine and Camille arrived back at Threshold Farm and went to hang the laundry out to dry in the garden, laying the bedlinen out on the grass in the meadow. Exhausted by hours of rinsing in the wash-house and dazzled by the reflection of those huge white expanses of cloth, Camille stretched out on the ground, between the wet sheets, and fell asleep. She slept until evening. It was La Fine who woke her, calling her in for supper. She stood up, her body feeling pleasantly lethargic after her long siesta in the sun, cradled in the earth's warmth, amid the scent of the grass and flowers and the smell of the sheets. She had slept in the gentle warmth and roundedness of the day, as though in the curve of a shoulder. As she walked past the farm buildings, she passed Simon-the-Hothead coming out of the cowshed – she, all pink and golden, almost stumbling like a sleepwalker in the fading light of day; he, standing in the cool shade of the cowshed doorway. She stopped, uncertain, her eyes still silky with sleep, and gazed at him in amazement. He simply stepped forward, caught her by the waist, and kissed her. Then she went back to the farmhouse to join La Fine.

She had not exchanged a single word with Simon. They had kissed at the end of the day, between shadow and light, coolness and warmth, sleep and wakefulness. But after supper, when it was time to go up to her room, Camille crept out secretly, and returned to the meadow. Simon was there. For a while, they stood face to face, not moving, just staring at each other. Then all of a sudden, as though in response to some lightning signal, still facing each other in silence, they undressed with swift, confident movements. They seized each other and now their movements became fumbling, too hasty, almost rough. They dropped to the ground, their bodies yielding beneath the weight of desire, overcome with wonder, in the hunger and splendour of their nakedness. Entwined together, they rolled among the sheets in the dew-soaked grass. They crawled upon the earth; they swam with their bodies pressed against each other, skin to skin, in the grass, among the sheets. They nestled together, each buried as deep inside the other as possible, in the damp warmth of their flesh, an ardent, liqueur-like warmth. They tasted each other's skin, savouring all the moisture exuded through their skin, and all the smells. They kissed passionately, hungrily, and with mouths scalded by saliva and burning with thirst they licked and nibbled and clasped each other, suffering the anguish of the most impulsive tenderness.

Exhausted by their wild lovemaking, they sank into a deep sleep, locked together. The sheets' chalky whiteness lay spread all around them in the darkness, like a pure and tranquil nudity: the earth that night was crazed with nudity; it was a paean to naked flesh, a hymn to desire. They slept until daybreak. Then they hurriedly dressed, but their movements were clumsy and they dressed in confusion, getting tangled in their clothes as if they had not regained full command of their bodies. But at that moment they were neither in command nor possession of themselves, nor did they know any more which of their two bodies was their own. The only thing they both knew was that their true body from now on was the other's.

They went home furtively, she to her room at Threshold Farm, he to Upper Farm. But these were vain precautions to protect their secret, for someone had already seen them. And that someone was Huguet Cordebugle, who stole into the Mauperthuis' garden during the night, coming to plunder the washing-lines. As he was stuffing one of Camille's petticoats into his pouch, he had glimpsed a strange shape, moving in an even stranger manner, over on the far side of the orchard, in the chequered meadow. Without making a sound, he had gone up to the low wall at the bottom of the garden and taken a good look. It was a dark night, but the sheets spread out on the ground broke the darkness with a dull gleam. And it was by the murky brightness of these sheets that he had recognized the couple entwined in the grass: Camille and Simon Mauperthuis, from the two enemy farms – Camille the Serpent, La Corvol's daughter, the granddaughter of the fugitive from the valley, the same impudent Camille who, that very morning, had been laughing her head off with the women at the wash-house. The Mauperthuis girl – my, what a fast one she was! While the old man and her parents were away burying her grandfather, that old crackpot down in the valley, she took the opportunity to mate like a bitch with the farm's cowherd! The wanton little hussy! He had seen her body, and how beautiful and supple it was. He had seen how that body could abandon itself, and swing its hips, and arch its back, and lay itself open. How that body contrived to embrace its prey, and then suddenly clamp round it, holding it between its limbs with a voracious and terrible gentleness. He had seen, too, above all, Simon's body – the movements of his body, how it gripped the other and held her, driving into her with increasingly rapid thrusts of his loins. He had watched the couple, even to the point of enthralment and grief, then gone away without a sound, clutching his cotton booty in his pouch and treasuring his carnal secret in his madness.

Ambroise Mauperthuis, his son and daughter-in-law, together with Leger, returned at nightfall the next day. And Camille had to keep silent her joy and desire, to contain the surge of this new happiness welling up inside her – in her heart and in her flesh – like a cry, like laughter. Yet she had not been able to suppress a dazzling smile of joy at the sight of Leger. But this aged child had come home much too overwhelmed by the gloomy ceremony he had just attended to be able to catch this beamingly happy smile and grasp its meaning. He had had other dreams since the one he gave to Camille. That dream belonged to no one but her now, and she had already shared it with somebody else. That dream had become incarnate, invested with a dual, crazed body.

The next night, Marceau had left the farm to go in search of oblivion, deliverance and peace, from the branch of the angel-with-the-heart in the clearing of Our-Lady-of-the-Beeches. Then a few days later, it was the turn of her mother and Leger to leave. The farm was emptying. As if Camille's new body were driving everyone away – everyone that was not Simon. As if the happiness that had carried her heart by storm were sweeping through the house with the unruliness of a great wind, chasing out all those with hearts too bruised to withstand the rigours of joy, the clamours of desire. Time, which had seemed to stagnate all these long years, drip-dripping away with heedless monotony, was suddenly surging ahead, swirling

148

and mounting. Time was racing on with the utmost swiftness, like the waters of the streams and rivers at the time of
year when the logs were floated down, and the sluice-gates
of ponds and lakes were opened to hasten the flow.

Away they went, those chilly, morose and timorous
bodies, like dead wood swept along by living waters.
Away they went, going to ground, taking refuge at the
bottom of the valley. Away they went, those poor bodies,
crackling with loneliness, worn out with boredom. They
fled to rooms more bare and bitter-cold than those where
they had slept night after night for dozens of years, those
austere rooms at Threshold Farm, with their beds like
wooden boxes. Scattered by the wind like dust, all those
destitute bodies fled. They fled – and good riddance to
them! That very same night after her mother left, Camille
joined Simon again, for yet another carnal feast, another
celebration of flesh and nakedness.

'And the Temple of God was opened in heaven.' It was the
earth, time, and the world that had just opened. And
beauty had appeared, close to the skin, deep in the flesh, on
the face of the earth.

'And there appeared a great wonder in heaven.' A great
wonder had struck the earth and marked their bodies. A
wonder as forceful as the living water and the living wind,
as keen as hunger, as violent as the midday sun in summer,
at once bitter and sweet, thirst and drunkenness, dancing
and sleeping: desire.

'A woman clothed with the sun, and the moon under
her feet, and upon her head a crown of twelve stars.'
Camille was that woman. A naked woman clothed in her
desire for the weight of a man's body upon her own,
happy in the smell of a man's body on her skin, and with
the wet pleasuring of a man's body for her kingdom. A
woman so much in love that she was naked even when
clothed, so desiring that she was naked to the point of
distraction. And her heart, too, was bared, and her gaze
distracted – radiant with distraction.

Camille had become the woman she had seen in a dream after the ceremony of Our-Lady-of-the-Beeches. She transgressed reality – thought and desire were fully endued with substance, life, and energy. She confused Blaise-the-Ugly's recital, Leger's dream and the days of her love. She confused her body with Simon's. She confused words, images, and flesh. Everything was sensation; she saw words, and touched them; she smelt images, laid hold of thoughts, and embraced dreams; she walked among recitals as though walking barefoot in dewy grass, running and dancing. To her, everything was voluptuousness, infinite tenderness, and strength – the light of day, night, silence and noise, the taste of food, the smell of the earth, the least thing that she brushed against. To her, everything was Simon.

Simon had taken Camille to see his brothers. They had all met up one evening in Jalles Forest, near the Morning brothers' cabin. They had eaten and drunk, and laughed and sung, and Blaise-the-Ugly had told stories. It was a clear night, twinkling with stars. Martin-the-Sparing, not being one for words, had lifted his arm to the sky, pointing out to the others the Milky Way, of luminous whiteness in that moonless night. His brothers fell quiet at his gesture: a slow, precise gesture, wordlessly indicating where beauty lay. For him, gestures took the place of words.

They all looked up, and Adrien-the-Blue soon broke the silence with his tremendous laugh. 'All those stars shining up there are bursts of laughter. It's God who's laughing. On the last day of Creation, He laughed to see the world looking so beautiful. Maybe when He saw the forests rising from the earth?'

'Look,' said Ferdinand-the-Strong, 'it's like a long beam supporting the heavens. It's a giant oak-tree felled across the sky, and those are its acorns shining, thousands upon thousands of them. God wields the axe.'

'Do stars make any sound? Could there be music up there?' asked Germain-the-Deaf.

'Certainly, but no one can hear it,' replied Blaise-the-Ugly. 'It's a music too violent for us, a music so violent that it becomes visible. And it's a beautiful sight. It's like a swarm of white bees flying over the earth, marking a trail. It's the path taken by souls returning to the next world. We need to be shown that path.'

'It also looks like a great flight of white birds,' said Leon-the-Loner. 'It's the path of dead birds. Up there is the land of solitude. No one has a name up there, or a body, or a house – nothing. Everyone's light and transparent, flying through emptiness and silence. We all become birds of eternity.'

'I see fish,' said Eloi-Elsewhere, 'fish like those that swim in that lake over there, that transparent lake . . . they're the footsteps of those that walk on the waters of that lake . . . one day we, too, will walk up there . . .'

'Walk?' echoed Loulou-the-Bellringer. 'But of course those are footsteps! Footsteps in the sky. They're the Virgin's footsteps. She runs up there over our heads.'

'It's a great river,' declared Simon-the-Hothead. 'Up there, too, perhaps, there are oxen, and at night they go and drink from this river. They're the oxen that draw the sun across the sky during the day, the oxen of light. At night they rest. They go and bathe in this river.'

'It's a mountain stream,' thought Camille, 'a mountain stream like the one in Leger's dream. Its icy waters flow through space. And I'm looking up from the bottom of that water. Like a pebble. And I move in the waters of that stream. I see the sky, the earth, Simon. My gaze travels in the stream. The world shines brightly. It's Simon's body.'

Camille was with the brothers. She sat leaning against Simon, watching the Milky Way shimmering in the sky. She saw her thoughts and dreams everywhere, assuming shape, light and movement. She seemed to hold eternity in her hands, like a fine fruit, still hanging from the tree and all warmed by the sun, placed in her palms before being picked. Her joy had the fullness and sweetness, the smell and the taste of a ripe fruit. It had the earth's roundedness, the roundedness of the day encircled by the sun, the roundedness of a body caressed in love. Her joy yearned for eternity. And each moment spent with Simon made keener that yearning even while it satisfied it.

THE SMELL OF MIST

Camille's joy yearned for eternity, and that eternity was resplendent in Simon's body, in his smile and in his name. But Time also had a name – that of Ambroise Mauperthuis.

As soon as his widowed daughter-in-law was reinstalled in the valley, old Mauperthuis returned to Oak-Wolf. He was in a hurry to get back, because from now on, Camille, his Spark of Life, would be truly his, and belong to no one else but him. Although Marceau, Claude and Leger had never been very close to Camille, or made any great claim on her, yet their departure was a relief to him, and his jealousy-crazed heart leapt with joy. He would live with his Spark of Life at Threshold Farm till the end of his days. He could not imagine anything other than that – he and his Spark of Life, day after day, season after season, year after year. For he gave no more thought to his own age than he did to Camille's. He was already old – but since age had no dominion over him, and he remained as robust and strong as in the days of his youth, as if the years had been arrested one spring morning on the banks of the Yonne – what did it matter? He felt strong enough to survive several decades more. Camille was now a woman, and her beauty drew men's eyes and attracted their desire, but what man would dare consider himself worthy of such beauty? He knew of none, and refused to admit of any. He alone would enjoy Camille's beauty and presence. He desired nothing more than to keep her by his side, to watch her live. Was he not entitled to this? It was he who had created Camille, who had seized from death Catherine's beauty and given it life and light. It was he who had cancelled the crime committed by Vincent Corvol, who himself was irreversibly dead, without remission, for ever – and would that the black devils of vengeance clawed his soul to shreds, as his heart and hand had been devoured by swine. It was he, Mauperthuis, who had buried Catherine's body, and who by force of will, and stubbornness, had caused that body to rise again. It was he who had wrested from the desiccated womb of grey Claude Corvol this much-desired body, this glorious body: Catherine-Camille. His Spark of Life.

In the joy of returning home, old Mauperthuis forgot how much Camille's attitude and behaviour towards him had changed in recent weeks, how distant and withdrawn she had become. He was unaware, as he entered the yard of Threshold Farm, that Camille had actually forgotten about him, as she had forgotten about her father and mother. He was even more unaware that she was prepared to repudiate him if he tried too quickly to break the spell of that forgetfulness.

He found her with La Fine, both busy tidying the linen away in the cupboards. When he came into the room, gaily greeting her from the doorway, Camille did not turn round. All she did was to start slightly. That excessively loud and rough-sounding voice that was always domineering, even in joy, struck her like a stone thrown at her back.

'Well, aren't you going to come and kiss me?' asked the old man.

Since she still did not stir, he went over to her, seized her by the shoulders and, forcing her to turn round finally to face him, he added in a tone of triumph, 'The two of us are alone now. So we'll have to be friends, like before – even more than before.'

Camille kept her eyes lowered, her face set. The old man put this coldness down to the sorrow that Camille must be feeling at having lost her father and, after all, perhaps, too, at having been abandoned by her mother.

'Now then, my lovely, don't look so miserable. Your mother never liked this place, or this farm, that's why she left. She's back down in the valley now. So, let her stay there, if that's where she wants to be! Your father's resting in peace now. It's not your fault, and it's not mine, that he was never happy, that he didn't like being alive. But this is

154

your home, and the farm, the forests, the meadows and the land are just as much yours as mine. You're the queen here, you're my queen! So don't look so sad. There are good times ahead of us!'

She let him talk, at once relieved by this misunderstanding and ashamed of being credited with a grief that she ought to have to felt but did not. He offered his brow to her to be kissed, as she always used to kiss him. But the kiss she placed on her grandfather's forehead made her want to weep, to scream. She was no longer the adoring child, no longer the affectionately filial young girl as he still liked to think of her. She had turned into somebody different – somebody in love and jealous of her love, fearful for her love, and capable of every violence to safeguard that love. And it was the person whose brow she kissed of whom she was apprehensive for her love.

After Ambroise's return, Camille at first managed to be careful. Only with infinite precautions did she leave her room to go and join Simon. She would wait until the middle of the night, when she was sure that La Fine and the old man were fast asleep, before creeping away from the farm. She would meet Simon at the bottom of the meadow or at the edge of the forest. But autumn was setting in, and the rain and the cold drove them off the land. They stole into barns and cowsheds, their nakedness accommodating itself as well to straw and hay as the grass and leaves. They made love in silence, as if the least moan of pleasure might have risked waking the old man asleep on the far side of the farm buildings. And this silence they imposed on their mouths enveloped them in a physical delight even greater, more unsettling and profound. This silence was like the very integument of their pleasure: a second, invisible and almost impalpable skin born each time of their two entwined bodies, coupling them with a bond so sweet, so violent that it was as much a wonder as a terror to them. On moonlit nights a faint brightness shone through the skylights and their bodies took on a slightly blue-tinged milkiness. Their bodies became glimmerings, moving reflections, and their hands and mouths frantically sought to follow these glimmerings, to seize these reflections. These were their true bodies, and when the time came for them to part, to rush off in opposite directions, having dressed in all haste, they felt then as if they were naked, and the cold penetrated their flesh with a searing pain that made them quake.

Camille managed to evade the old man's vigilance, and he had never yet caught her escaping or coming home, a fugitive shadow in the night. She managed to betray nothing of her love and desire, training her gaze to remain impassive and her face to wear an expression of cold ingenuousness, so that the old man might not detect the least sign. She pretended to be as before, and the old man was duped. But one evening, he returned home from Château-Chinon, where he had been for a few days attending a timber sale – without Camille, who had claimed to have a temperature in order to stay at the farm – and bending down to kiss her, he detected the smell on her skin of the cold and mist, mingled with another smell.

He straightened up again. 'Where have you been? If you're ill, why did you go out?'

'I haven't left the house. Ask La Fine!' Camille replied at once, knowing that La Fine would never have the heart to contradict her in front of the old man.

'Then why do you smell of the mist, as if you'd been out?' he insisted.

'I just went out into the garden for a moment. I don't like staying cooped up inside all day. And anyway, I'm already feeling better. I haven't a temperature any more,' Camille replied calmly.

But the old man persisted.

'In the garden, eh? So the mist in the garden has the smell of a man on it? Where have you been, you slut? Tell me, who have you been rubbing up against?'

This time Camille did not say anything. She suddenly turned pale and darted him a look so terrified and at the same time so defiant that the vague suspicion that had insinuated itself in him all at once crystallized into certainty. There was nothing more to be said: they had just toppled beyond the realm of words. Without further reflection, he slapped her across the face. As in the summer, in the clearing of Our-Lady-of-the-Beeches, she held her own against him. She did not lower her gaze, and her gaze was that of a lover suddenly meeting a threat to her passion and all armed to counterattack. At that point Ambroise Mauperthuis' heart froze. He had just seen the look that Catherine Corvol had given her husband on the road to the station that ran alongside the Yonne; that vibrant look of a woman in love, a look of splendour, pain and anger. A look he had only seen fixed in death, and which he had usurped, as though he were the lover that Catherine had been running to that morning. And he was seized with terror.

'But ... but ...' he stammered at Camille, 'tell me, what's wrong with you? It's me, don't you recognize me? It's me ... me ...' He sank to his knees.

'I'm the man you were running to. The man you've been running to for so many, many years, for ever and always. The one for whom you left your home, your family, your wealth, and your name. I'm the man you love. I'm the one you've been running to. Don't you recognize me? Who hit you, my Spark of Life, my love? Who's been trying to keep you away from me, to turn you against me? Who is it that has tainted you with another man's smell? I'm the one you love, the one you're seeking, it's to me that you're running, and yet you don't recognize me?'

Collapsed in a heap at Camille's feet, he began to sob, while she looked at him with terror and now pity. For the first time in his life, Ambroise Mauperthuis wept. He held Camille by the heels, his head resting on her feet and his tears spilling over them.

'Come on, get up, get up,' she kept saying, bending down and trying to force him to stand. All her anger had died, but a strange fear choked her. She did not understand anything any more. She wanted to help her grandfather, to calm and console him, and at the same time she wanted to run away. His hands on her ankles were strangling her, as though gripped round her neck. His tears spilling over her feet scalded the skin on her face. Her heart whirled dizzyingly with pity, fear and disgust. The old man kept cringing on the ground, his face buried against her legs in abject despair, as he cried, weeping and moaning.

At last he released his grip and stood up, bowed and stooped, then went off without saying any more, still sobbing. He climbed up to his room, and went to bed. That night he was overtaken with a fever. He who had never in his entire life been ill before had to stay in bed for more than ten days. His fever lasted day and night all that time, and the doctor that Camille had sent Toinu Follin to fetch from the neighbouring village could not bring down his temperature, or explain the reason for it. Camille spent hours at her grandfather's bedside, watching over him and taking care of him. Shame, remorse and pity for the old man now kept her beside him in a constant state of alarm. All the fondness she had felt for him until the last few months came flooding back into her heart, and her memories returned: memories of her childhood and adolescence, still so close in time, yet suddenly so distant now, since the arrival in her life of Simon. Recollections of herself with her grandfather flashed through her mind in no particular order, like a randomly leafed-through picture-book. He had always been there, close at hand. The earth, the seasons, and the forests – he was all these things. He had taught her everything about the land, the weather, about animals and the forests. He had laid out his riches for her; he had only worked so hard for her benefit. He had never loved anyone but her. She now understood all this, and she took full measure of this man's presence in her life. And she felt a terrible anguish to see him so ill, perhaps dying.

This anguish was all the more terrible for not being pure. However deep and sincere her distress at seeing him so poorly, the remorse she felt for having caused him such despair and for having provoked this fever, and the childish fear that knotted her stomach at the thought that he might die, she was none the less possessed by quite another sentiment. A bizarre sentiment that she could not define and dared not admit to herself so much did it resemble hope – a hope as ignominious as it was bold and grasping: the hope that he would die, freeing her from the burden and menaces of the too-possessive love of this grandfather who ruled as all-powerful lord and master.

Camille felt as though inwardly split in two. There was the child full of affection, gratitude and concern, seated at the bedside of the patient she devotedly watched over and cared for, and there was the other one: the one who was madly in love and wanted only to rush from this bedroom, to run far away from the old man lying here, delirious with fever, and to return to Simon. And the earnest, loving child who had at every step to battle secretly and relentlessly with this headstrong lover, to force her to remain silent, to keep calm. But as soon as La Fine came to relieve her at Ambroise Mauperthuis' bedside, the lover would at once leap up and overcome the anxious child, gagging her in turn, supplanting her filial heart with the reclaimed heart of a woman in love.

When she was with Simon, Camille did not talk about her grandfather. The hours spent at the sick man's bedside were hours of recollection, pain and distress. The hours spent with Simon were hours of forgetfulness, happiness and peace. They spoke no more of the future than of the past, and least of all of the present. For them, it was as if time had become snared in a solidly opaque darkness, broken only by an archipelago of bright moments – sparkles of eternity. The past would have been too painful to evoke, because behind them reared the same man, the same irascible, close-mouthed grandfather, who had disowned his elder son, treating with contempt Ephraim's whole family and leaving them destitute; and who had overshadowed his younger son and daughter-in-law so as to have to himself their only child, his love for whom had grown oppressive. They could not imagine or talk of the future, for before them loomed the shadow of the same man, the same grandfather, who would eventually be gone. As for the present, it oppressed them with all the weight of this man who lay shivering with fever in his bed. A weight all the more heavy because this man, still this same man, was continually deepening the mystery that had surrounded him for so many years. In his feverish delirium Ambroise Mauperthuis dwelt on the same incoherent, disconnected phrases, on the same words and names, and Camille was unable to make any sense of his gibberish. One name kept recurring like a fervent, sorrowful incantation: a woman's name that she had never heard mentioned before - Catherine. And Camille could not understand why her grandfather linked this name with her own, which he repeated almost as often. She asked La Fine who this Catherine might be that her grandfather invoked in this way, but La Fine knew no more than she did.

'His wife's name was Juliette,' La Fine told her. 'She died when your father was still a boy. Not that I knew your grandmother – she wasn't from these parts, she came from Clamecy. In any case, she certainly wasn't called Catherine. There weren't any Catherines in the village or round about that I knew of. As for the master's mother, her name was Jeanne. And your grandfather's never been known to have had any other women in his life. There's never been talk about anything like that.'

Camille made no further efforts to find out more. She had quite enough anxieties of her own to cope with, to want to get involved with her grandfather's as well.

With Simon, she forgot about everything else, in the rediscovery of the repleteness and savour of her joy. And Simon shared this same desire for oblivion, this same impulse to relish the moment – a moment out of time, which was too fully occupied by old Mauperthuis. Come nightfall, they would slip into the sheet of silence they had fashioned for themselves at the back of the barns, and wrap up together in the splendour of that covering in which their nudity exalted.

Ambroise Mauperthuis' illness lasted ten days. As suddenly as he had collapsed with fever, he got better. He opened his eyes one morning as if nothing had happened, amazed to see La Fine at his bedside, working at her embroidery, half-asleep in her chair. He immediately chased her out of the room and got up. La Fine hurried off to Camille's bedroom to warn her of her grandfather's recovery, but she could not wake her. Camille had only a little while ago got back from the barn, where she had met Simon, and she had just fallen into a deep sleep.

Ambroise Mauperthuis went down to the kitchen and demanded his breakfast. He was ravenously hungry, and felt endowed with increased energy and strength, as if this illness, which had laid him low with such a fever and made him sweat so much, had served only to reinvigorate his body and stimulate his blood. He sat at the table and gorged himself with an appetite that appalled La Fine. He did not ask any questions, either about his illness or about Camille.

This silence worried La Fine even more than his fit of gluttony. Eventually she said, 'Camille's still asleep, poor thing, after having sat up all night with you. I'd just taken over from her when you suddenly woke up . . . She's been so worried. To be sure, we've both been worried. You've been very ill, you know. Camille even sent for the doctor. But the doctor couldn't find out what was wrong with you, and he went away baffled. So we . . .'

But Ambroise Mauperthuis cut her off in mid flow. 'So what day is it today?' he asked curtly.

La Fine told him, and took the opportunity immediately to resume her chatter in the hope of softening him, for she sensed that he was, as she put it, full of nastiness.

But again he testily interrupted her. 'Stop gabbling!' Then as soon as he had wolfed down his breakfast, he left the farm and went up to the forest.

It was already well into November. It was freezing cold.

The earth crunched under his clogs, the frosty air seemed to vibrate and the birds were silent. As he passed Middle Farm, he caught a glimpse of Alphonse at the window. The old cockerel was shaking his limp comb, flopped over one of its eyes, and trying in vain to give a loud crow. Huguet Cordebugle, like all the other woodcutters in the village, was already up in the forest. Ambroise Mauperthuis walked at a steady pace. The chill, morning air invigorated him even more. He felt calm, armed with a calm as ice-cold as this white November morning. He passed Follin Farm, where he heard children's voices whingeing, then Upper Farm, where Loulou-the-Bellclinker was sweeping the doorstep, all wrapped up in thick woollens, and singing softly under his breath. He entered Jalles Forest.

His forest, his village. It was all his. These trees, this land, and these men that he employed – they all belonged to him. He was master here, and he felt as though he were master of this beautiful, frosty morning, resonant with the sound of footsteps and the creaking of branches. Master of everything and everybody. The tears he had shed over Camille's feet, the first tears in his life, and the last, had washed clean his memory and his heart. His memory was clearer than ever, limpid, and tinged with the wonderful green of Catherine-Camille's eyes. His memory chimed: troops of logs went by, round logs of a luminous grey, while a bell at the heart of a sun rang out. C for Catherine, C for Camille. The letter rang out in the heart of the morning. The sun and his own heart were one. They turned like a grinding-wheel, whetting the C for Catherine, the C for Camille – these two were one and the same. The Spark of Life, the Serpent, his inveterate passion reared between tenderness and violence like the splendid move-ment of a tree, of the light, the wind. The Spark of Life, the Serpent, his crazed, green-eyed virgin – a slut smelling of mist and of a man's skin.

He would unmask this man. He could only be a local man, one of those whose master he was, from Oak-Wolf or one of the nearby hamlets. He would hunt out this dog, this thief of beauty, this debauchee who had dared to lay his filthy hands on the Spark of Life, and strip him of these monstrous rights that he had treacherously usurped. He would banish him from her heart and soul. He would drive him out, and keep him far away from here, where he was master. He would keep him away for ever.

Ambroise Mauperthuis went deeper into the forest, making his way between the trees that glistened with frost. His heart sparkled with calm and patience – a fierce, bitter patience.

IN THE ATTIC

As Ambroise Mauperthuis entered Jalles Forest, his heart steeled with glacial patience, in her room at Threshold Farm Camille slept, a happy, dreamless sleep. She no longer dreamt while asleep: there was no room for dreams in her sleep. What had been a dream was now alive, with a real body, a name and a smell. There was no other dream but Simon, no other reality but Simon. In him, dream and reality came together; in him, life was living and dreaming. Apart from him, there was nothing but boredom and insignificance. Without him, life no longer had any vitality or movement, but flagged and faltered. When she came home from the barn, with the taste in her mouth of Simon's lips and body, with the marks of his embraces and the smell of his skin on hers, with the echo of his groans and the wet traces of his pleasure inside her, she was in a hurry to get back to her room, to slip into bed and curl up under the sheets, and fall at once into a deep sleep. The flames of desire, and its eagerness, the surges of pleasure, the impetuousness of heightened senses, the exaltation of a body that relentlessly and without restraint assailed the other with touches, caresses and kisses, cast like a huge net of avid tenderness – slowly, in the course of this deep sleep, these abated, easing to suffuse her body with greater mellowness and to penetrate more profoundly her heart and her flesh. Sleep worked an unseen and silent alchemy in Camille and Simon's parted bodies; in this crucible took place a transmutation of their senses, their breathing, and their gaze. Each became the inner lining of the other's body, the other body's sensitivity and delight. And on waking, desire overwhelmed their being in a rush and entwinement each time more enduring and happy.

When Camille saw her grandfather again, she was amazed at the calm he displayed. Not only did he refuse to discuss the clash between them, but he evaded any allusions that might be made to the sudden fever that had confined him to bed for ten days. He behaved towards her as in the past. He seemed just a little distracted, as if he had decided to shut his eyes to the entire matter, and let Camille conduct a secret love affair that in the long run he did not mind. Once she had overcome her initial surprise, Camille was quick to set aside her earlier fears, and she went along with her grandfather's game with blithe insouciance. But this game turned out to be a double bluff. For, reassured by her grandfather's apparent calm, Camille ceased to be distant with him, and was just as affectionate as ever before, which somewhat restored old Mauperthuis' confidence in her. After all, he occasionally found himself thinking, perhaps nothing had happened, and everything could yet be saved. Nevertheless, deep down inside, he remained coldly vigilant. The merest trifle was enough to re-arouse his jealousy.

The day came when his jealousy was exposed, passing from muted alarm to attack. This happened in early December, in the middle of the felling season, in Jalles Forest. The woodcutters were taking a rest. Seated around the fire on which they heated up their soup, they ate in silence, reluctant to talk with old Mauperthuis there. The arrival of three women – Rose Gravelle, her daughter Louise, and Marie Follin – accompanied by Loulou-the-Bellclinker, broke this gloomy reticence. They brought the men buckwheat pancakes made with bacon, cooked fresh that morning, which they produced from their baskets, wrapped in linen. The presence of the women and Loulou-the-Bellclinker, and the smell of the pancakes, still piping-hot, raised the men's spirits again. They bantered with the women. Adrien-the-Blue's great laugh kept prompting laughter in response. There were only two men who did not join in this merriment: Ambroise Mauperthuis, whose expression remained hostile and suspicious, and Huguet Cordebugle, who had moved away as soon as the women appeared, with a vicious look on his face.

As ever, the men made fun of him.

'Well, where's your wife, then, Huguet,' they gibed. 'Are you waiting for Alphonse to bring you your pancake? But that Alphonse is as much in need of a wife as you are. So who does the cooking in your house?'

'That's the reason why you're both so filthy dirty that no one would want to touch you!' said the women, needling him further.

'Come on over here, Huguet! We won't tell Alphonse that you've eaten some pancake without him – in the company of women, what's more!'

'Ah, well, perhaps virgins like you, who can't appreciate any of the good things in life, don't eat bacon pancake!'

'Huguet doesn't like women, dressed or naked, either at close quarters or from a distance. He prefers their petticoats and knickers with no one inside them. Is that not so, Huguet?'

'Tell us, do you make pants for Alphonse out of all those women's undergarments?'

'Or perhaps you've a woman hidden in your castle? So where are you hiding her? In the bread bin? Among the ashes in the grate? Under the dust or behind the cob-webs?'

'With all the clothes that you've been stealing from people's gardens, your spider-woman must look like a queen dressed up to the nines.'

'Your spider-queen's arse doesn't get too cold in winter, does it? It's a bad time of year for gathering knickers!'

Huguet Cordebugle's prurient and cantankerous prudery always incited the other men to bawdy raillery, and that day they enjoyed themselves heartily.

Ambroise Mauperthuis, who listened without joining in the fun, eventually said in a gruff voice, 'I'm warning you now, Cordebugle, if I ever catch you nosing around my garden at night, looking for clothes to filch, I'll take my fork to you, and set my dog on you!' Not only was Ambroise Mauperthuis not amused by all this light-heartedness about Huguet Cordebugle's thieving, he was irritated by it, for he could not bear the thought of this old peeping-Tom laying hands on Camille's undergarments.

So far, Huguet Cordebugle had endured in silence the

barrage of ridicule that his companions had loosed on him, but when Ambroise Mauperthuis made this threat, he flew into a rage.

'Well, truth is, master, it's another fellow's arse that you'd better stick your fork into and set your dog on – a fellow that bares his arse, in your meadow, too, and not just to let the moon shine on it, that's for sure! And don't think that he's alone when he does it! Truth is, master, that when your back's turned, there're mischief-makers at work in your back garden!'

Huddled in his corner, with his soup bowl held between his knees, Huguet Cordebugle delivered his tirade without a pause. All laughter and quipping died. Proud of this effect, Huguet snickered and noisily emptied his bowl.

Ambroise Mauperthuis rose to his feet, white-faced.

'What are you talking about? I'm going to make you take back your filthy lies, you old dung-heap.'

But the other man became even more enraged.

'I'm not lying! It's the absolute truth I'm telling you. I saw them! I saw them with my own eyes – your granddaughter and that swinish lad of hers. They were even rolling in the grass, and stark naked, as well!'

'If you don't shut your mouth, I'll smash it for you!' shouted Ferdinand-the-Strong, beside himself.

Ambroise Mauperthuis instinctively leapt at him, but with a quick shove the younger man pushed him away.

Unruffled, Huguet muttered in his corner, 'He's not the one. It was Si . . .'

He did not have time to finish. Martin-the-Sparing threw his bowl at Huguet's face. In a frantic rage, Huguet stood up and yelled, 'You see! You see how it is, and it's all because of women! Whores, they are, the whole lot of them, sluts and whores. And Camille's no different from the rest. She and her grandmother from the valley are one of a kind. Sluts, the pair of them!'

And with that, he spat, picked up his bowl and his pouch, and went off, back to work, cursing.

Then all the others gathered up their belongings in silence, while the women hurried to retrieve their empty baskets and return to the village.

Ambroise Mauperthuis was left standing by the fire, as though nailed to the spot and left speechless and stunned by the revelations that Huguet Cordebugle had just made and by the insults, levelled at both Camille and Catherine, voiced in front of everybody. The bitter patience and watchful jealousy that Mauperthuis had recently brought into play, in order to discover Camille's secret without anyone being the wiser, had just been thwarted and turned to ridicule. This secret that despite all his suspicions he had persuaded himself not to believe in, that he wanted to penetrate merely in order to quash it in the clandestine darkness of his jealous passion, had only ever been kept secret from him. Everybody else already knew. They were all accomplices to it. He felt cruelly betrayed, deceived and humiliated, publicly, by everybody. He realized how deeply he was resented and how great the indignity he had just suffered. He had been insulted – he and that dual creature that was his love, his light, his pride and sole joy in this world.

Simon. It did not matter that Cordebugle had not finished what he was saying; Mauperthuis had understood. And he was amazed not to have been aware from the start, not to have realized that the robber of Camille's beauty was actually the very person practically living under his own roof. The one who was most like Camille. Ephraim's fifth son, the Cowherd, the Hothead. The one whose breath had blasted through the clearing of Our-Lady-of-the-Beeches – a scintillation of brass and sunshine amid the intensity of that long ago August noontide, a scintillation of brass and insolence that had beguiled Camille as a necromantic spirit enchants those that have strayed into the depths of the forest. This was theft, abduction, a dark spell meant to subjugate Camille and turn her against him – he who had forever and always claimed an exclusive right to

Camille's love, who considered himself Camille's destiny. It was a crime: a crime of sorcery; a crime against nature, a crime against him, Ambroise Mauperthuis.

He stood stock-still before the fire, his eyes vacant, staring into the already sinking flames. The dual image of Catherine and Camille, whom he had always confused with each other, now focused into a single image of perfect clarity. As the fire on which the men had heated their soup died, this single image became more and more sharply defined before his hallucinating eyes. Everything inside him – his memory, thoughts and passion – had just been consumed. Cinders and ashes: a grey heat in which the old image was purified of the instabilities that had previously marred it. Cinders and ashes: an incandescence in which a new image was forged. He had already forgotten how he had been publicly affronted, as he was repossessed of the pride and strength as master of this place that he had felt on entering the forest that first morning of his recovery. Already he had forgotten the insult, and the lies fabricated by everyone around him, and the threats made by the Morning brothers in their readiness to defend Simon. He was afraid of no one. He had even forgotten Camille's betrayal. He forgave nothing – he forgot. He forgot the old image that by its instability had eventually grown obscure and deformed and allowed itself to be sullied. All that he could understand was that his Spark of Life had to be snatched with the utmost urgency from the dark spell to which she had fallen victim. Camille did not matter any more – only his Spark of Life, only the image that dwelt in her, pervaded her, and emanated from her. He had to save this image whose splendour belonged to no one but him, for he alone was capable of seeing it. He had to unshackle this image so that it might continue its progress, gathering the impetus to culminate in a vision, a pure transfiguration. The Spark of Life needed to be rescued from a fallen Camille, from the murkiness caused by Camille and Simon. And to achieve this, their bodies had to be disentangled, and the Spark of Life's image and soul safeguarded from everyone, even Camille – especially Camille.

He returned to the village. When he came into the yard of Threshold Farm, he found Camille standing under the magnolia tree, waiting for him. The women had rushed over to forewarn her as soon as they got back from the forest, and told her to beware of the old man. But Camille had replied resolutely, 'Very well, so now he knows, and perhaps it's for the best. I'll wait for him to come home, and I'll talk to him.' She did not know what she would say. All she knew was that she had to talk to him, to put an end to the fear, mistrust and lies.

As soon as she saw her grandfather, she walked towards him. She held her arms folded across her chest, hugging the big woollen shawl that covered her head and shoulders.

'I want to speak to you!' she cried sharply.

'Why's that?' replied the old man in a calm, almost detached voice. 'What have you got to say to me? I know everything there is to know. Now, get back indoors. It's too cold even for the animals to be out. You'll catch a chill.'

They entered the farmhouse.

'Go and fetch my pipe and tobacco pouch from the table in my room. I'm numbed through with this cold,' said the old man.

Camille was increasingly suprised. Not only was he not angry when he came home, but now he was asking her to go up to his room to fetch a pipe that he only rarely smoked.

'In your room?' said Camille doubtfully. 'But you don't like us going into your room – either La Fine or myself.'

'So what? When I was ill, you both came in anyway, didn't you? I've nothing to hide. And besides, I feel like smoking, but my limbs are all numb – you'll find the things quicker than me. Go on up and fetch them, now.'

And Camille went upstairs.

While she was hunting in her grandfather's room for things that were not there, Ambroise Mauperthuis silently climbed the staircase and crept up to the door of his room. He walked on tiptoe, in his stockinged feet, holding his breath. As soon as he was close enough, he rushed for the door, slammed it shut and locked it.

Camille had no time to react. She walked hesitantly, almost unsteadily, towards the door, not daring to comprehend what was happening. But when she tried to open the double-locked door, she understood in a flash.

'Open up!' she yelled, banging her fists on the door panel.

'Now, then, my girl, you're very impatient!' Ambroise Mauperthuis responded. 'I'll open the door, but not just yet. You'll have to wait a bit. I've things to do, but since you only misbehave and carry on the moment my back's turned, I've really got to lock you up for a while.' And he went back downstairs without paying any attention to Camille's shouting.

He collided with La Fine at the foot of the staircase, as she came running up, alarmed by the racket that Camille was making upstairs. The old man roughly pushed her back.

'That's the end of it, La Fine, do you hear? No more lies, and filthiness, and treachery. And you've come to the end of your time here, too. I don't need you any more. You're of precious little use. You didn't keep your eye on Camille, as I asked you, you let her run around like a bitch on heat. I'm going to teach her the way to live. She's going to have to watch her step, the little slut! And you can go and pack your bags. Go home to your daughter, or son — wherever you like, I don't care! I don't want to see you — or anybody else — here ever again.'

La Fine wept and begged and argued to no avail. Ambroise Mauperthuis was not to be swayed. In fact, he made her hastily gather her belongings and clear the little cubbyhole that she had occupied in the kitchen, and then marched her out to the road.

'And don't ever come back!' he shouted after her, as he pushed her away. 'Never again, do you hear? And let no one dare set foot in my place again, or even come prowling around it.'

Then he went back into the farmhouse, and climbed up to the attic. He cleared a corner, where he installed a mattress and laid out some linen, a bowl, a jug of water and a bucket. He reinforced the door of the attic, cut a peep-hole into it, stuffed the cracks in the ceiling with wading, and brought up an old footwarmer and a lantern, which he lit. Camille's new room was ready. He went down again.

Camille was no longer shouting or banging on the door. But he knew perfectly well that this did not mean that she had already resigned herself – on the contrary. He opened the door to his room, where he had locked her up, and immediately blocked the doorway to prevent her getting out. Camille rushed at him, attacking like a cornered animal. She pummelled him in silence, with her jaws locked, and with a strength increased tenfold by her anger. Her blows had no effect. The old man felt nothing. His strength – a solid, stubborn strength – had been forged so long ago. He stood, immovable, in the doorway. He grabbed Camille by the hair, forcing her head back. She started screaming again, with pain and impotence. And it was in this way – pulling her hair – that he dragged her up to the attic. Again he shut the door on her. Up here, she was secure. As soon as the door was bolted, he opened the peep-hole a fraction, and saw Camille standing still by the mattress, with her arms hanging at her sides. The day was already drawing to a close and a wan, cold gleam filtered through the dust-blackened skylight. The lantern-glow flickered, a faint, reddish halo at the head of the mattress, and the footwarmer was cast in wavering, orange-coloured reflections. These two dim lights – subdued and without radiance – set on the floor, were the only splashes of colour in this place of greyness: grey with dust, grey with cold and boredom, grey with silence, loneliness and oblivion. These two pools of colour, of red and orange, were like two sick flowers, a rose and rust-diseased peony that had grown out of the filth on the floor: two cankrous growths of colour in this prison cell under the eaves, two open wounds of beauty at Camille's feet. She stood there, motion-less, her face livid, her mouth blue with cold – a coldness that rose from her heart. Her haggard eyes stared into space, into the grey emptiness of her gaol. Her shoulders were trembling. And he watched her, his eye glued to the peep-hole and his heart beating against the door as he gazed at that slim figure who looked so frail, so magnificent in her distress and dismay. Here was his Spark of Life again, saved from Camille, disentangled from Simon's body – delivered to his sole gaze at last.

Suddenly rousing herself from the torpor of her plight, Camille moved to the centre of the room.

'I'll let myself die if you don't let me out,' she told him. He did not reply.

'Die . . .' she repeated without emotion, murmuring rather than speaking. 'Die . . .' It was a very soft whisper that seemed to emanate more from the sick flowers, of red and orange, than from Camille's mouth; a whisper that originated from a long way back, a very long way.

Then from the other side of the door he shouted in a now frenzied voice, at once imploring and full of hatred, 'Die! Die! But you've been dead for nearly thirty years! You can't die again. You're going to come back to life. You're alive now. You're going to live. To live again! You've come back! Oh, I've been waiting so long for you! And now at last you're here. I've got you! I've got you! My beloved has come back, as lovely as she was the day she died! All right, go on and die, then, if you like. Die again and again, as often as you please – you look so lovely when you die!' He slammed shut the peep-hole and went downstairs, still talking to himself.

Up in the attic, silence descended on Camille, a new and terrifying silence – that of reason. She had just realized that her grandfather was acting not so much out of anger and revenge but insanity. He was mad. She had never had suspicion of this inveterate madness that knew no bounds, and now all of a sudden she realized the extent, virulence and intransigence of it. She shivered. It was a shiver that stopped her breath for a moment and chilled her entire body. The old man's madness had now penetrated her own consciousness, blinding her with its evidence, transfixing her with its violence. The old man's madness assaulted her reason. She looked around: she was not so much locked inside a place as pinned down in the heart of this madness that had just been revealed to her. This attic, grey with dust, and these dark beams, this grimy skylight, these heaps of old junk piled everywhere, the whistling of the wind over the rooftop, the cold dampness of these walls, the creaking of the floorboards, and that peep-hole in the triple-locked door – all these things were actually the frame and furnishings of old Mauperthuis' soul. She felt shut inside his skull, like a fragment of a bullet lodged in a wounded man's head, a fossilized tumour.

THE NAME OF ROUZÉ

Along with Ambroise Mauperthuis' madness went a perfect lucidity and efficiency. Since his return from the forest, he had managed to confine Camille in a secure place, to get rid of La Fine, and to declare his farm a forbidden stronghold. He now had to get rid of Simon-the-Hothead, who would soon be arriving at the farm, for it was already time to rub down and feed the oxen.

He waited for him in the yard, in front of the entrance to the cowshed. He had armed himself with a mattock. He had selected from the tool-shed the mattock with the sharpest cutting-edge and the longest handle. He held it firmly across his chest. Simon arrived. Loulou-the-Bell-clinker had told him, before he reached the farm, of the row that had broken out in the forest at lunch-time. Simon walked resolutely towards Mauperthuis, but when he was a few steps away the old man brandished his weapon and shouted, 'You'll not come in! You'll never set foot on my farm again! There's no shortage of cowherds round here. I'll be hiring a new one tomorrow. You'll be leaving – not just my farm, but Oak-Wolf. You'll be leaving the area. Go and find yourself a job somewhere else. Go and look elsewhere for girls to debauch. And if you don't leave this very night, I'll go to the police. Camille's under-age, you've no right to her. I'll say that you forced yourself on her. I'll have you sent to prison, is that understood?'

'No,' said Simon. 'Camille will tell the truth. I've never forced myself on her. If I go, it'll only be with her.'

'So you set your face against me, eh? Tell me, just who do you think you are? You forget that you're nothing, nothing but a pauper, a peasant. I can have you arrested by the police if I want to. I'm the one with all the power, not you! And do you know what? If you don't leave this very night I won't give any more work to that worthless father or those ruffian brothers of yours. Make no mistake, I mean what I say, and I'll waste no time about it. I'll put you all out of work. And then where will you go? Where will you find work? What will you live on? You'll all have to leave that shack of a farmhouse. So you'd better disappear, for good, or I'll do as I say. You've been warned. I'll do it, for sure.'

Simon was abashed. He was not afraid of the police, but the destitution of his family, already so poor, just managing to survive – that, he could not take. He could not bear the idea of seeing them all driven off their farm, away from the village, forced to go and beg for work elsewhere. He felt trapped, defeated before he had been able to put up a fight. The old man would not hesitate for one second to carry out his threats. When seized with anger, he had never hesitated to do harm, without pity or remorse.

'Where's Camille?' asked Simon in a faltering voice.

'She's where she ought to be! In my house. She's behaving herself now. She understands now, too. Nobody makes a fool of me, far from it. Nobody sets their face against me. She does as she's told. She'll stay inside. You can shout your head off, she won't come. The little fool thought she could deceive me, but I've taken her in hand now. She's told enough lies and done enough carrying-on as it is. That's all over now, and a good thing, too! Go on, clear out, and don't ever come back. Otherwise it's the whole lot of you – your entire pack of brothers, your father, his fat Verselay wife, and the old woman – that I'll be turning out to find other work and somewhere else to live. And you'll have to go far from here, way beyond my forests. Is that clear?'

Simon, who usually lost his temper at the slightest provocation, just stood there, three steps away from the old man, with his head bowed and his arms dangling. His hands were shaking, not with anger but distress. It was his courage and his entire strength that he had lost. The old man's threat against his family forced Simon straight away to submit to his will, with no appeal, and he was crushed by his powerlessness. In a hollow, almost trembling voice,

176

he said, 'I'd just like to see Rouzé . . . one last time . . . Can I at least say goodbye to him . . . let me go into the cowshed for a moment, to see Rouzé.'

Rouzé was one of the oxen he looked after, the one he favoured most. He felt so bereft, so lost all of a sudden, so painfully alone, defeated and humiliated, that he had to find some kind of comfort. He felt an urgent, passionate need to put his arms round the animal's neck, to rest his face against its head, to bury his sorrow in the sweet, warm smell of the beast, and to let the tears already scalding his cheeks trickle down its breast.

But the old man snickered, keeping a firm hold of his mattock. 'Ah, so you're snivelling now, are you? Well, you'll get no pity from me! When you were having your way with Camille behind my back, you cared as much about Rouzé as you did about me. Isn't that so? So that's enough of that. Go on, clear out. You'll no more see Rouzé than you will Camille. I can look after both of them by myself. I don't need any help from you. You can save your tears. With this cold, they'll be cutting into your face. As far as I'm concerned, they just make me laugh.'

It was not only his face that his tears were cutting into; they racked his entire body, biting into his flesh, right through to his heart. The old man laughed nastily, and the more he laughed, the more his breath condensed into a white vapour that obscured his face. Ambroise Mauperthuis suddenly appeared to Simon to be at once terribly close and terribly distant – a creature that was no longer completely human, but bewitched and baneful. As if the darkest spirits of the forest had taken possession of his soul. As if by so obscuring himself in the mist of his malevolent laughter, not only was his face going to disappear from sight but his whole body as well. As if he were about to dissolve in the frosty evening air, and become the coldness of the night: the damp coldness that pervades the under-growth, that seeps from the trees, stones, and paths; that seeps into the dreams of those unhappy wretches whose sleep is not even a respite but further perpetuates their sorrow, hunger and care. The coldness that seeps into the anguish of the poor, into the hearts of the downcast.

And Simon was downcast, thwarted in love, and in his pride, joy and even anger. Until that day it had been no hardship to him to be poor. He had never even really thought of himself as poor. He had work, he was happy in this village and these woods where he had always lived, and he loved his brothers. He was the middle child, the brother of Noon, born auspiciously when the great August sun was at its zenith, surrounded by his elder brothers' strength and then by the dreams and tenderness of the younger ones. Favoured in birth, he was born in the middle of the day, at the height of summer, endowed with a beauty that was all radiance and verve. And he was the loved one – his beauty was his father's pride and his mother's wonderment. He was loved by Camille. He had found in her his female double, the response to his desire, the true locus of his joy. But now, all of a sudden, Mauperthuis was turning all this upside down, trampling it underfoot, and throwing his poverty in his face, making him see that he had never been anything but an impecunious wretch, even more at the old man's mercy than at his service, and now he was nothing but a vagabond.

Simon was no longer swept by rushes of happiness or anger, desire or infatuation, towards the outside world and other people. He was swept in on himself – to the deepest, emptiest, darkest part of himself – swept inwards, to the loneliness of his heart that had been snatched away from everything and everybody; plummeted inside himself, without issue, driven to a non-place of silence and nothingness.

Three paces away, over there, on the other side of the world and the far side of Time, stood Ambroise Mauperthuis, his face clouded with evil laughter: a man he did not know, having once known him too well, and run foul of his power and rage. A man of commanding presence, a man bewitched, brandishing a great mattock with a blade that glistened in the evening mist like a sparkling flash of hatred; the supreme, incisive flash of an ever-mounting hatred.

Ambroise Mauperthuis laughed. He laughed as he had never laughed before, with a deep irregular laughter. He laughed at having subdued Camille, and driven out La Fine, and defeated Simon. He laughed at being master of this place and the destinies of those living here. He laughed at having cut in two that hideous and obscene, double body that Camille and Simon had dared to form. He laughed at knowing that Camille was locked in the attic, the prisoner of his jealous, magic love. Up there, Camille was going to recover her true body, her sacred body: Catherine's body. He laughed with joy and power, with satisfied revenge and gratified anger. He laughed at having found Catherine-Camille again. He laughed at having saved his Spark of Life.

Old Mauperthuis laughed, and with the blind force of buffeting winter wind, his icy, cutting laughter drove Simon back. It was as though he had sharpened his laughter on the edge of his mattock. Simon staggered back, reeling, feeling that the night was opening up behind him like an abyss that he was going to topple into.

Simon was about to fall. The ground was giving way under his feet, and the abyss of night growing dizzyingly larger behind him. He had not the courage to turn round, to confront the gaping darkness into whose depths the old man's laughter banished him. He was going to fall. Already his hands were flailing the air. He needed someone, something, to cling to. It was Rouzé's name that he caught at. He started yelling Rouzé's name, modulating his cries, dwelling on each syllable, and Rouzé's name became drawn out, pliant and hollow. It rolled and swept into the evening, pressing back the night – the fear of night. Rouzé's name resounded, noble and solemn, heavy and slow, like the tolling of a great bell to signal alarm, sorrow, and grief. Rouzé's name, yelled continuously in a plaintive, imploring tone, acquired the weight and volume of the animal's body. Rouzé's name filled the void, travelling through the night like a sob, a sweet, warm surge of blood.

And Camille up in the attic at the far end of the

buildings heard this long drawn-out cry, this call. It wrested her from her torpor. She cried back. She called to Simon. But no one heard her. Her voice beat against the walls, the beams and the door like a frightened bird unable to find the gap through which it entered. Rouzé's name drowned her cries, muffled her voice. Camille banged on the door, and broke her fingernails on the lock.

The ox Rouzé, tied up in the cowshed, strained his neck, stamped the ground with his hoofs, and tugged at the chain that tethered him, gathering his strength. He heard his name, bellowed with bestial distress, and he responded to this call. He began to bellow loudly, and soon all the animals in the cowshed joined in this mournful din. Ambroise Mauperthuis was no longer laughing. The low, violent clamour coming from the cowshed in answer to Simon's cry had got the better of his laughter. He was now menacingly brandishing his mattock at Simon. But Simon continued to retreat, staggering backwards and bellowing in unison with the oxen.

The cattleshed door burst open. Ambroise Mauperthuis just had time to leap aside. He dropped the mattock. Having broken his chain, Rouzé came rushing out into the yard. Simon threw himself at the beast, flattening himself on its back and flinging his arms round its neck. Rouzé careered on, head down. He did not try to dismount Simon, who was crouched on his back, clinging to his neck. He bolted from the yard. And the ox with its human burden that bore down on it with the distress and pain of a man humiliated and defeated, disappeared into the night.

Ambroise Mauperthuis did not try to go after them. What mattered was that Simon should disappear, even at the expense of one of his oxen. In order to keep the Spark of Life all to himself, and nobody else, he would have sacrificed even his forests, if need be. He picked up his mattock, carried it into the tool-shed and then returned to the cowhouse to calm the oxen and feed them. Then he went back to the farmhouse to have his supper. He closed the shutters and barricaded the door. Silence reigned over the farm and all around – the yard, the cowsheds, and the whole village. The oxen were still now, and Simon had been swallowed by the night. The old man took a lamp and climbed quietly up to the attic. He stood for a moment listening at the door. He could not detect a sound. He opened the peep-hole and saw Camille cowering in the silence, at the far end of the attic. She did not look up at the door. She was staring at the ground. The reddish glow from the lantern at her feet was already failing. The gloom filling the room was deepening, encroaching on Camille's pallet and gathering in around her. Camille was slowly fading into the darkness, swallowed up by the same night that had just engulfed Simon. Ambroise Mauperthuis slammed shut the peep-hole. This sound rang out in Camille's heart. She was only slightly startled – just enough to apprehend the immensity and the coldness of the night of her captivity, just enough to fathom how boundless was the terror in which her love languished. Her eyes widened for a moment in shock.

Simon had gone, devoured by the night. Who would come and free her? But could she really be freed? Prisoners were freed, but she was even less than a prisoner. She did not exist, had never existed. She was dead long before she was born. The old man had told her so. She was surely just an image, nothing more: an image pinned up inside the old man's madness, an image snatched from death that the old man would come and gloat on, through the peep-hole, morning and evening. She was surely just an image, since her body – her true body – had just been stolen from her. It was fleeing deep into the night, flattened on the back of an ox. Then she remembered what Leger had told her the day he had given her the dream he had described, as he sat beside her on the garden wall. He had spoken to her of the strength of images, of their enduringness and reality. He had said to her, 'We have lots and lots of eyes. And all these eyes open at night. Dreams are our night-eyes.'

She distinctly remembered every word. And even more vivid was her recollection of the yellow tufts of saxifrage that sprang out between the stones of the wall. The old man had reduced her to a superficial image, with death's seal on it. There was only one remedy: to delve into that image and break the seal on it, to split it apart and daub it with vibrant colours. Yellow – the bright yellow of the saxifrage bursting through the stones, the sunshine yellow of that brilliant high noon on 15th August, when the brothers had sung, the brassy yellow of the trumpet that Simon played, the saffron yellow of the brass sound and Simon's breath, the straw yellow of the Morning brothers' hair, the acid yellow of Loulou-the-Bellclinker's carillon, the golden yellow of Blaise-the-Ugly's bees, the amber yellow of Simon's eyes - yellow, ad infinitum. She had to fight the old man's madness step by step, with image against image. She had to defend with great splashes of colour her reason against assault by the old man's madness, and her heart against confinement in the dust of the attic and the grey shadows inside her grandfather's skull (whose all-powerful eye slammed shut like a peep-hole).

And so she fell asleep, curled up on her mattress, by the dying gleam of the lantern. 'I'll let myself die,' she had told the old man. No, she would not. She did not want to die in the old man's madness. She would drift into a sleep, a dream, among images and colours, and she would sleep for as long as this night, this terror, lasted.

ENDURING LOVE

PSALM

Blaise-the-Ugly's melodious voice carried down the road, floating in the morning blueness, between the tall grasses. All the orchards were in blossom, the air was fragrant, and the birds in the trees and hedges shrilly twittered their amorous trills.

> *Hearken, o daughter, and consider, and incline thine ear;*
> *Forget also thine own people and thy father's house;*
> *So shall the king greatly desire thy beauty . . .*

Blaise-the-Ugly sang, his voice so sweet it brought tears to the eyes. Old Edmée toddled along, holding his arm. Her head and shoulders swayed very slightly as she walked, and her lips quietly mouthed the words that Blaise sang. 'Hearken, o daughter, and consider, and incline thine ear . . .' They both led the way, the others following in silence. Everyone advanced as though in a dream – like pink-eyed sleepwalkers meekly led by that clear voice.

> *For he is thy Lord; and worship thou him.*
> *Even the rich among the people shall entreat thy favour . . .*

Thy beauty, thy favour, old Edmée repeated under her breath. And at the thought of this beauty, this smiling favour, she almost smiled herself – such a tender, sorrowful smile, all spent with tears and vigils. And she nodded her head as she sang softly to herself, as though to mark her acquiescence with each word, to acknowledge in humility and wonder the splendour of the beauty celebrated by the psalm, to give thanks once more to the Virgin for having blessed her with the gift of Regina – her daughter with the wondrous smile! She was constantly grateful to the heavens for the miracle of this smile, and would constantly seek to find it in the invisible from now on.

The king's daughter is all glorious within
Her clothing is of wrought gold.
She shall be brought unto the king in raiment of needlework . . .

Daughter of the Most Pure and Most Chaste Queen of Heaven; of the Most Holy Mother of Our Saviour, Most Merciful Mother of Mankind and Comfort of the Afflicted; daughter of the Queen of Angels, Queen of Virgins, Queen of Queens – Regina Verselay, Mauperthuis by marriage, was brought before the king of this world all decked in the blueness of that spring morning, arrayed in the tears and love of her family, and fragrant with the smell of the orchards and hedges.

The virgins her companions that follow her shall be brought unto
*   thee.*
With gladness and rejoicing shall they be brought:
They shall enter into the king's palace.
Instead of thy fathers shall be thy children,
Whom thou mayest make princes in all the earth.

Fat-Ginnie's sons were there – the sons that had come to her like so many gifts of the Virgin Most Venerable, Mother of Divine Grace. They were all there but one. At their head walked the last-born, whose mouth bore the mark of the angel's fiery finger; whose heart knew that the world was madness, that men had so little reason, patience and goodness that their lives were but tales fraught with violence that might see the sweet miracle of mercy, love and forgiveness occur at any moment. The one whose twisted mouth knew the gravity of words, the melody of sounds; from whose deformed mouth came inflexions of absolute clarity, of overwhelming sweetness.

I will make thy name to be remembered in all generations:
Therefore shall the peoples praise thee for ever and ever.

They, her sons, would make their mother's name endure.

It would live on in their memories. It would pervade their lives. They would instil it in the hearts of their children.

The last-born led the way, tracing another brightness in the blueness of that morning with the descant of his song. And little old Edmée, with her failing sight, kept gazing up at this other brightness, seeking in it her daughter's smile – the favour of her one and only, and so dearly beloved, Regina, who came after them, resting on the shoulders of her Morning sons. And Ephraim walked with them, bearing his share of the weight of the coffin that he himself had made. His Morning sons had cut down the tree of the angel-with-the-fruit, in the clearing of Our-Lady-of-the-Beeches – the one they had sculpted in honour of their mother. And out of the wood of that beech-tree, Ephraim had carved Regina's last bed, which had no room for him, her husband. He would never again sleep at Regina's side, nor bury his face and arms in her hair, nor find that miracle of peace, happiness and oblivion in the moist depths of her body. Fat-Ginnie's fabulous, superabundant body was to sleep alone for evermore in this narrow beechwood bed. And he, her husband, still with the heart of a lover, brought his beloved to the King of this world who had summoned her back. His grief was so great that he found neither the tears nor lamentation to express it. His grief gaped inside him, like a boundless space, an inward desert in which he was now lost. A desert so vast and empty that it exceeded the confines of his body, his reason and his thoughts. And Ephraim the widower, as he walked, in step, with his sons, beneath the weight of the beechwood bed on which his wife lay, had the calm, exceedingly vacant gaze of those who wander the desert wastes without refuge, the gaze of those who know that they will never find their way home, that they are lost for ever, in loneliness and hunger, and yet keep walking, with head held high – the transparent gaze of idiots.

Ephraim the widower had that imbecilic look of absence in his eyes – not defeated but resigned. For he had felt no sense of rebellion when Fat-Ginnie closed her eyes, as only the dying close them, with a slowness suddenly bordering on eternity – that eternity where the Father reigns, the King of this world, and his Lord. In the course of his life he had rebelled only against his earthly father, his father of flesh and anger, but never against his heavenly father. His faith was too simple, too stark, to experience the throes of doubt, the temptations of despair, revolt and denial. God had given, and God had taken away again – and it was the one, same God, of clemency and mercy. And this was why he, the inconsolable servant, so meekly brought to the Lord, their Creator and Redeemer, His handmaiden Fat-Ginnie, while looking forward to the day when his turn came to be summoned. He was resigned to his grief, he accepted his loneliness. In his heart, devastated at being parted from Regina, he murmured a song of offering and renouncement. While Blaise-the-Ugly continued to give voice to the melody of the psalm, Ephraim put his own humble words to the song:

'Look, Regina, look and rejoice, forget the earth and your anxieties, the King shall desire your goodness and gentleness.

For he is your Lord, and you must worship him! He is our Lord. I bring you to him. Even the poorest of the people that are burdened with suffering shall seek your favour. And those, like Marceau, who have come to a bad end, will beg you to help them.

The daughter born of hope and prayers, you lie in this beechwood box, in all simplicity, clothed in a shroud. You shall be brought to the King adorned with our love.

In sorrow and hope, in grief and gratitude, these young men, your sons, escort you. In your sons' stead, and mine, angels shall approach you. You shall watch over your sons throughout the world. And you'll send for me, won't you? You'll send for me . . .'

Of the same cast and the same austere and enduring simplicity was his sons' faith – the faith that Edmée, in her devotion to Our Lady, had grafted on to the souls of the whole family at Upper Farm. They were all there: mother, father, and sons, with the last-born leading the procession, the Morning brothers carrying the beechwood bed, and the other Evening sons following behind. There were all there but one.

And it was because of his absence – the absence of her Noon son – that Fat-Ginnie had died. When Simon disappeared, with that winter's night closing in, driven away by Ambroise Mauperthuis' evil laughter, as though by a great dark wind, carried off on Rouzé's back (the ox crazed by his sobbing), a lamentation had risen from the middle of the forest. A lamentation had risen in the clearing of Our-Lady-of-the-Beeches. There, too, the wind was blowing, flurrying round the trees, with their tall, smooth trunks and bare branches, gusting in the angels' wings and between their fingers, in which one held fruit while others bore an heart, trumpet, axe, or bells. It whistled in the folds of their grey bark gowns; it growled at their shoulders, which were graced with birds, bees, or fish; it shrilled as it skimmed their eyelids and grazed their lips that were either smiling or stern. There, too, the wind was blowing – a wind not dark, like Ambroise Mauperthuis' laughter, but grey, almost white; not violent but sad. As if the soul of Marceau, who had hanged himself, in the autumn, from a branch of a beech-tree, the tree of the angel-with-the-heart, had suddenly taken fright and begun to moan. And this grey lamentation that roamed round the statue of Our-Lady-of-the-Beeches had come all the way down to the village of Oak-Wolf, had slipped under the door of Upper Farm, and penetrated Fat-Ginnie's heart. That same night the snow, so late in coming that year, had started to fall. In the morning the countryside, paths and forests were buried under snow, as though to cover up even more effectively the traces of Simon-the-Hothead, of Simon who had gone missing. Some people later claimed to have caught sight that evening of the figure of an enormous white ox with a man clinging to its back, hurtling through the fog down the road to the valley. But it was already so dark and the fog so thick that no one could really tell where this great spectral ox was going, nor what exactly it was carrying on its back. And then the snow came down just after it had gone by – light and white and soft, like a child's dream.

The snow had fallen on the forests, in the clearing of Our-Lady-of-the-Beeches, on the angels' brows and wings, and the wind had dropped. The lamentation was stilled. But the lamentation had continued its murmur in Fat-Ginnie's heart. What had happened to her son? What affliction had driven him far from home and all his family? What new curse had the old man laid on him? Fat-Ginnie, whose body was a kingdom unto itself, who had always dwelt within this fecund body as within a palace, and who had never left the hamlet except to go down to the nearest village, could not imagine living anywhere else. There was Oak-Wolf, where the farm that had belonged to her parents and that was now hers nestled on the edge of the forest. And on the farm, there she was: there, the domain of her body. There, the long story of her hunger had unfolded; there, she had endured the attacks of her ferret-like famine, and the torments and distress due to this unreasonable, insatiable appetite. There, thanks to her mother, to Ephraim's love and the presence of her sons, she had drawn and eventually tamed the voracious little beast inside her. Beyond these few concentrated landmarks, the world was unknown to her – it was no doubt a wild place, full of dangers and wickedness. And surely there was hunger abroad, a nasty hunger, that attacked men's souls.

She was thoroughly acquainted with this hunger's mischief. She knew better than anyone how this hunger could cast into despair those it seized upon. It had taken her so many years, and so much love to realize that in truth this hunger was nothing else but a passion for tenderness. The countless prayers that her mother had kept making to the Blessed Virgin had hollowed out inside her this chasm of feeling. She was born with this wound, this insane tenderness gaping in her innermost heart and flesh. She was born consumed with an infinite care for the world, and for others – for their bodies and skin, their faces and voices, for the look in their eyes, their gestures, their sleep. But for a long time this had remained an unfocused dream inside her. For a long time she had been unable to name her hunger, and she had tried to deceive it with great quantities of food, attempting to suppress it. Her hunger had only grown more frantic. Then Ephraim had turned up, and she had given birth to nine sons. And all these bodies that had come to surround her, that had looked to her for their own nourishment, seeking peace, gratification and the sweetness of oblivion, or the strength to grow up, to become men, had helped her to name this hunger. She had only swelled to such vast proportions the better to give of herself, to bestow herself in sweetness, smiles and caresses; the better to glorify the beauty of the flesh.

She knew the vulnerability of the flesh and the frailty of the soul – these were things to which she was even painfully, fearfully alive. She knew that it took almost nothing at all to wound or destroy, to inflict suffering or drive a person mad. A bramble thorn, a viper's bit, meadow saffron or a laburnum pod, a splinter of glass might be enough to taint a man's blood, causing it to run dry, sapping him of life. A cruel word, a spiteful look, a scornful smile, a betrayal, a lie might suffice to sour a man's heart, to blacken his thoughts, to lay waste his soul. She knew this as an animal knows by instinct which is its habitat - its lair, or nest, or den – and which its manner of movement – running, swimming, creeping, flying; what it feeds on, and what its enemy. She had an instinct for human vulnerability, of body and soul. She was gifted with an aptitude for tenderness to match that instinct. She had nourished her sons with this tenderness; she had safe-guarded the integrity and brightness of their hearts. Even her sons of Morning and Noon, who were so quick to anger, kept pure in their hearts that tenderness. Even her sons of Evening, sometimes inclined to melancholy, kept pure in their hearts that brightness.

Yet Simon had now been carried off into the night, into

the cold, driven away by the darkest of winds, the wind of hatred and despair. One of her sons had been snatched from her tenderness. Where had he gone? Who would take care of him? Where would he find food and shelter? And was there not a danger of evil taking root in his heart overwhelmed by distress? She so dwelt on these questions that doubt insinuated itself inside her. Her anxiety for Simon began to gnaw at her as her ferret-like hunger once used to – in silence, unknown to anybody else. All her tenderness was thrown into alarm. She had to continue to safeguard her son without even knowing where he was or what he was doing. Day and night, her thoughts went out to Simon – thoughts woven into prayers as though into some invisible foliage meant to reach her missing son, to protect him from a distance.

Fat-Ginnie had spent all winter tensed with this anxiety, this vigilance, waiting for Simon to return. But there was no return, and no news came. Winter passed, the snows melted, the water began to flow freely in the streams again, and the birds came back. The felling in the forests was over, the timber-marking was done. It was time to start taking the wood down to the river. Fat-Ginnie watched as the heavy, open-sided carts, filled with logs, went past, drawn down the road by pairs of oxen. But Rouzé was not among them. Simon did not walk alongside any of these carts. She listened to the tread of the oxen, the men's footsteps, the squeaking of the carts' axles beneath their load of timber. She listened to the cowherds urging the yoked beasts to their task, with a cadenced, rough-voiced chanting of onomatopeic sounds, punctuated with animals' names. And she kept intoning the name of Rouzé, the name that no one chanted. But neither Rouzé nor his herdsman came. Then she took to her bed.

It was not that she was again overcome with the flaccid indolence that had once kept her dozing all day long. She lay in wait, in torment. She stopped eating. The hunger, the terrible hunger, that had been the bane of her childhood now returned, gaping inside her. Fat-Ginnie lay in bed, her blue, doll-like gaze fluttering in space, imbued with tears – a gaze that seemed to flit about like some delicate insect with transparent wings, made frantic by excessive light or darkness; an insect trying to escape from the glass shade of a lamp that had grown too hot, into which it had strayed. Fat-Ginnie's gaze tried to escape, to wrest itself from her body and gather the impetus and speed to fly off in search of Simon, the son carried off by the blast of a wintery wind. Edmée nursed her all day long, relieved by Loulou-the-Bellclinker and Blaise-the-Ugly. Used to serving her daughter with enormous platefuls of food, Edmée bent over her, dismayed that she now had to spoon a little water between her closed lips.

Blaise-the-Ugly wondered at his mother's gaze.

'What are you searching for?' he asked her in his gentle voice. 'Where do your eyes want to travel?'

This restless gaze that would not settle worried him. It reminded him of the crazy flight of bees when they are about to die.

'What have your eyes seen that has so panicked them?'

But it was because they had seen nothing that her eyes were so troubled. It was because they had not seen Simon among the herdsmen, because they had not seen his face again. It was because she was in the throes of despair, her tenderness unable to reach the child she yearned to console.

At night Ephraim held her even more tightly in his arms, as if he might detain her with his human strength. He placed his hands over her eyes to still her gaze.

'Go to sleep, Ginnie, go to sleep now. I'm here.'

But he felt his wife's eyelids beating against his palms; her eyelids were wet. He fell asleep with his hand stretched out to cover her eyes. One morning when he woke up, he had not felt the damp flutter on his palm. Very slowly he had removed his hand. Regina's eyes were calm again. She lay, peaceful at last, with her eyes half-open. He bent over her face, and she smiled at him – a ghost of a smile, already very distant. Then slowly her eyelids closed. Ephraim felt a light caress skim his palm. He looked down. A blue gleam shimmered in the hollow of his hand. The blueness of Regina's eyes stole upon the surface of his skin one last time – a teardrop radiance.

ROUZÉ'S BODY

The son who had been missing for such a long time reappeared. He had fled far from Oak-Wolf on the back of an ox. He had wandered from village to village, hiring himself out, with Rouzé, to farms that had need of him and his beast. And every night he had gone to bed with this sombre hope in his heart: that in the morning he would hear the great, magic news of old Mauperthuis' death. But this news never came. Other news reached him – it was not even news really, but more of a sign. One morning he felt a draught on his hands and face; a very slight draught that had nothing to do with wind or breeze. A draught so tenuous, it was like a breath with the smell of fruit on it – his mother's breath. And he had suddenly rediscovered all the forgotten sensations of his childhood: how he used to fall asleep in his mother's arms amid the delicious fragrance of her skin, with his head resting against her throat; how he delighted in his mother's voice, her gentle purls of laughter, and the limpid blue of her eyes. When he woke, he suddenly felt his mother's tiny hand caressing him, and thought he saw her smile and her tranquil, always rather dreamy gaze. He felt that she was watching him, looking into the very depths of his soul, and he thought he heard a murmur right against his ear: 'Here I am, my child, I've found you at last. I'm with you now . . .' His mother's voice whispered inside him, close to his heart, soothing him.

His mother's gaze and his mother's voice were so present in him, so enveloping, that the desire to see her again, and to see his brothers, his house, the upland forests, and Camille made him resolve to go home. He set out to return to his village. His desire to see his mother again, and all his family, increased with every step. With every step his hope of seeing Camille again raced faster and faster. In his eagerness to be back, in his longing for this reunion, he

195

forgot about the old man. He reached his village after several days' long walk – days so slow that they seemed to him even more interminable than all those months spent away from home. He returned with Rouzé.

He met no one on the way through Oak-Wolf. Nor was there anybody at Upper Farm, when at last he reached it. He called his mother, then Edmée, then Loulou-the-Bellclinker and Blaise-the-Ugly – usually, they did not leave the house, or stray far – but none of them responded to his calls. Then he was struck by another silence, an even bleaker silence than that of absent people: a silence that subsumed all other silences, compressing them, imparting to them an edge of violence. The big clock was quiet; its pendulum hung still. Had time, then, stopped since his departure? He dared not look around him further, for fear of detecting other signs. For he knew well that clocks were stopped only in a house where death had slipped in. The silence of the clock tightened round his throat; he felt choked by this silence. Yet he finally made a move towards his parents' bedroom. He opened the door very slowly. He only need to open it a chink, and he knew. The silence of the clock rushed into his heart, swept through his blood, chilled his senses and his reason. His parents' bed was empty; the mattress had been removed – to burn it, of course, since it was customary to burn the mattressess of the deceased. The wardrobe mirror was covered with a sheet – so that the deceased's soul should not linger, seeking the reflection of a body that it had ceased to inhabit, so that the disembodied soul should not panic at being destined henceforth to remain invisible.

The bedroom was empty, and this emptiness cut his legs away from under him. He collapsed in the doorway. He knew. Only his mother's demise could have so desolated the room. Before the gapingly empty bed, before the veiled mirror, he felt the loneliness and grief that had now become his father's fate. It was a loneliness to match his mother's defunct body – of fabulous immensity, but cold and harsh, not warm and gentle; not one that took you to its bosom, but a knee-buckling, back-breaking immensity. It was a grief to match the happiness that his mother had continually bestowed. Everything turned; all of sudden everything became hollow. The light that bathed the room seemed to Simon ugly and chalky, and the air grew harsh, odours rank, and the silence unbearable. Even the saliva in his mouth acquired a bitter taste. Never again would he see his mother, for whose sake he had returned, and whose prodigious body was an offering, representing goodness and consolation.

Then he remembered the old man. It was Ambroise Mauperthuis who had driven him away from his family and all those bodies that, once parted from, his own body had lost its vigour, radiance and joy. Old Mauperthuis was the one that had stopped the clock and set fire to the mattress; he was the one that had brought death into Upper Farm.

Though he felt his father's grief, it was quite a different mood. There was no resignation or submissiveness in Simon, but a wild burst of anger. He stood up, walked through the house, and grabbed an axe. The light in the yard blinded him. And in that end-of-May morning light, he saw Rouzé. The animal was waiting placidly in the middle of the yard. But Simon did not recognize Rouzé, his companion in exile. He saw a colossus of terrifying whiteness. A colossus that looked like a ghost, standing there before him, in broad daylight. A terrible colossus – death's mount.

So, where was death now that had sat astride this colossus? Perhaps it had stuffed his mother's body inside the entrails of this enormous beast? Or perhaps it was hiding in the beast's heart? Simon rushed straight at the ox. The axe came down on Rouzé's brow. He collapsed in a heap, with no time to make the slightest movement, without even a bellow. Simon set upon the felled carcase. He cut off its head, then its limbs, he opened its belly. He attacked, he attacked death's mount, he attacked old Mauperthuis' ox. He dismembered the body, he lacerated its

197

flesh, he drained it of blood and eviscerated it. He destroyed Rouzé's likeness; he flayed a spectral ox, he cut into pieces a colossal draught-animal, a colossal beast of burden, so that it might no longer be a vehicle for the old man's evil laughter, so that it might not carry death and sorrow any more. Simon flayed the old man's hatred, he cut up his evil laughter.

When Simon returned through the deserted hamlet and entered the yard of Threshold Farm, he was naked, covered with Rouzé's flayed torso that he carried on his shoulders, his skin smeared with the animal's blood. Then he shouted the old man's name. He summoned Ambroise Mauperthuis out into the yard, to come and fetch the colossus' carcase, the carrion of the mount that had brought death to Upper Farm. He summoned Ambroise Mauperthuis to come and answer to him for his mother's death. But only two big dogs chained to the trunk of the magnolia tree responded to his calls, by barking furiously. Mauperthuis was not there. He had left at daybreak, long before the tribe at Upper Farm emerged, carrying the fat Verselay's woman's coffin, to take her down to the cemetery in the village below. He no more wanted to meet the son he had disowned than he did the grandchildren that he had always regarded as savages, and, more importantly, whom he knew to be all in league against him. He had closed the doors and shutters of his fortress farm, which he always left guarded by his dogs, and had gone off to his forest of Failly. He would not be back until evening, or nightfall. All the men and women of the hamlet had joined Fat-Ginnie's funeral procession – all except Huguet Cordebugle, from whom everybody had been keeping their distance, even more assiduously than Huguet had always kept his – ever since that scene in the forest that he had caused the previous winter. And Huguet Cordebugle, ensconced behind his dirty window-panes, with the ancient cockerel Alphonse in a heap on his lap, was yet again the only person to see Simon.

He had seen him go up the road, at Rouzé's side; he had heard the impact of the axe as it landed on the beast's brow, the thud of the body as it fell to the ground, and the renewed whistling of the axe as it cut the animal to pieces. He had heard all these sounds from inside his house, without quite understanding what was going on – what was the meaning of those sharp whistlings of an axe slicing through the air, all those dull, hurried thwacks, and the heavy panting of a man hurling himself without restraint into some violent physical labour? There was a note of madness, of fury, to all these sounds, which he could not explain. And these mysterious noises in the deserted village scared him. He huddled over his old cockerel with the bobbing head as if he needed to shrink, to make himself extremely small, to escape the anger of the man who was chopping away nearby, frantically, breathlessly – at what, he did not quite know.

It seemed to him that all those axe blows were soon going to attack him, too, that they were going to break down his door and come and chop him to pieces as well, here on his chair, with Alphonse. He moaned with terror. But silence descended once more. Then he saw Simon go past again.

Simon, or Simon's ghost? He saw him come down the road, naked. Naked, as he had been that September night, on the far side of the meadow at Threshold Farm; the night that was illuminated by the whiteness of the sheets spread out on the grass. Naked, but with no whiteness illuminating him now. Simon's skin glistened with blood. His entire body was streaming with sweat and blood – the sweat of his own body and the blood of the ox Rouzé. He carried Rouzé's flayed torso on his shoulders, walking bowed beneath the weight of that torso. He walked bowed beneath the burden of his anger, grief, and lost love – and of his desire stripped bare. Simon was on his way to Threshold Farm.

Huguet Cordebugle remained seated at his window, his eyes riveted to the filthy panes long after Simon had

199

disappeared. He could still see Simon's naked body on the empty road; Simon's splendour – his body reddened with a blood that was not his own, but became his by mingling with his sweat. Simon's splendour under the spell of the beast's blood. The splendour of his body in its new nakedness – not just of the skin, but of the flesh. All streaming with Rouzé's blood, Simon himself looked flayed. Nakedness of flesh and heart, nakedness of anger and desire; Simon's body was more than bared, it was excoriated. Rouzé's blood glistened on him with the brilliance of flame. Huguet Cordebugle stared at the hallucinating image on the deserted road, of Simon-the-Flayed, Simon who had become a man-beast, a god of flesh and blood, a walking torch. He kept gazing with a bewildered look of admiration and stupor at the body that had appeared on the road, shining with sweat and blood, a fulgurating vision in the morning brightness. Simon-the-Hothead, Simon-the-Flayed, going his way with his body in flames. And Huguet Cordebugle would not betray this image, this nakedness of flesh and heart, this nakedness of blood and fire. He would not own to anybody what he had just seen. He would jealously guard in his heart this image that only he had seen. He would go and dream about it in his white room, in the comfort of that bed with its fancy sheets made out of women's lingerie.

The old man was not there. He was attending to business. He had become even more ruthless in his affairs, looking after his wealth as a bitch looks after its pups. He argued over every centime when selling the timber from his forests, and was warily suspicious of being robbed by anybody, whether by his own employees, woodcutters, log-drivers and herdsmen, or by the timber merchants. He wanted to be wealthy, wealthier still, fabulously wealthy. He built up his wealth like a vast, invisible mausoleum dedicated to the dual body of Catherine and Camille, to the one's deceased body and the other's confined body; a dual body that had become one, an ever-growing body.

The body of his wonderful Spark of Life. He never tired of reading and rereading his big account books; he was intoxicated by figures. Every new sum that he acquired embellished his imaginary mausoleum. His happiness was great and solid; he had striven hard for it, he had wrested it from a horde of determined swindlers that were his enemies. But he had been harder and more stubborn than all of them, he had overcome his enemies. Corvol was rotting in the earth, his daughter-in-law and her dwarfish brother were holed up in their house in the valley, Marceau's etiolated shade was for ever laid to rest in silence, Simon had disappeared; and he held Camille prisoner, by force, with a master-hand, and he would never, ever let her go. She was his possession, entirely his creature. It was to him that she owed her advent into the world, and she would not live except by virtue of him. He brought her food, her water, her clothes, the embers for her footwarmer, the fuel for her lamp. He cared for her as for a bird in a cage, a bird far too lovely, far too rare, to go flying through the sky. A secret bird that had no right to spread its wings in flight except within the space of his gaze. He spent hours watching her through the peep-hole, endlessly talking to her with his mouth pressed against the wood of the door.

THE WHITE ROOM

Camille did not let herself die. She let herself float on the surface of sleep, on the surface of dreaming. She swam among colours, drifted through images, with her eyes wide open. And she listened. She listened to every sound. She was familiar with the slightest stirring in the attic, the creaking of the beams and the floor, the squeaking of the door when the old man opened it just wide enough to pass in her food and her jug of fresh water. She was familiar with all the inflexions of the wind, all the sounds and rhythms of the rain; with every bird that nested under the eaves, and the pitter-patter of mice, and the faint rustling of insects. She had no other knowledge of the world now, beyond these few noises – of wood, wind, rain, leaves, insects, mice and birds. There was nothing that she hated more than some of these noises – those that the wood made: the quiet creak of the staircase under the old man's tread, the slam of the peep-hole when he opened and closed it, and above all those murmurings that seeped through the wooden panels, oozing down the door like dirty water, like a greasy dankness – the old man's voice whispering his litanies of love to a dead woman. Every time the old man came and pressed his eye, with its crazed pupil, to the peep-hole, and his mouth, all clammy with death, against the wooden door, she buried herself under the blankets, and put her hands over her ears. When the old man did not come up and torment her from the other side of the door, she resumed her listening. She endeavoured to discern sounds beyond the walls and roof of the attic. From day to day, from night to night, she had trained her hearing to detect sounds that were ever more distant and faint. She listened with a beating heart to the footsteps of the men and beasts that climbed the road. But none of them were Simon's, none of them were Rouzé's. Yet she waited. Her life was concentrated on this waiting, her life was nothing but this straining to hear. She slept with her eyes sharpened.

That May morning, long after the old man had gone, she heard a strange cohort of men and women coming down the road. The rhythm of their steps was slow and heavy, of the utmost gravity – the steps of those that accompany the dead. She heard Blaise-the-Ugly's voice singing in a steady voice on the verge of tears. She caught only the first words of his song: 'Hearken, o daughter, and consider, and incline thine ear . . .'

Who was being taken to be buried? And who was signalling to her, putting her on her guard, reviving her vigilance. Who was telling her to listen, watch, and be attentive?

'Hearken, o daughter, and consider, and incline thine ear . . .' She listened to the voice singing, the footsteps that kept their funereal pace, and the silence of the men and women of the hamlet answering the silence of him or her that was to be buried. The song died away, out there, among the grasses, the footsteps faded, and only the silence remained – that of the dead and the living. 'Hearken, o daughter . . .' And she had listened, lying on her bed, completely still and holding her breath so as not to disturb, even by the slightest stirring, the silence that encompassed the farm, and all the farms in the village. But the blood was pounding at her temples, and she could hear the racing thud of her heart-beat. She listened from deep inside her body.

'Hearken, o daughter, and consider, and incline thine ear . . .' And then suddenly, out there on the road, had come the sound of approaching footsteps, the dual stride of man and beast, of a cowherd and his ox, climbing slowly up the hill. They were getting nearer; they were going to come into the village, and pass close to the farm. A dual stride – that of Simon and Rouzé. Camille listened from deep down inside her body as from the bottom of a lake whose waters are just about to burst forth as the flood-gates are opened. It was joy opening up in her heart, but with such violence that her heart ached. The tumult of the lake waters and of the waters from the reservoirs rushing into rivers to swell their flow and speed their course, and sweeping along the drove of logs crammed between the banks, rose inside her, filling her body – as if all the dams in the area had burst, and their waters were surging through her. Her body, lying still and silent on the pallet in the corner of the attic, was invaded by a tremendous tumult. A roar of rampageous, living waters stormed through her body, flaying her flesh from within.

'Hearken, o daughter, and consider, and incline thine ear . . .' Listen, watch, and be attentive . . . She listened, frantically. She could not see any more – the undammed lake waters filled her eyes, and swept away her gaze – but her whole body was attentive.

Simon had gone by without stopping at Threshold Farm, without even slowing his pace. He had gone on his way. Then, there was silence again. But the waters had continued madly coursing through her; nothing could stop them now. Blows had resounded, out there, on the edge of the forest. They came from the yard of Upper Farm – Camille recognized the resonance that distinguished every place in the village. The blows had ceased.

'Hearken, o daughter . . .' Listen . . . Was that someone walking down the road? Was that someone coming to Threshold Farm? From the depths of the tumult and swell inside her body, Camille strained to hear.

She thought she could detect the tread of a man walking barefoot. Someone was coming, someone was entering the farmyard. The dogs were on their feet, barking furiously, their chains rattling on the stones. And suddenly Simon shouted. His voice drowned the dogs' howling. He threw something at them, a sop to their rage, and they fell silent, avidly devouring it. Simon shouted the name of Ambroise Mauperthuis, the name of the man who was master of the farm and master of the dogs; master of hunger, anger and death. The name of Rouzé's master.

Up in the attic, Camille leapt to her feet. All the waters that had invaded her body now drained away. She tried to cry out Simon's name, to call him to come and free her, but she could not utter a sound. After remaining silent all these months, living in isolation, locked up under the roof, her voice had gone. She tried to shout, but her throat remained constricted and her mouth mute. Simon was there, in the yard, close by, and she could not call him. And he just kept repeating the old man's name.

Even in his absence the old man continued to hold her prisoner – not just behind a bolted door, on a farm guarded by two dogs starved by their master to make them more ferocious, but within herself. And there was Simon, down below, only able to cry the old man's name. Had he forgotten her name? In his flight and exile, had he even lost the name of Camille? Had the old man so entirely robbed them of everything? She beat against the door, hurting her fingers on the lock. She could hear Simon shouting. But it was no good listening any more, now was the time to speak, to shout back. She was unable to. Then she had an idea.

She took the lamp with the low flame burning in it that she would turn up at nightfall. She broke the lamp glass and set fire to bits of material from her bed, and placed them against the door. She blew on the flames to set the wood of the door alight. The fire wavered for a moment, then finally leapt all over the door, licking at the wood, until it took hold, and the wood began to burn. Camille stepped back. She took a blanket and poured over it all the remaining water in the jug, and wrapped herself in it. The wood of the door cracked, as wider and wider fissures appeared in it. Camille suddenly began to laugh. She had regained her voice. She laughed to see the door burning, the door she so hated, this monstrous door with its lewd eye and hideous murmurings. The fire reached beyond the door, travelling along the walls, rising towards the ceiling, and attacking the beams and floorboards. It was getting stiflingly hot, the air unbreathable. Camille rammed the door, and the wood went flying in all directions. She rushed down the staircase.

The old man had, as usual, locked all the doors leading out into the yards, front and back. But the shutters, which he had also closed, opened from the inside. Finding the doors bolted against her, Camille hastened to open a window. The fire had followed her. The whole attic was in flames. She heard them devouring the roofbeams and attacking the walls with a loudening roar. The fire raced on above her, consuming the ceiling; it swept down the staircase, the flames already entering the kitchen, setting alight the table and benches, and smoke clouding the room. Camille climbed out of a ground-floor window and jumped down into the yard.

She saw Simon, standing under the flowering magnolia tree, watching the roof collapse amid the rising flames. He was no longer shouting the old man's name. He was naked. But Rouzé's blood that stained his body from head to toe formed a dark red crust as it dried. Crouched at his feet, the two dogs were tearing at the remains of the ox's torso, unconcerned by the fire writhing above them. The bones of the carcase cracked between their jaws, just as the beams cracked. At last Simon noticed Camille, but he looked at her in the same way that he stared at the fire, his gaze distant and stupefied. He still saw the body of the colossus he had slaughtered in the yard at Upper Farm. That dismembered, flayed colossus loomed before him now, looking even more enormous and terrifying. The fire rose from its entrails. And the colossus bellowed, its bellowing becoming increasingly loud and sonorous. Its flanks opened, and from its belly, ripped apart by the flames, a kind of female ghost emerged. But this woman was not the one whose bed was empty, and whose mirror was veiled. So in what depths of its belly had the colossus buried Regina's body? Simon continued to seek his mother's image, to await her appearance. But it was Camille that had just appeared – or was it? He seemed not to recognize this thin figure wrapped in a completely scorched blanket, her face blackened by smoke, her hands blistered and burned.

It was she that made the first move. 'The dogs,' she said, 'we must free them – and all the other animals . . .' Her voice was faint, breathless, almost inaudible still.

They freed the animals, lurching about like sleepwalkers in motion.

'We must go . . .' Again it was Camille who spoke.

The fire raged over the whole house, sweeping into the rooms, bursting through doors and windows, devouring the furniture and furnishings, consuming the beds, and then racing ahead, ever onwards, ever more voracious. The cowsheds and barns caught alight. The branches of the magnolia tree began to twist. The ivory-white of its flowers that had only recently bloomed, turned bright red and purple. The magnolia waved its flame blossoms. Then the flowers shrivelled, curling up in the fiery blaze. The air quivered in the blast of heat; it rippled, red, and shimmered. This suffocating air filled the yard, driving out the animals. Even the dogs had fled, carrying off in their chops the tattered remains of what they had been feasting on.

'We must go . . .' Camille repeated quietly. Simon could not tear his eyes from the blaze. And what if his mother were in turn to emerge from the colossus' belly? What if his mother were to appear from this gut furnace and come towards him with her little dancing steps?

'Let's go now,' Camille said again. 'We must.'

They left, with Simon backing away. Threshold Farm was burning, sending its roar in the direction of the forest. Was this Ambroise Mauperthuis' response to Simon, who had come shouting and cursing his name? Was this the howling of old Mauperthuis' anger? The flames rose in a spiral of black smoke at the entrance to the village. Was this the old man's body – his body of hatred and jealousy – that was blazing away, soon to be consumed? Camille threw over Simon shoulders the scorched blanket that she was wrapped in. She seized his hand. She tried to drag him away, to tear him from the sight of this fire that seemed to have cast a spell over him.

'Don't look back, hurry up, quick, quick . . . don't look back,' she kept saying. But she stumbled along, slow in her movements. She had no strength left. After those months of being locked up in the attic, all this space around her suddenly made her feel dizzy.

'Come on, hurry . . .' she said, but her voice was faint and weary, and her legs were trembling. Already she was not so much dragging Simon along as leaning on him. 'Quickly, we must get away . . .' she said, but she was not moving any more. 'Help me . . .' she murmured at last.

When Huguet Cordebugle saw their silhouettes on the road, he stood up. These were not the bodies of living human beings, but silhouettes, nothing but silhouettes, driven by the dark, fiery wind blowing from Threshold Farm. Two lost chimera that wanted to run, but whose footsteps were quagmired in immobility. Two chimera the colour of ashes and singeing, the colour of blood and dust.

He emerged from his house. 'Come in,' he shouted to them.

Simon and Camille were so weak, so distraught, that they obeyed. At that moment they would have been capable of obeying any order. They had no strength or defences. Their reason seemed to have burned in the fire that raged behind them. They entered Cordebugle's farm. Without a saying word, Huguet Cordebugle led them to the back of the room and pulled out a big wooden tub, which he dragged across to them. Then he went to fetch water from the well. He filled the tub, and brought some soap and towels.

'Wash yourselves,' he told them. And then he went away, to sit guard again at the window, where Alphonse was dozing on his chair.

Simon and Camille obeyed the new command they had been given. They bathed in the tub, washed their skin clean of the sweat and blood that sullied them, then dressed in the clothes that Huguet had laid out for them on a stool by the tub – shirts made out of women's lingerie, and men's trousers of rough velvet. When they were dressed, Huguet rose and crossed the room. He opened his secret room to them. 'In here,' was all he said. Simon and Camille came over. Dressed similarly like this, half in men's clothes and half in women's, the resemblance between them became uncanny. And at that moment they both had the same expression, of children exhausted by tiredness, fear and loneliness. With a wave of his hand, Huguet indicated the bed to them. 'And now lie down and sleep.' Then he left the room and shut the door behind him.

They obeyed Huguet Cordebugle's last instruction once again with the same docility. They lay down on the bed, with its pillowcases and sheets trimmed with lace and embroidery combining the initials of the first names of all the women in the neighbourhood. They lay down among these soft, white letters, these monograms of oblivion. And stretched out side by side, they fell asleep straight away. They dropped into a still and dreamless slumber, free of all anxiety. They held hands. In the boundlessness of their sleep they clung to each other with this single gesture whereby all their distress drained away and the bonds of their love were renewed. In the afternoon Huguet Cordebugle noiselessly entered the room again. In the darkness he discerned the sleepers lying still and silent, shoulder to shoulder, side by side. For a long time he gazed at the dual reclining body. He bent over their faces, with their eyes and mouths closed, and he wished that their sleep might last for ever. His sheets – the sheets that he had fashioned out of women's undergarments – and all this lacy finery, that for so many years he had spent evening after evening sewing together, had at last found this quiet and innocent twin body.

For them, Huguet Cordebugle went out thieving from gardens again – stealing not washing but flowers. He brought back armfuls of flowers – peonies, roses and lilies, irises and amaryllis. He even picked slender branches of apple and plum blossom. He filled the room where they slept with all these flowers. The air was permeated with their mingled fragrances. He covered the sleeping pair with flowers. He kept plying their twin body with gauzy fabrics, lace and flowers – with whiteness and softness.

He was constantly dazzled by the transformations of these two bodies in one. He had seen them one late-summer night bounding naked through the dark grass. He had seen how they swam upon the ground, among sheets of chalky brightness. He had seen how they rushed towards each other, and enfolded each other in their embrace, how they entangled their arms, and hands, and legs. He had seen how they kept binding and unbinding their two bodies, and how they seemed to keep endlessly dying and reviving, to the abrupt, and sometimes gentle, rhythm of the movement of their loins and hands, accentuated by their mouths. He had seen all this – this twofold, single body, this twin body all crazed with nakedness, desire and pleasure, a body that was both self and other, in the ecstasy of its own metamorphosis. He had watched even to the point of amazement and sorrow. But on a day of anger he had betrayed this vision, he had betrayed his secret. Out of vengeance and spite, he had cast his secret, like some crude denunciation, at the one person that could not, should not, learn of it. He had let out his secret as one might let loose a raging dog, a wounded dog, to attack the old man, his arrogant, hard-hearted master, to defy his power and pride. But really, it was an admission not so much of what he had seen as of the pain of having seen a beauty that to him was madness, terror and bitterness. A pain, too, that had become something he treasured, even more than his secret room. And in the strength of this secret treasure he had humiliated old Mauperthuis.

But old Mauperthuis had rent asunder this twin body. Autumn, then winter had passed. Spring was already drifting towards summer. And the earth and the days were destitute of beauty, the fabulous torment of beauty. But then Simon had reappeared, accompanied by his ox, as though by some spectre – no, not a spectre, a sorcerous spirit and body. And Simon had killed and dismembered it, chopped it up and flayed it, and garbed himself with its torso, as if armouring himself; he had then appropriated its sorcery. Huguet had seen this: he had seen Simon become a man-beast, a blaze of flesh, sweat and blood; he had seen him in turn become sorcery embodied. And this body had undergone another transformation, turning itself into tall and roaring flames. Huguet had seen the sky redden in the full light of morning, and the trees turn purple in the middle of spring. Then the body had become a silhouette – a silhouette holding its shadow by the hand. An exhausted silhouette and shadow.

ROCKING-STONE ABBEY

After Fat-Ginnie's burial, the men and women went to the village inn. Only Edmée returned to the church to pray in the shadow of the Madonna's blue mantle, now that the Madonna had summoned back to her the miraculous child she had bestowed on Edmée half a century ago. Edmée did not weep. Her grief was too pure to thrill to the taste of tears. While her daughter was dying, she had sometimes wept. But when she saw Regina's face on the morning of her death, she had stopped crying, for then she had stopped seeing suffering and death. All had been consummated – human happiness as well as distress and pain: the Most Merciful Mother had taken her daughter by the hand again, to bring her to God, and she in turn, the old earthly mother, stretched out her hands into the silence and emptiness of the invisible. And in her outstretched hands she offered up her sorrow, so that this sorrow might be purged and relieved of all despair. Edmée knew that the souls of the dead should not be upset with cries and sobs; she sensed that the departing soul is frail and bewildered, and that it does not fall to the living to be able to guide it. The mystery of death remains closed to the living, who must simply allow the souls of their loved ones to be entrusted to those blessed by God who have already penetrated this mystery and abide within it for ever. Edmée sensed this, and she entrusted her daughter to Her that was blessed among all men and women, and whom all generations called blessed.

Edmée did not weep. She strove to make her grief accord with her faith, to reconcile the invisible with transparency, silence with song, and to attune her heart, of one who survived, to the soul of her departed daughter. Already she existed only to have loved, and to love still more, in a void, in relinquishment and bereavement.

And similarly Ephraim the widower existed only to

have loved. As he sat with his sons at the largest table in the inn, he had ordered a plum brandy. He drank as he had done that long-ago evening when, with face branded by his father's fury, he had come to ask Jousé Verselay for his daughter Regina's hand in marriage. But this spring morning he asked for nothing. Regina's hand had just been taken away from him. He asked for nothing – he gave. Just as Edmée resigned herself, so he yielded to the transformation of his sudden loss into a gift. But for this, he had to learn to forget himself, to deny himself and his love, as that of a living man who felt desire. So he downed one glass after another to hasten the onset of oblivion, to sink to the underlying depths of his being, and get below his body's vigour and its rushes of desire, which though still keen were now destined to meet the void. He had to plunge as quickly as possible deep into self-forgetfulness, to drop far below his vigorousness, to quell from the outset all rebellion, all onslaught of desire.

Without a word, he drained one glass after another, in a single swig each time, surrounded by his sons who let him drink as he pleased. None of them would have dared tell him to stop, just after returning from the cemetery. Only Loulou-the Bellclinker was upset by it: this mechanical gesture that his father kept repeating, raising his glass to his lips and emptying it, terrified him. He had the impression that his father was killing himself before his eyes, that he was going to drink until his heart failed. But Ephraim was only trying to drown his suffering, and it was the man who felt desire that he was trying to suppress within himself.

While he was drinking in this way, the other men and women seated at the tables in the inn spoke among themselves, eating and drinking as well. They spoke of Fat-Ginnie, thinking back, and reviewing her life, now that she was dead. And in doing so, they were put in mind of others that had died. They reminisced about their dead, recalling past funerals. The names of Marceau, Jousé, Firmin Follin, Pierre and Lea Cordebugle, and Guillaume

Gravelle acquired renewed force and resonance. Their images emerged from the shadows. Memories were interwined, one leading to another. The collective memory of the small population of the hamlet was stirred into full flood, as the tide of time retreated with an ever-increasing surge. The small population of the hamlet grew, as they sounded the call for all the dead, for those of Oak-Wolf and the other hamlets nearby, and those of the larger village. The small population of the hamlet rallied its deceased flock, and became a crowd, a vast tribe.

And the living who recalled their dead forded the present as if it might have been a river, and went sauntering in the past, laughing and weeping. They sighed, nodded their heads, poured themselves another drink, then resumed their rambling reminiscences and became animated once more.

At the Mauperthuis' table, no one spoke. Grief, there, was stiff and silent. They all stared vacantly at their glasses, or at their ungainly hands, lying flat on the table. Ephraim had drunk more brandy than a man is capable of. The moment finally came when his grief ceded, when the man that felt desire was defeated, and his heart overturned – directly above the void. He set down his glass, and stood up, resting on the shoulders of Martin-the-Sparing and Adrien-the-Blue, who were seated beside him. And he said in a dull, resounding voice, 'I shall never go back up there. Never. Take me this very day to the monks at Rocking-Stone Abbey. This very day, I tell you. Do you hear, my sons?'

They had heard, and understood. They understood their father's dread at the idea of returning to the farm forsaken by their mother, and of lying in that empty bed. And they also sensed that along with this dread went their father's refusal to go back and work under the old man's orders. The old man who was still alive. The old man who had anathematized his elder son, raised his hand against him, and kept him necessitous, in his employ and at his mercy. The old man who had so persistently dogged his younger son's footsteps with unhappiness that it led to his death. The old man who had separated Camille and Simon; who had kept Camille locked up and driven Simon away, so far and to such effect that Fat-Ginnie had gradually worn herself out keeping vigil on the fringe of this banishment, in the chill of her alarm. The old man who with great sweeps of anger, hatred and vengeance kept mowing down the happiness of others around him.

They heard everything their father had said, and sensed everything that he was unable to express, that was too painful to him. And so also did the others at the tables nearby, who had been talking from every distant horizon of their collective memory. All fell silent.

'Do you hear?' said Ephraim.

But before his sons could find it in them to reply, he had collapsed in a heap across the table. His forehead struck the wood.

They laid Ephraim on a bench at the back of the room. Then his Morning sons went looking for someone in the village who might let them have a horse and cart to take their father to Rocking-Stone Abbey. Their father's request had been: this very day. They found the cart, laid their father in it, and set off. Ferdinand-the-Strong, Adrien-the-Blue and Germain-the-Deaf sat in the cart around their father. Martin-the-Sparing led the horse. The others stayed behind in the village, waiting for Edmée to return from the church and rest for a while before going back to Oak-Wolf.

Ephraim did not come to until they reached the gates of the abbey. He told his sons to return to the village and then go home. He told them that he would never leave this place of solitude, this enclosure of oblivion, and that Ferdinand-the-Strong was now the head of the family. After which, he embraced them and said goodbye to them all. His sons left. Then he went and knocked at the monastery's door. It opened, and closed behind him – behind Ephraim the widower, who had come to learn self-denial. The monks welcomed him, and he remained with them. He was doing what he had to do, just as in the past, for the love of Fat-Ginnie, he had renounced his wealth along with his rights as the elder son. In the past, he had broken free of his father, now he was breaking free of himself.

The younger sons did not get back to Oak-Wolf until late. Evening was closing in. But at the bottom of the road they saw a strange redness in the sky that did not come from the sunset. When they entered the hamlet, they discovered the source of this glow. Threshold Farm had been burning down. The other inhabitants of the hamlet, who had arrived home earlier, were trying to extinguish the last outbreaks of the fire. The roof of the house had completely fallen in, leaving just the blackened walls standing, with their doors and windows shattered. The interior of the house was in total ruins – the walls, ceilings and floors had collapsed, and not a single room existed any more. The barns and cowsheds had burned down. The magnolia stood over the charred remains of its final flowering, shed by its bark-stripped, broken branches and strewn over the ground. A flowering of cinders and ashes.

RAINS OF MAY

Ambroise Mauperthuis was the last to turn up. The fire was dying and some people were already beginning to search among the ruins despite the acrid black smoke rising from them. Everyone was anxious to know whether Camille had perished in the blaze. Old Mauperthuis stood stock-still in the middle of the yard, seized with terror. He gazed at his devastated farm, the retreat that for months he had so zealously kept locked, which the flames had forced their way into, and completely gutted. His retreat whose charred innards were revealed to everyone. He realized what those floundering among the steaming entrails of his farm were looking for – Camille's body. But he knew right from the start that Camille could not be lying under this debris, that she was safe. That she was the one who had started the fire, and that she had escaped. And it was Camille's escape that terrified him. He also realized that Simon must have come back. Only Simon's return could have given Camille the idea of setting fire to the attic, and the power to do it. He vowed that he would find them. If necessary, he would rebuild with his own hands his entire farm, he would construct a castle, like Vauban Castle at Bazoches, he would dig a crypt like the one in the basilica of St Madeleine in Vézelay – he would raise fortresses, he would excavate underground caves and deep cellars in which to hide Camille, and bury her, and keep her prisoner for ever. If need be, he would immure Camille, he would put a leash round her neck, to stop her from escaping and robbing him of his Spark of Life.

During the night, rain fell. The last embers still smouldering beneath the wreckage were extinguished, the ashes turned to mud. A stream of black water ran across the yard of Threshold Farm. Ambroise Mauperthuis had refused to leave his disaster-stricken domain. He had found shelter in the shed at the bottom of the vegetable garden behind the house. He had cleared it of all the tools and implements cluttering it, and made a bed for himself there. This shed was enough for him. He decided that he would stayed there as long as it took him to rebuild the farm. He would not admit defeat, he was not at all despairing. His wealth was considerable; he would have even bigger buildings constructed. His patience was even more considerable, and it was stubborn. Now more than ever, it was hardening round his anger. He decided to go to town the very next day, and denounce Simon-the-Hothead, and accuse him of every misdeed − of having raped and abducted Camille, stolen his cattle, and finally set fire to his farm. He would denounce Simon the thief, Simon the arsonist. He would have him declared an outlaw and set the police after him, have him arrested and thrown in gaol. He was sure of his power, sure of his rights.

He vowed to Simon the hatred he had borne Victor Corvol, just as he vowed to Camille the passion that bound him to Catherine. In his mind and in his heart, the dead kept their grasp on the living, beauty had a constant taste of anger, and desire was called vengeance and strife.

Lying on his makeshift pallet, he listened to the rain pelting on the branches, stones and tiles all around him. It was a violent downpour that lashed the leaves and bounced on the ground. He fell asleep amid the noise of this rain. And this noise invaded his dreams. He saw himself floating on one of those huge log-rafts that went back to his adolescence, when he was an apprentice raftsman. But the logs kept growing larger, each acquiring the length and thickness of a tree-trunk. He was sailing on a raft of tree-trunks, a couched forest. And the riverbed gradually grew deeper and wider, the waters swelled and flooded and flowed ever more strongly. The river was in spate. And alone aboard his giant raft, he poked at the banks with his long steering pole. And at each thrust the banks receded.

The river became as vast as a lake, its waters as heavy as the sea. Then whole sections of the raft detached themselves. The trunks that broke loose plunged into the water, righted themselves, and became trees again, whose branches turned green. The trees that stood on the bottom of the water were of the same green as Catherine's eyes, Camille's eyes. A serpent-coloured forest sprang up all along the river-bed.

Bells pealed under the water. Bells boomed in the tree-trunks. They burst the bark of the trees. Catherine's name was graven in the bark, with brutal resonance. Catherine's name rang out from the hearts of the trees, and strange, round, sun-coloured fruit, bristling with thorns, matured on their branches. Fruit that sparkled in the water's depths, like suns.

Camille ran along the bank. He heard her laughing. The suns on the branches of the trees burst like overripe fruit. The light trickled, mingling with the water. Lying on her back, Catherine floated on the surface of this swelling, golden water. She drifted alongside the raft, now reduced to a few separated logs.

He had lost his steering pole. Instead he held a tall cross, like the one carried by the St Nicholas, made of painted wood, decorating the banner of the guild of raftsmen, to which he had once belonged. And with this cross he tried to row, crouched over his craft that kept contracting in size. There were thousands of burst sun-rinds in the water. Camille was still running along the bank. She was not laughing any more, but shouting, or singing. She uttered a continuous cry in a deep, rough voice, a man's voice – Simon's voice, when he had bellowed Rouzé's name.

He was stretched out on a raft composed of Catherine's multiplied body. The forest had disappeared, the light in the water had died, all the bells had fallen silent. All he could hear now was the thud of a heart beating against his own – Catherine's heart, whose throbs reverberated in every one of her bound together, multiple bodies.

Ambroise Mauperthuis woke with a start, his heart pounding. The first glimmerings of daylight were beginning to appear. The rain had just stopped. Water dripped from the branches and roofs. Some birds in the bushes shook themselves. He emerged from the shed. It was cool outside, and the damp earth gave off an invigorating, bitter smell. As he passed by the raspberry canes, he heard the sweet twitterings of a warbler. He crossed the vegetable garden, skirted the ruins of his farm, and set off up the road. Sleep abandoned him. The confidence he had retained the previous day, even in the face of disaster, had been overshadowed. The dream that had suddenly woken him had thrown him into confusion. He felt tired. All at once his age weighed heavily on him. He climbed up to the forest. He felt the need to walk, to go in among the trees. All the inhabitants of the hamlet were still asleep. This was just as well: he certainly had no desire to meet another living soul. He had never liked people, but at that moment less than ever. He moved towards the trees, their silence and their shade. Their strength. They were his only comfort now. The sound of the rain, when it began to fall early in the night, wakened Simon. He half-opened his eyes and was amazed to be lying in this strange, unfamiliar room, all crowded with flowers and permeated with their heady smell. Camille was asleep beside him. Her presence at his side further amazed him. He had for so long yearned to see her again and to hold her in his arms, it had grieved him so much to be parted from her – and now suddenly, one morning, he woke up right next her, in the freshness of a white room filled with a greenhouse fragrance. Then jumbled memories of the previous day came back to him. He saw again the deserted hamlet, the forsaken farm, his parents' bedroom given over to the desolation of mourning – the empty bed, and the big hanging sheet. He saw Rouzé with his gentle eyes and warm muzzle: he had so often slept against his flanks that winter, and lain in his warmth. He saw Rouzé, looking huge and white, and suddenly terrible in the morning brightness, in the middle of the deserted yard. He saw an alien beast, overtaken with frenzy and madness, by the blinding flash of light that death cast from the doorstep. He saw this colossal beast collapse in a heap beneath the axe. He saw the road streaming with the blood of the flayed animal that he carried on his back. He saw the façade of Threshold Farm, hostile and silent, with its closed shutters and two thin dogs that leapt up, howling amid a rattling of chains. He saw the black smoke rising from the roof, and the flames climbing into the sky. He saw the figure wrapped in a scorched blanket appear through a window. He saw the great wooden tub that someone filled with water, and himself plunging into this water, with Camille.

He saw all these things in a quick, chaotic succession of images. But before trying to make sense of them, and to sort them out, he turned to Camille, held her face in his hands and sought her eyes and lips. He found her again; at last he recognized her. And they once more took possession of each other, with the same gestures, the same impulsiveness and hunger as during the autumn.

Within the room were the flowers with their opaque whiteness, the silence, the rustle of lace; outside, the violent downpour of rain beating against the walls and shutters. Everything reawakened their senses, revived their memory, intensified their happiness at being reunited. In the middle of the night they quietly slipped out through the window. Huguet Cordebugle was asleep in the next room. They stole away to Upper Farm. Simon knocked softly on the door. Almost at once Edmée opened it. She hardly ever slept any more – this old lady, who for a long time had not kept count of how many years her neverending life had numbered. 'Hearken, o daughter, and consider, and incline thine ear.' Echoing Blaise-the-Ugly's singing, she had mumbled these words of the psalm all along the way, the previous morning, as she tottered ahead of the big beechwood bed in which her daughter lay. She listened, amid the worldly hubbub attentive to the silence of God.

When Simon saw his grandmother, so small and tiny at the half-open door, he momentarily forgot the terror and pain he had felt that morning on finding the house empty. His grandmother – who had always known how to relieve the body's suffering and the heart's anguish – was there; the little old lady was still there, gentle, retiring, and true.

221

They both went inside. Edmée made them sit at the table and prepared them a meal and gave them something to drink. The brothers that were in the house came and joined them at the table. All the Evening brothers were there. The Morning brothers were spending the night in the village, not having returned from Rocking-Stone Abbey until after dark. They spoke little. Blaise-the-Ugly said simply, 'Mother looked beautiful. Father and Ferdinand cut down the tree that we'd sculpted for her in the clearing of Our-Lady-of-the-Beeches. We carried her, laid in the hollow of the tree: there was a crowd of people to accompany her. Father won't be coming home again. He's gone to the monks at Rocking-Stone Abbey. He wants to stay there, by the waters of the Trinquelin, by the big stone that rocks in the wind. We'll go and visit him soon. We'll tell him that you came home. He'll be pleased. And now, what you are both going to do?'

'We're leaving, tonight, before the old man starts looking for us. We'll go far away, to a place where he can't find us. I'll certainly be able to get a job anywhere. We'll come back later on, when the old man's gone. We'll walk all night – I know the forest, I shan't lose the way. We'll head towards Avallon.'

They both felt equal to taking the route through the forest and walking all night long, and all of the following day – walking until the old man lost track of them.

They got ready for the journey. Edmée wrapped some food for them, and a few clothes. Loulou-the-Bellclinker called Camille and led her into his parents' bedroom. He wanted to look in the wardrobe for one of his mother's shawls to give her. He was so fond of wearing skirts himself, and did not like to see Camille clad in a rough pair of men's trousers. He wanted to dress her in one of his mother's shawls, to wrap her in his mother's memory. As he was opening the door of the wardrobe, the sheet covering the mirror slid to the floor, and Camille saw herself in the looking-glass. For the first time her resemblance to Simon took her by surprise. She accepted the shawl that Loulou-the-Bellclinker offered her, and folded it at the bottom of the bag that Edmée had given her.

'I'll wear it when we get there,' she said. She did not know where 'there' was – a place where the old man would not be, that was the important thing. 'There' was wherever the old man's jealousy could not reach them, where his madness and anger would no longer be a threat.

Camille slipped into an old jacket of Simon's, tucked her hair up under a cap, and put on some tough shoes. She thought it was better to go through the forest dressed in this way, it being easier for a boy to walk through the undergrowth than a girl hampered by a skirt. Anyway, she did not actually have a dress or a skirt any more – she had lost all the clothes and belongings she had once owned. Everything had been burned in the blaze, and her dress, dirtied by the smoke from the fire, had been left at Huguet Cordebugle's farm. And besides, dressed like this, she looked like Simon's twin brother, and this pleased her. It even reassured her, for it meant blotting out the terrible resemblance that the old man persisted in foisting on her: her resemblance to a dead woman that the old man had often invoked through the wooden door. But that door had burned down; the whole farm had burned down, and the past along with it – as well as the old man's madness.

Simon and Camille each slipped a bag over their shoulder, said their goodbyes to Edmée and the brothers, and slipped away from Upper Farm, hurrying towards the forest. Dawn was about to break.

A SONG

They entered Jalles Forest, and soon veered over towards the sound of the river. The Cure at this point was more of a torrent than a river. Its waters, swollen by the rain, leapt from boulder to boulder. Cold, living waters, that sprang from the rocks, among the trees. In the summer, Simon and his brothers would go down and swim in it. Listening to the flow of this water, Simon thought of his father – his father who was now living on the far side of the plain separating the two valleys, of the Cure and the Trinquelin. His father was withdrawing into himself, taking himself off into stillness and silence. His father was pursuing the invisible traces left behind by his mother now that she was gone. He was off into self-forgetfulness; he had no other place to rest now but on the very brink of the void, waiting, like the heavy stone balanced on a rock at the water's edge, which could be made to seesaw at the slightest pressure. His father trembled in remembrance of the woman he had so greatly loved, he let his heart quiver in loss, grief and hope. He waited, with patience and calm, to be summoned in his turn. Like a plant torn from the bank and carried along by the waters of a mountain stream, he meekly entrusted himself to the name of God, whose praises he sang day after day. His father was going into retirement on the banks of the Trinquelin, very close by as the crow flies. And his son, the child of Noon, was going away with Camille. They were both fleeing as far as possible from the old man's anger, and the noise of the torrent reverberated inside them, marking their progress – a light, exhilarating sound of cascading waters. The weeds, brambles and ferns, and the leaves of the trees were still glistening with the rain, and the birds were shaking their feathers in the branches and thickets, warbling shrill songs, piping fluty melodies and pretty chirping strains. Everything around the two fugitives took on an accent and flavour that was sharp, damp, and full of freshness. The sky was beginning to turn rosy.

Simon went first across the bridge made of a big oak tree-trunk laid over the ravine in which the torrent roared. He knew all the shortcuts through the forest. The mountain stream, swollen by the rain, could only be crossed here. They had to get away from the hamlet as fast as possible, leave Jalles Forest, and put the old man's estate behind them before it was fully light. The bridge that the woodcutters had rigged up here, was precarious, with no handrail: its mossy trunk was slippery. Simon ventured across cautiously. When he reached the other side, having made sure that the trunk was sound, he called to Camille, who was waiting her turn to cross.

'It's all right,' he shouted above the roar of the torrent, 'you can come across. Be careful, it's slippery.'

Camille approached the tree-trunk with careful little steps, but she took fright and stopped. Then to give her courage, Simon began to sing. Laughing and clapping his hands, he sang one of the songs that he and his brothers were fond of belting out when they were little and fear sometimes overcame them in the forest.

'*We'll not go to the woods any more, the laurels have been cut down. This beautiful young woman will go gather them up . . .*' He sang at the top of his voice, to drown the noise of the water and dispel Camille's fear.

Ambroise Mauperthuis, who had been disquieted by his bad dream and had come among the trees to buck his thoughts, started. He stopped dead in his tracks, like a pointer suddenly catching the scent of game. His heart was immediately cheered. He had heard a voice coming from the stream, a voice shouting amid the tumult of the water. Was it the stream shouting? What male voice had it torn from the granite rocks? What insane call was it making at this hour, when daylight was only just beginning to break? He hurried towards the stream, stooped so that he was just skimming the tall weeds, which wet his face. He held his breath, the sharpness of his senses at its most acute. The voice was very close now. It leapt among the trees and rocks. He recognized it. It was Simon's voice. He was singing.

The mountain stream was singing. It had taken on the voice of Simon the thief, Simon the arsonist. Words sung to a swift rhythm and a merry tune soared above the din of the water . . .

'*If the grasshopper's sleeping there, we must not wake her . . . Join the dance, see how we dance, Leap and dance, Kiss whom you will . . .*' Simon's voice splashed the rocks, and frolicked in the water. It seemed to be laughing at everything and everybody. It was laughing at him, Ambroise Mauperthuis – that was for sure.

. Encouraged by Simon's song, by his gaiety and enthusiasm, Camille was defying her fear. She had ventured on to the tree-trunk, and was already half-way across. She advanced with her arms slightly outspread to keep her balance.

'*The nightingale's song Will wake her . . . Join the dance, See how we dance . . .*'

The old man came to the edge of the gorge through which the torrent flowed, very close to the bridge. Crouched in the grass, hiding, he saw a figure, with arms outstretched for balance, nervously shuffling across the trunk that lay over the ravine. It was Simon; this funambulist that he could only vaguely discern from behind could not be anyone else but Simon: Simon the fugitive, Simon the vociferous, Simon the insolent. Squatting in the cover of the grass, Ambroise Mauperthuis could only see the figure crossing the bridge; he did not see the other person waiting on the far side of the torrent. He had eyes for nothing else but this figure that he thought was Simon's. He had eyes only for this funambulist absconding with little trembling steps across the old mossy tree-trunk, in the mist of water, singing at the top of his voice. And his eyes were fixed: hatred and the thrill of vengeance sharpened his gaze.

'*The nightingale's song Will wake her, And so, too, will that of the sweet-throated warbler . . . Join the dance, See how we dance . . .*'

Camille was only a few steps from the other side. A stone as large as a fist whistled through the air. It struck the funambulist right between the shoulders. Camille lost her balance and slipped, and before Simon had time to leap forward and catch her, she fell.

The singing stopped dead. At the same moment a cry pierced the tumult of the water. This cry seemed simultaneously to fall right to the bottom of the gorge and to spring from the rocks. This was not a man's cry, but that of a woman. Ambroise Mauperthuis stood up, with a wild expression. He could not understand any more. He had aimed at Simon, he had hit him, and sent him plunging into the torrent, and the torrent had immediately started to cry with Camille's voice, while Simon reappeared on the far side of the bridge. But already the voices of the torrent had fallen silent. There was simply the eternal sound of the waters, but no cry or song. Just opposite was Simon, standing by the bridge in a state of shock. He did not shout or move. He stared at the riverbed, at the body lying on the gravel, its face looking up at him from the clear depths of the water. He gazed in hallucination at this other body, this strange double of himself: his green-eyed reflection lying all broken on the pebbles at the bottom of the water. Again a stone whistled through the air. Another cry simultaneously rose and fell among the rocks. Another body hit the waters of the mountain stream.

Yet again Simon lay at the bottom of the water. There were two of them down there: Simon the thief and Simon the arsonist. There were two of them, the strong twin and the more delicate twin: one lying on his back, the other face down on the stones. One with his eyes open, their green gaze fixed on the patch of sky high above the forests, the other with his forehead buried in the gravel.

Ambroise Mauperthuis at last had done with Simon, with all the Simons: the thieves that stole Camille and the arsonists who burned down farms. He had brought down all the Simons. Let their broken bodies be swept along by the waters of the torrent, like logs destined to be thrown on the fire; let the waters of the torrent carry them far away from here, into some swamp.

But where, then, was Camille? Where was the Spark of Life hiding? Ambroise Mauperthuis went back to Oak-Wolf. He whistled under his breath the tune of *'We'll not go to the woods any more'*. His throat was dry, his lips rough, and his whistling was jerky. He returned to his house avoiding the road that led through the village. He went straight to the shed at the bottom of the vegetable garden, without even glancing at the ruins of his farm. He lay down on his pallet. He was still whistling the same tune, punctuating it with bursts of snickering laughter. Now and again he uttered some words of the song. *'We'll not go to the woods any more.'* And every time, his words were cut short by his snickering, as though by fits of coughing. Outside the rain began to fall heavily.

It rained all day. The road leading down from the forest turned into a stream of muddy water. The branches of the apple, plum and lilac trees bent beneath the weight of all this water that fell incessantly. Weighed down with their crumpled petals, the heads of the flowers in the gardens were bowed to the ground. The paths everywhere became streams, and the streams and rivers overflowed, like rushing torrents. The rain only started to slacken towards evening. A rainbow appeared on the horizon; three colours predominated: violet, green and yellow. A dark violet, a bright green, a straw yellow. The children finally emerged from their houses, waded in the muddy yards, and squealed with joy, admiring the splendid rainbow.

Simon and Camille's bodies were not found until the following day, considerably downstream of where they fell. The swollen waters of the Cure had so violently buffeted their bodies among the rocks that the marks of the stones that had been hurled at them, hitting one of

228

them in the back and the other on the temple, were no longer detectable. Their bodies were completely bruised, their bones broken, their skin marred and scratched. There was nothing else to be deduced from their bodies after they had been swept along by the current but the evidence of a twofold accidental death. They must have slipped off the slimy, moss-covered tree-trunk as they hurried across it.

No one came to tell Ambroise Mauperthuis of the death of his granddaughter, Camille. Besides, even if someone had found the courage to do so, it would have been pointless. The old man had taken leave of his senses. Since the evening of the fire, his mind had seemed to be wandering. He shut himself up in his shed at the bottom of the vegetable garden, showed not the slightest concern for his devastated farm, and appeared completely to lose interest in his affairs. He only emerged from his hut to go and walk up to the forest, but he never entered it. He would stop short of the trees, and skirt them. He was always whistling the tune of 'We'll not go to the woods any more', and punctuated his rendition with brief bursts of fitful laughter.

It was suddenly the end of Mauperthuis the rich and powerful, the Mauperthuis that was full of pride and anger; his time was now passed. He lost his reason when his farm burned down, and his strength when Camille left. He became so crazed and irresponsible that he had to forfeit his rights and property. Since he had disinherited his eldest son and all his descendents, and his own direct heirs were dead, the administration of his estate fell to his daughter-in-law, Marceau's widow and Camille's mother. Claude Corvol thereby recovered the forests that the old man had in the past usurped from her father. Like the trees that were felled and sawn up into logs, ownership of the forests resumed its age-old, rightful course, down into the valley.

The arrogant Mauperthuis, owner of the forests of Jalles, Saulches and Failly, master of Threshold Farm, seigneur of Oak-Wolf was soon forgotten. The dark secret of his past wealth no longer excited people's curiosity at all. He was of no interest to anyone any more. Mauperthuis the irascible, the violent, the jealous was just a poor devil now, lurking in a shed behind the ruins of a farm, in a corner of a vegetable garden that had turned into wasteland. A poor old devil who no longer recognized anybody, seemed not even to see them any more, capable only of roaming the edge of the forest snickering shrilly between two couplets of his endlessly repeated song. '*We'll not go to the woods any more, The laurels have been cut down, This beautiful young woman will go gather them up.*'

The beautiful young woman was no longer there, but the old man waited for her. He waited for his Spark of Life. He had been waiting for her so long now, she was bound to come back. '*The nightingale's song Will waken her. And so, too, will that of the sweet-throated warbler . . .*'

NOT ENOUGH TIME

Join the dance,
See how we dance,
Leap and dance,
Kiss whom you will . . .

Up at Oak-Wolf there were now three of them waiting.
Theirs was a mad waiting – waiting for what can no
longer happen, because it has already occurred.

There was Edmée, the gentle grandmother who went
on surviving the days, as tiny and frail as a sparrow. A
firefly. She was waiting at Upper Farm until it was time at
last to go and rejoin her daughter. She awaited the summons while saying her rosary to the ever-renewed glory of
the Most Holy Virgin and Most Merciful Comfort. She
awaited a summons that had always dwelt within her, she
awaited a call that had for ever summoned her, that she
had ever answered: the fulfilment and consummation of
her waiting, the assumption of her expectation.

As soon as the fine weather arrived, she was still to be
seen, all hunched and small, walking surefootedly down
the road leading to the cemetery. She tottered along without stopping, without turning her head to left or right.
Nothing could have distracted her or made her slow her
step – her tiny, mouse-like step, her devotional step. Holding a bunch of wild flowers in her hand, she made straight
for the graveyard where her one and only, beloved, miraculous daughter was laid to rest. All the way there, she
muttered the words of the Litany of the Virgin – words as
polished by her lips as her rosary beads were polished by
her fingers. Words that had become her saliva, boxwood
beads with the sheen of fingernails. Her grief had the
brightness of a rainbow after rain, her grief had the smell
of fields, meadows, orchards and gardens, and her grief had
the freshness of a breeze, the clearness of fountain water.
Her faith had purged her grief; her tears glistened in the
crux of her soul. They were the same blue as the Madonna's
blue mantle. Edmée tottered along in the blue of her soul,
the blue of her waiting. She trod on the very rim of death,

quietly singing and smiling. She already glimpsed the lovely eyes of death. They had the gentleness of Regina's gaze, and the blueness of the Virgin's mantle. She rejoiced that she would soon melt into this blueness.

There were just Loulou-the-Bellclinker and Blaise-the-Ugly living with her now. All the others had gone. After Simon's death they had left the hamlet. They did not want to work and live any longer in a forest marked by the death of one of their own; they could not. The forest had struck, it had killed the brother of Noon, it had cut through their midst. It was driving them away. And besides, their mother was lying in the earth now, and their father had retired into the shadow of a great stone that trembled like a lamb on the banks of the Trinquelin. They, too, had retired, they had gone to complete the journey at whose threshold Simon had fallen. Leon-the-Loner had gone down to the forests of Sologne – he was said to be living there as an outlaw, as Leon-the-Poacher. Eloi-Else-where had found his river: the Loire. He had settled where the waters of the wide river run into the sands.

The Morning brothers had journeyed much further still, far beyond their native land. They had crossed the seas and moved to a different continent. They had ventured all the way to Quebec. There, the forests stretched as far as the eye could see, the rivers were as broad as the sea and carried huge herds of logs for miles and miles. There, even the sky was more vast. There, the forests and waters were virgin, with no memories attached to them.

Even the last two still living at Upper Farm were awaiting the time when they could leave the hamlet. When Edmée went off to join her daughter, they would go and join their father. They would shut behind them the door of the farm, where the mirrors had long since lost their quicksilvering, and they would go and knock at the door of Rocking-Stone Abbey. They would become lay brother, like their father. They would go and purge their memories in the living waters of the Trinquelin. Loulou-the-Bellclinker had stopped ringing his bells three times a day. He spent his days up in the trees. He would climb the branches of the elm and stay squatting up there among the leaves, chirping with the birds.

There was Huguet Cordebugle, who had long since stopped filching laundry from the gardens and meadows. He hardly ever left Middle Farm, where he lived, more lonesome than ever. One morning the old cockerel Alphonse had fallen off his chair-perch, and dropped dead on the ground. No other cock had succeeded him. Cordebugle raided only the past now. He kept returning to spy on the images fixed in his memory: images of Simon naked in the grass, in the meadow at Threshold Farm; of Simon on the road at Rouzé's side; of Simon-the-Flayed with his streaming, flaming skin; of Simon duplicated, whom he had taken in and hidden, and covered his body with flowers. Simon who had gone by the morning, leaving empty the bed strewn with faded flowers. Simon dashed by the rain and the forest to the bed of the river that was rugged with rocks. Simon-the-Hothead, Simon the twin, Simon who never stayed put, who kept turning up unexpectedly, each time endowed with a new and astounding beauty. Simon of whom he expected a new appearance, a new transformation. Simon who had disappeared in a trail of flowers, who had plunged into the waters of the torrent. Simon who would return with the current. In another season. Huguet Cordebugle awaited his return. The room was ready. When Simon came back, he would give him the key to the room, he would watch over his sleep, he would be the guardian of his dreams. Would he come back again holding his green-eyed double by the hand? No, that double was just a reflection of Simon that had wrested itself from the troubled water of some pond to follow him whose image was so beautiful. That reflection must have been lost in the waters of the torrent.

And there was Ambroise Mauperthuis, waiting for his Spark of Life. His Spark of Life with Serpent eyes and

Serpent body. That beautiful young woman, lying there, on the banks of the Yonne, in the waters of the Cure. The beautiful young woman who sallies to and fro, who swims in every river and runs through every forest. Who sleeps in the dawn dew, in clear waters. Who rests beneath the undergrowth, lying on gravel. *'If the grasshopper's asleep, We must not hurt her. The nightingale's song Will waken her. And so, too, will that of the sweet-throated warbler. The beautiful young woman will be back again With her white basket, Gathering strawberries And wild roses.'* Serpents do not die, they do not even grow old. They enter the world as though joining a round, they enter on Time as though joining a dance. *'Join the dance, See how we dance!'* It made the old man laugh, it made him laugh all the time.

Serpents do not die. They enter men's hearts; they dance in their palms, sing in their dreams, swim in their blood. Serpents are immortal Sparks of Life. The beautiful young woman that was here before will be back again. *'Grasshopper, my grasshopper, Come, we must sing. For the laurels in the wood have already grown again.'*

The woods had turned to wasteland and depredation was rampant. The hamlet was emptying. The Mauperthuis boys had all left, except the last two, but they were already at the threshold, ready to go. Then the war called the menfolk of Gravelle Farm and Follin Farm, and kept nearly all of them. No one went to the woods any more; people went to war and never came back. Those that did return left again soon afterwards with their families. The days of log-floating were over. No one went to the woods any more, no one went to the river. Everyone was moving to the towns.

The rain fell, melting the snow. All traces disappeared – all traces of the departed year, inscribed in the snow and frost, in the frozen earth. All traces of the departed century – of centuries never to return. The rain fell, and the writing – the footprints of men and beasts – was washed away. To be started anew. But there was no one left to enter into fable once more and set memories dancing.

The land began to stir, and a new light appeared in the sky, a vibrant brightness with the barest tinge of straw-yellow. And the bird-song took on a more lively, slightly warmer modulation – the song of the first migrant birds to return, giving voice to their choice of territory from the tops of the branches, still almost bare, and the roofs of abandoned cowsheds and barns. At the break of day, their shrill voices tinkled in the silence like cracking glass. But always towards evening, there came the raucous clamour of rooks passing overhead on their return to the forests – a streak of sound drawn across the sky, between day and night, between past and present. A distant past, a lonely present.

Then, his beautiful darling had been there. Where is she now? 'She's sleeping,' says the dying old man. But he still strains his ears, trying to pick out among all the bird-song that of the nightingale and the sweet-throated warbler, nesting in the thorny bushes and clumps of nettles around his tumbledown shed. Right to the last, he listens out for the song of these two little birds that will surely be able to waken her.

'My Spark of Life,' murmurs the old man, 'come now, you must sing.'

He has lost his wicked laughter, his pained laughter. He grimaces a smile. For his Spark of Life is returning, here she comes now, passing through the walls of his hovel, gathering strawberries and wild-roses. She passes through the walls and through the old man. She stoops slightly and with a delicate gesture plucks his gaze, his trembling smile, his faltering breath. Here she comes, his beautiful darling, and already she is gone.

With old folk, death's progress is effortless. It is simply a matter of plucking a breath that has long since lost its strength and roots, of gathering the few seeds of madness that have fossilized in their hearts and minds – those dried and withered husks. And yet, at the final moment, the old man bucks one last time, because for him, not enough time has passed. And never will. At the final moment, he will not let go of those hard, shiny seeds of his madness, which he has polished in his anger as Edmée polished her rosary beads saying so many prayers. Edmée has gone now, melted into the most radiant blueness of death. But the old man is still resisting. He is desperately chewing on those sharp and bitter seeds of his madness. He has always loved gnawing at them. But his beautiful darling snatches them from him and all of sudden crunches them up. The old man is left with his mouth open and empty. His beautiful darling escapes through the window. Death, which is here now, only took on the look and appearance of the beautiful young woman who has just left. Old folk can no longer distinguish properly between then and now, between Serpent and Spark of Life, between love and anger. Ambroise Mauperthuis had always been old.